D1132521

THE BOXER
AND THE
ROSE

Lily M. Winter

Book Cover design by Monica Thomas and Evgeniia Freeman

First paperback edition December 2023

ISBN 9798870543123 (paperback edition)

For Patch

Contents

Phrases and Tidbits

Some of the words and phrases used are from the era and aren't used much these days; some are still used in parts of Scotland and England. Here are the ones that might stick out to you:

anointing – a thrashing, beat someone up
at sixes and sevens – in a state of confusion or disarray
bairn – baby or small child, Scottish
balmy – deluded, insane
bampot – idiot, fool, Scottish
blackguard – scoundrel or villain
bout – a boxing match
cannae – can't, Scottish
chit – a young woman, sometimes one who is impertinent, usually said unflatteringly
clyse – clothes
couldna – couldn't
deep into one's cups – drunk
dicked in the nob – crazy, insane
dinnae – don't/ didn't, Scottish
doxie – prostitute
dray horse – horse used for hauling heavy loads
eejit – idiot, Scottish

fall (in terms of clothes) – front panel of men's trousers, fastened with buttons

fash, as in 'dinnae fash' – don't worry, don't fret yourself, Scottish

flimp – thief, pickpocket

for certs – truly, indeed

gaol – jail, British spelling

gig – a light two-wheeled carriage

grease my fist – bribe

hale – strong, healthy

haversack – a long bag with a strap at the top and bottom worn crossbody, often favored by soldiers and sailors

hie – hurry, go quickly

high dudgeon – bad mood

in a trice – quickly, right away

ken/ dinnae ken - to know or understand/ don't know, Scottish

knick – steal, take away

mill – a boxing match or where boxing matches were held

mo chridhe – term of endearment, literally my heart; pronounced: moh HEE-ah, Scottish

nae – no, Scottish

pettish – childish or bad-tempered

pinch – steal

pink – a man at the height of fashion

posh – elegant or fashionable, slang uses it as a noun

puling – crying that is soft, weak, pathetic in its sound

quim – a vulgar, derogatory insult

redshank – Scotsman or specifically Highlander

reticule – a lady's purse

shite – shit, Scottish

shouldna – shouldn't, Scottish

sit-upons – pants or underwear

swell – elegant or fashionable, slang uses it as a noun

the noo – right now/ for the moment, Scottish

toff – derogatory slang for someone with aristocratic background

togs – clothing

tulip – a man who dressed well

vinaigrette – a small hinged metal box with a decorative metal grate on one side, contained sponge soaked in aromatic substances dissolved in vinegar, used to carry perfume, often used when lady felt she might 'swoon' or faint

wanker – a vulgar, derogatory insult

ye/ yer – you/ your (or you're), Scottish

yourn – yours

If you aren't familiar with the Regency or early Victorian periods of England, some of the customs and situations may seem strange or confusing. Here's a glimpse at what I have learned about their time. Please note that if there are errors, it is due to my own ignorance and not intentionally done; I try to make my historical novels as accurate as possible.

The early- to mid-1800s was a time of transition. Within a span of less than twenty years, four different monarchs sat upon the English throne, finally ending with Queen Victoria, who ascended in 1837. This period also marked what many believe to be the peak of the Industrial Revolution with huge advances in science as well as innovation. The first railway appeared on the scene in 1825, and the Liverpool and

Manchester Railway—the world's first inter-city railway—opened in 1830.

The 'Season' was still adhered to during this time of transition. It refers to a stretch of months when the aristocracy and their families returned to London (often referred to simply as 'Town' with a capital T) for the sitting of Parliament. With so many wealthy citizens in Town at once, there was a need for entertainment, so the Season was littered with balls, lavish parties, and a very active marriage market. By 1822, those months shifted from fall through spring to February through the end of July or beginning of August. It was rare for families to remain in London outside those months, but not unheard of.

Much of the old customs of high society, previously known through the Regency as the Ton, continued for a short period, but they slowly became less prominent as the size and wealth of the middle-class boomed. Things that would have only been available to the wealthy aristocracy even a few decades earlier were becoming accessible to the middle class as they began earning wealth that had been, up until then, impossible for their status.

Men and women in "good society" still used a title with one another and it was only in intimate and familiar situations and relations that a first name, or "Christian name", was used, and then most often only between women. Even men who grew up with one another as cousins or other close relations called each other by their surnames rather than by their first names. From what I've learned, women almost never called a man by his first name unless they were married, and then only if they were alone.

Bare-knuckle boxing had been around as a sport since the mid-1700s and was still quite popular, though it evolved over the decades and received new rules in 1838. Those who participated in the sport as competitions were mainly from the middle and lower classes. While gentlemen from the aristocracy often excelled at and practiced fencing and boxing at various clubs around London, they rarely competed. In competitions, men fighting would have a handkerchief in their chosen color tied to the top of the center stakes; the winner was entitled to take their opponents "colors" as a trophy.

Gentlemen's clubs, such as White's and Brooks's, were well known places for wealthy members to come and socialize, play cards, and commonly placed bets on anything and everything, from card games to when a man might marry. Many of these club practices continued for years after the Regency period turned over to the Victorian era, and as time went on, those elite clubs became accessible to the middle classes and, eventually, to women as well. Some are still standing and in use today.

Chapter One

Margaret Everleigh, a prominent gem in the crown of London's aristocracy, a lady whom any member of court would quickly recognize, was without friend or ally for the first time in her life, and more frightened now than from any fantastical nightmare her dreams might have attempted to invent before this. Fear like a noose tightened around her throat, a great lump that she could not swallow, one that hindered even a single full breath to reach her lungs. Instead, she was left panting with short, shallow puffs of air that made her head feel too light and her thoughts disjointed. Or was the addlement due to her fall upon leaping from the moving train? Her head throbbed even still from the impact of it.

Hurrying through dim alleyways crowded with the dredges of society, her usually proud, erect posture was replaced in favour of a forward hunch with the hopes it might hide her as she stumbled along. Her mind continued to reel in panic at the plot she had overheard on the train, and as a lock of hair whipped across her face, she reached up to re-secure her bonnet. She pulled up short and shot a look behind her as her hand continued to grope about her head for the missing article. She must have lost it in her tumble from the train! Now scandalously unpinned ribbons of tawny hair lashed her face as the wind tore through the hamlet's tightly packed avenues. The cacophony from the intermingled clash of day labourers hurrying to home and hearth and those creatures of the night out to peddle their evil wares threatened to overwhelm her, and Margaret ducked into the opening of an alley, fairly collapsing against the wall in momentary respite and sense of sanctuary. A glance down at herself revealed just how much like a vagabond she now resembled. Her gloves were torn and showed splotches of blood where jagged cinders from the railside had pierced the tender skin of her palms. Ash smudged the primrose-coloured travelling coat, several places torn through, and a good length of once fine trim hung lifelessly by a thread. The silk carnation pink gown beneath was torn at the knees and it felt as if the shoulder seam had popped open. Nevermind what state the usually fair skin of her face must be in now.

Her mind spun with disbelief. How could her friend have done such a thing? She would never have imagined it possible! She had been so certain of his presence in her life, in his role as a dear and trustworthy friend; he had always seemed so genuine and sincere since the very beginning of their friendship! Never had she been so mistaken in determining a person's character, and the fact that she had so misjudged a person in her inner circle created a sickening hole in the pit of her stomach. He was as bad as Marcus Brutus! Or Judas Iscariot!

A fresh wave of horror crashed over her as a new thought occurred to her: was every one of her friends a party to this wicked scheme of his? Must she doubt each of them? Could he have been successful in turning every one of her beloved friends against her? If that were so, what would she do? What *could* she do?

One thing shone clearly in her mind: she needed to return to Brookshire, the country estate of her cousin, Michael Saxon. He was not in residence at the moment, but Brookshire was safe; it always had been. Even before she was orphaned, before her uncle's home was hers as well. Many of her happiest memories were created upon the backdrop of the sprawling, four level estate. Michael was, after all, her acting guardian despite being of age and means, herself, and he had been like an older brother to her for as long as she could remember. He could not come to her aid now, however, and she had no information besides the bits gleaned from the conversation she'd overheard on the train on her trip north with the, and no way to prove it was so.

The wickedness of her false friend's betrayal hit her anew, and she fought back the tears threatening to rise into her eyes. No, she refused to give way. She could mourn her lost friendship later with tears and heartache, but for now, she would focus on how deeply this betrayal cut and allow that anger to focus her as she searched for her next course of action.

Which led her to another problem: where was she?

She closed her eyes against the dilemma she faced. With a sigh of exhaustion, she fell back against the wall and allowed it to support her. It would be for but a moment, she told herself. Then she would continue on and find a private carriage to take her home.

"Yeh poor little thing! Yer all done in, ain'cha?" crooned a soft feminine voice with just the slightest edge to it. The face was shadowed beneath the ridiculously wide brim of a pompous hat at least a decade beyond fashion. "Just come with me, my sweet. We'll fix yeh right up, draw yeh a nice warm bath and inta some nice clean clothes."

Her nerves were so frayed and her situation so desperate that Margaret willingly permitted the woman to take her arm and tow her through the milling crowd before she even took stock of the woman's appearance.

"Where are we going, if you please?"

"Safest spot 'round fer th' likes of a pretty little flower like yerself," the woman replied.

Safe! Oh, was any word more heavenly? That was enough of an answer to ease Margaret's mind at present, so she continued to follow in the wake of the woman, her eyes on the somewhat bedraggled feathers that bobbed from the old, made-over hat. The woman's hair was a dull, mousy brown, and stringy as if in grave need of a good, thorough washing. With a more discerning eye, what she'd first assumed to be a fine garment now revealed its many reinforced stitches, places where tears had been mended time and again, and a few splotches of deeper mulberry hue where the new dye hadn't quite covered a previous stain. The hand which firmly clasped her elbow was none too clean, with dirt beneath the longish nails and black, fingerless lace gloves which were obviously several years old.

Fatigue weighed on her and her steps slowed, but the woman continued to drag her along until they arrived at a nondescript brick building with garish red curtains pulled closed over the windows. A shingle overhead bore the name *The Flower Garden*, of which Margaret barely caught sight before she was ushered firmly through the door.

"Who's this, Mis' Marigold?" came a sharp, metallic voice off to one side.

"A guest, Violet. Off wi' yeh!" snapped the apparently-named Miss Marigold as Margaret's long yellow coat was quickly unbuttoned and shoved back off her shoulders.

"A moment, if you please," Margaret protested, righting her coat and casting a glance about the room.

The parlour in which she stood had the appearance of a pauper trying to convince the world it was a prince. Every bit of furniture looked as if it had adorned the manor of a duke... once upon a time. Now the pieces were as worn and tired as the woman who'd brought her here. The silk paper might have been fine once but was now sun faded and tattered in places. Cheap, still life paintings of flowers and fruits crookedly adorned the walls in frames that had lost all but a few smudges of their gilt paint.

"Come now, luv, we ain't got all day t' tarry," Miss Marigold coaxed, tugging at Margaret's coat again. "We need t' get yeh cleaned up."

She'd begun to shrug out of her sleeves when a rhythmic thumping sounded on the stairs, and a man came trotting down, buttoning the fall of his trousers as he did so. Margaret caught her breath and scuffled backwards in shock.

"Who have we here, Mis' Marigold? New girl?" said the man as he reached the bottom of the stairs and paused to further straighten his clothing.

"Possibly," Miss Marigold answered cryptically. A hand passed over Margaret's hair and the girl shuddered before straightening to her full height. *New girl?*

He closed the distance between them and looked her from head to toe impertinently. "She's a looker, alright. Wouldn't mind a taste of 'er before she—"

Margaret's eyes flew wide open a split second before her palm connected with the man's face in a resounding slap. "How dare you speak to me in such a manner!"

The man raised a hand to rub his cheek, humour dancing in his eyes. "Found yerself a fiery one this time, didn'cha, Mis' Marigold?"

Miss Marigold's fingers seized her arm in a punishing grip and shook her until Margaret's teeth clacked together. "That's not 'ow we treat our generous patrons! What's th' matter wi' yeh?"

"S'alright, Mis' Marigold. I like a bit of snap in me snapdragons," he chuckled.

The purpose of the establishment struck her like a bolt of lightning, and nausea flooded her senses. Wrenching her arm away, she shoved at whom she assumed now was the madame and made a dash for the door, only to get caught up in a pair of arms stronger than iron bars.

"Aw, yeh can't leave now. We're just getting started, we two," and his mouth came down on hers in a bruising kiss.

Margaret yelped and thrashed wildly against him. In an act of sheer desperation, she bit down hard on the man's lip.

He stumbled back as he shoved her into the wall, anger flashing in his eyes. His hand shot out and slapped her across the face with such force that she crumpled to the ground.

She stayed where she was, cradling her face in utter shock, dazed from the impact, the second in as many hours.

Hard hands grabbed her by the shoulders and yanked her to her feet before she was slammed back into the wall with enough force that her head bounced off its surface. The man glared into her eyes and was close enough that she could smell the alcohol on his breath. Blood trickled from his lip where she'd broken the skin with her teeth. "Yeh stupid quim! Yeh'll live t' regret that." He grabbed her by the throat and began to squeeze.

Oh God, help me! Please! Her fingers clawed at the hand and wrist that steadily choked her. How was she going to get out of this? What was it that her cousin had taught her? She was so certain she'd never need it, but now... Oh, what was it?

Her entire face lit up as the memory surged to the forefront, and with all her might she brought her knee up between the man's legs.

With an oath and a groan, the man dropped to the floor before her. While the madame screamed behind her, Margaret flew to the door, wrenched it open, and raced outside to freedom.

She ran blindly for what felt like miles, tears streaming down her face as she sobbed. Her jaw ached and her cheek stung; her throat was sore where his hand had gripped her and in the back of her mind she wondered if there would be bruises. What would her cousin think? How was she to explain all this? It was madness! She had to get home! She never knew such danger and evil existed outside civilised society! Once she reached Brookshire, all would be well; her cousin would know what to do.

Her legs burned in protest at the distance she'd run and her lungs bellowed frantically. She finally slowed to a stop and, bracing a palm against the nearest wall, she let her head fall forward as she struggled to catch her breath.

What a mess she'd found herself in! But her cousin couldn't sweep in and carry her home; it was up to her.

With new determination, she lifted her head to strike out once more... and came face-to-face with the horrifying visage of an ancient drunkard, his toothless mouth gaping in an empty grin while his putrid odour of urine and old whiskey choked her entirely. It was all she could do to keep from retching.

Unintelligible words garbled up from his throat as filthy hands reached for her, and with a cry she flung herself backward in an effort to escape. The mad clattering of wheels and hoofbeat upon stone didn't penetrate her awareness until it was too late; a pair of horses bearing a coach careened straight toward her. Screaming, she threw herself from the path of the coach toward the factory wall to keep from being trampled alive. Her head cracked against the cobblestones underfoot, and a blinding light burst behind her lids. With a soft moan her body crumpled to the sidewalk as darkness enveloped her.

Chapter Two

The tall, broad-shouldered Scotsman wove his way through the milling masses. His nose wrinkled at the mixed aromas of liquor, cheap perfume, body odour, sewage, and various foods wafting from street-side stalls and open storefronts. It was in moments like this that he missed the wide-open spaces of the countryside. The fragrances to be found in memory were those of flowers carried faintly on a soothing breeze, of fresh air and long grasses. Although he made a living as a bare-knuckle prizefighter these days, he'd spent his childhood and young adulthood working in country villages and hamlets, from farm to field, blacksmith shop to carpentry. A quiet sigh escaped him as he ignored the sultry, brassy offers of doxies lurking in doorways and the deltas to alleyways. Their cloying perfume was nothing compared to the crisp, clean smell of the Scottish Highlands. Even the aromatic memory of shovelling dung out of a stable was preferable to that of the sickly, artificially floral pungency that filled his nose now.

Apart from his unusually tall stature, there was little to mark Arran MacDougall as much different from the people he sauntered past and around. He wore a sandy-toned wool coat that sported mismatched patches on the elbows and its shoulder seams had been obviously repaired by a less-than-expert hand, namely himself. Beneath that, he wore a raw linen shirt paired with a twill waistcoat that was as faded and worn as his jacket. His loose fitting trousers were soil brown, and his boots were scuffed and weather-worn. An old haversack was slung over one shoulder, the single strap grasped firmly in a large fist. A few pickpockets had toyed with the idea of trying to snatch it and running off, but the man carrying it didn't seem the type to be trifled with.

He had lean, rugged features and was handsome in his own way, although certainly not in the present close-shaven, aristocratic style. His cheeks, chin, and jaw were usually scruffy with thick stubble if not a full, short beard, and hair the colour of dark roasted coffee fell in ungroomed waves to the collar of his coat. He had been told on more than one occasion that he resembled a highwayman, whatever that meant, and had caused several women to fairly swoon around him for reasons unknown to him.

The most intriguing aspect of his countenance was a pair of penetrating, nearly black eyes, something that surprised nearly everyone with whom he came in contact. He was adept at hiding his thoughts and more often than not wore an almost fierce expression on his face, one meant to deter conversation rather than invite it.

Those arresting eyes currently searched for the shingle of an inn or a hotel. He had a fight scheduled for the next night, and was planning on leaving town right after the match. MacDougall tended not to stay in one place for very long; a rolling stone gathered no moss, it was said. Although he had established a rather successful career as a bare-knuckler, he wasn't after fame and glory, only the purse. He'd scrupulously avoided signing on with any one group or handler. He was able to do this by taking fights on short notice, wherever, whenever. He would blow into a town, find manual work, fight a bout or two if there were any to be had, collect his cut, and then he was gone. With his unnatural size and abnormal strength, he was a valued commodity anywhere he landed, whether it be at the docks, on a farm, hauling wood, even factory work on occasion. He rarely socialised with anyone, and never put down roots. Life was easier and much less complicated that way. Growing up, being passed from one family to the next, he learned that relying upon anyone but himself was a risk, one he had little interest in taking as an adult. People died, or left, or were killed; there was less danger on one's own. He was free as a bird, following the whims of the wind, landing wherever he felt inclined and flying off as soon as the mood struck him.

The sharp sound of a woman's shriek snatched his interest from storefronts and shingles. Up ahead of him, perhaps a few rods away, a small crowd gathered, but they seemed to mostly mill about, peering curiously at something he couldn't yet see. Quickening his pace, he shouldered his way through the knot of onlookers.

On the street before him was a crumpled young woman bedecked in finery that far exceeded the attire of anyone else in the immediate vicinity, dirty and rumpled though it was. Long locks of warm brown hair were haphazardly strewn across and over her face, so he was unable get a good look at her. What he did get a good look at was a young man rifling through the fallen woman's clothes, looking to steal something of value, no doubt. His brows furrowed at this. He had been told more than once that his was an old soul, that he had clung to a code long ago abandoned by civilised, sophisticated people. Whether that were true or not, he detested cowardice and injustice above all else, and to see this ne'er-do-well attempting to take advantage of the young woman on the ground riled him.

"Get off, ye bastard," MacDougall growled, and a swift, well-aimed kick caught the pickpocket squarely on the backside. The force of the kick elicited a sharp yelp of pain and surprise, and actually lifted the sneak thief up and landed him on the ground in a deep puddle of mud and melted snow a good ten feet from his intended victim.

"Oi!" the grimy youth shouted in protest. "That's my—"

"Yer what?" MacDougall snarled in response, glowering at the would-be thief.

The hard stare from black eyes stilled any further utterance from the now sodden youth. Picking himself up, he shook off as best he could, and then darted away, red-faced.

MacDougall bent over the woman on the ground. "Ye all right, lass?" When there came no reply nor movement, he levelled his glare at those still lurking nearby. "What happened?" he barked.

Silence followed his question, and when it became apparent that no one was stepping forward with the information he wanted, he fished out a penny and held it up between his thumb and forefinger as a bribe.

A small urchin, showing more dirt than skin, darted out and snatched it from his hand before anyone else could start forward. "Lady stepped right in front of a gig an' near got runned over!" the boy rushed out, his broken, street-rat speech so thick the man could just barely understand him. "She frew herself out an' smashed 'er head." His duty done, he scampered back through the small knot of people and vanished with his treasure.

As there didn't seem to be much else to do, the remaining onlookers ambled away in disinterest. He watched the crowd dissolve, then turned his attention to the young woman on the ground. A large hand settled onto her upper arm lightly.

"Can ye sit yerself up?" MacDougall asked quietly.

An odd whooshing filled her ears, as if she were on the shore as the tide rushed in, but she didn't remember going to the seaside. The sound gradually receded and gave way to a soft ringing, then that, too, faded away. There was an argument of gibberish above her, and laughter drifting from an open pub window, and the aroma of savoury meat laced with the putrid stench of waste. Something hard, cold, and wet pressed against the side of her face, and one arm felt as if a thousand needles pricked her skin. Dampness seeping through her layers of clothing brought things into hazy focus, as did the curious warmth settling over her arm just under her shoulder. Her eyes blinked open and quickly settled upon a pair of worn, sturdy boots, followed by knees as someone nearby crouched at her side. Why was she on the ground?

"Lass? Can ye hear me? Open yer eyes, lass."

The voice and its words ever so slowly registered. Both hands were set to the ground and she pushed up with a whimper and a wince. "Brick," she moaned softly. The world tilted and her arms collapsed beneath her.

"Aye, looks as if ye took a dive into the brick here." The thick Scottish brogue brought an odd sense of comfort and peace, and she blindly groped in the direction of the voice, a shaky hand brushing the hard leather toe of his boot.

His hand covered hers in a warm clasp for a moment before he shuffled closer, setting one knee to the cobblestone while his hands gently slid to her shoulders. "I'm going to raise ye up," the man murmured close to her ear before slowly urging her to a gradual seating position. "Nice and slow, the noo."

Margaret's eyes flickered to his face, and dull, bleary eyes struggled to focus upon the concerned features hovered above her. Again, she reached for him, this time her hand making it as far as the lapel of his jacket before she crumpled against him. "Brr-brick… waaa-ter," she whispered. *Brick water?* That was hardly what she meant to say. Even as she said it, her brain groped for the reason her words sounded so foreign to her own ears, and part of her questioned whether she had spoken at all, or merely imagined it.

"Let us get ye on yer feet, then see about a drink of some kind," the man offered quietly, evidently guessing at what she meant. As slowly as a mother helping a babe to stand for the first time, strong hands clasped hers and guided her carefully to her feet. She moaned and felt herself pitch forward. In the next moment, her world twisted and she was suddenly in the arms of the dark stranger, borne across his chest, and she was obliged to rest her head against the flat of his shoulder. He stood still for a moment, rocking this way and that, as if deciding what next to do. She felt him start forward, evidently deciding where to go, and though his gait was even and steady, each step was punctuated by a throb in her head and a roll deep in her stomach. Her small hand curled around a fold of his jacket and she held on as if it were her only lifeline, then her entire form wilted in his arms as she fainted once more.

MacDougall felt the petite body in his arms go slack and he cursed himself for having intervened. He didn't really have time or the patience for this, but he couldn't have in good conscience left her to the human vultures he had found pecking at her. A glance up at the shingles hanging over the various doorways announced a public house, the Crown and Thistle by name, and he strode toward it. No one really paid him much mind even as he shouldered the door open and entered with his pretty little burden. As far as they were concerned, she was naught but a working girl who had imbibed a few pints too many. The soiled condition of her clothes lent her the worn look of a doxie trying to appear as fetching as possible, giving the impression that she was successful and attractive beyond her true station. He dipped his head and gave a cursory sniff, finding no trace of liquor lingering about her, which rather dispelled his first assumption.

He bore the limp young woman to a nearby closet booth and deposited her onto one of the bench seats as carefully as he could. Once she was propped up against the back of the seat, he used his fingertips to gently brush the hair back and away from her face.

His heartbeat stuttered as he took in the details of her face. What first caught his eye, and aroused his anger, was the pinkish handprint marring the side of her face. Besides that, her skin was smooth as porcelain beneath the dirt of the streets. Her cheekbones were high but not garishly pronounced; the gentle line of cheek and jaw gave her an unspoiled, innocent look. Fine, rose-petal lips tugged downward at the corners in pain and slender brows were furrowed together in a troubled pucker. She wasn't just pretty; she was unnaturally beautiful. But when her lashes swept upward and the woman's rich amber eyes locked with his, he felt as if he had taken a solid punch to the stomach.

MacDougall looked away with a clearing of his throat and focused his attention on locating one of the establishment's girls. Spotting one and waving her over, he quickly ordered a bowl of fresh water, clean towel, and a small glass of whatever brandy the place had on hand. She nodded at the order and went off to fetch the requested items. When his focus swung back to the small woman, her eyes were closed again. Just as well.

Once the serving girl brought the requested items, he began to carefully clean the inert young woman's face with the damp towel. As he did so, his eyes drank in the sight of her. His touch seemed to soothe her; he noticed that the furrow in her brows eased until it smoothed into peaceful repose. He was careful and gentle with the side of her face where someone had clearly struck her. He sighed and shook his head sadly that she had been treated thus, perhaps by a cruel mistress.

With her face as clean as he could manage, a light touch upon her chin directed her face away so he could focus his attention on the next matter at hand: the sticky mess of mud and blood congealing in her hair on the left side of her head.

He knew head wounds were known to bleed more than most other injuries, thus it was a good sign that what little blood there was had already begun to clot. The woman's head lolled to one side while the rest of her slumped unceremoniously in the seat, as if keeping herself upright took more strength than she had. It was then that the light illuminated her neck enough for him to see what he'd previously missed. If he'd been angry before, the outline of stubby fingers and wide palm around the slender column of her neck fairly made his blood boil. He gauged the size of his own hand against the print which circled her throat, and he bit back a growl. Only men had hands that size, and his own fists clenched as fury swept through him afresh. What had this woman endured before he happened upon her? He had an intense desire to spend the rest of the evening hunting for the useless waste of a man that had done this to her.

Clenching his jaw and locking away his desire for vengeance, he returned to the slow task of cleaning the wound. It was only when the sodden cloth touched the injury directly that the woman gasped sharply, her features contorting with a hiss as she jerked her head back, which cracked with a solid thunk against the wall behind her, bringing forth a fresh grimace and whimper.

"Cannae imagine that felt very good," he muttered. "Easy, lass; I'm just cleaning ye up. I mean nae harm to ye." He paused and watched the expressions of pain, discomfort, and confusion play openly across her unguarded features. "Do ye ken what happened?"

The young woman's brows pinched together in concentration, as if trying to solve a difficult equation just beyond her reach. "Brrr-ick." The tone of her words was cultured, despite her speech itself coming slowly haltingly, and her dialect was clearly not of the present locale. As it was clear now that she wasn't any sort of street girl, her clothing suggested a high-borne aristocrat. "Rose..." She paused and inhaled shakily, her gaze skipping here and there with uncertainty. "Rose... no... brick." She gave a soft grunt of frustrated anger.

He fought back a small grin at the sight of what had to be a usually picture-perfect gentlewoman in a fine fit, and possibly too deep into her cups for clear speech. "Ye've had a bump on the head, lass; confusion's right common. Take a slow breath, and try again," he urged gently, briefly patting the back of her hand before he went back using the cloth and bowl of water to rid her hair of some of the mess that had matted near the unseen injury. "Where'd ye hail from?"

"Ro-rose. No," she stammered, then scowled. "Brick waa-water, no..." Her brow puckered again, this time in what appeared to be frustration and confusion alike.

His movements slowed, his mind beginning to arrange and rearrange the scant pieces of information he'd gleaned in an attempt to make sense of the nonsensical. "How about yer name, instead, then?"

"Rose... rose. No. Rose. Brick waaa-water. No. Red. Red rose." The frustration in her features gave way to slow rising panic; her eyes glittered with tears, and her chin began to quiver. "R-rose..." Soft whimpers of distress came between quick, shallow gasps, and her slender form began to tremble until he felt the very bench beneath him shake. Her hand groped within her sleeve until she pulled free a delicate handkerchief and held it to her nose and mouth in an effort to hide her emotion. His gaze narrowed upon the threads of pink and yellow that decorated the edges, and he blinked in surprise. Setting the blood-tinged water and soiled towel aside, MacDougall tentatively reached for the edge of the cloth in her hand, leaning forward to get a better look.

Roses.

His thumb traced the tiny, hand-embroidered flowers and slowly shook his head. Perhaps the woman wasn't entirely off her rocker, after all.

The young woman continued battling with her sentiments, and a pang hit him in his core. He certainly didn't need the trouble, but far be it from him to leave her alone in such a state. With a sigh, he wrapped his hands around hers and held them in a steady clasp. "Breathe, wee lass." One hand slid to the table and, using his fingertips, he nudged the snifter of brandy towards her. "Take a sip or two, if'n ye feel up to it. Might help clear out the cobwebs."

The look of disgust that immediately crossed her features drew a low rumble of amusement from him. "Suppose yer not a fan of good strong drink then."

She wrinkled her nose, answering his supposition by her very expression.

"Nor am I." He pushed the glass a little closer, noticing with pleasure that the distraction had lessened her shaking. "Might try it anyway."

After a moment's hesitation, she finally reached for the snifter. But she paused and stared at her gloved hand, then spread her hands, palms up, to study both. The palms of the fine material were in tatters now, and she eased each off and set them on the bench beside her. Another moment of study revealed that her skin, while red and a scraped, didn't seem to have any gaping wounds that needed tending. Glancing to the brandy again, she slowly reached for it with a trembling hand that didn't obey her commands. Finally, she gave up and used her left to lift the glass to her lips, and promptly set it down with a grimace of distaste.

While she'd taken a slow appraisal of her own hands, he took that moment to move to the bench on the opposite side of the table, giving the clearly distressed woman a bit of room and space to herself, and himself as well. He was fairly certain she wasn't entirely mad or of any danger to him, but the woman had yet to speak even a single logical word in response to his questions. Better to be on the safe side for now. "Suppose there's little reason to introduce myself. Would be a sight more proper to have someone else introduce us. But the name's MacDougall, Arran MacDougall." He paused, then peered curiously at her. "Can ye say MacDougall?"

Her brows furrowed in concentration. "Doo, no. Maaa… madudle," she slurred. A crestfallen expression flashed across her face then, and he shrugged a shoulder and sat back.

He fought a smirk. "Never ye mind; I've been called worse in my day." The serving girl came back then to check on them, and when she did, he ordered a plate of roasted chicken and potatoes, a bowl of strong broth if they had it, bread, and some tea. The poor woman across the table had the glassy look of one still dazed. "Think ye could eat a bite?"

"Hm?" Her attention refocused upon the man across the table. Perceiving that he waited for an answer, her brows lifted and she gave him a faint smile.

"Good enough," he replied.

She smiled distractedly as she slowly searched the confines of her coat, and her eyes suddenly lit up. After a moment, she produced a small pouch that appeared to have been fastened to the inside of her garment using a ribbon. Easing it open, she peeked inside with the enthusiasm of a small child opening a Christmas gift. One by one she removed the contents: a coin purse evidently full, a lace fan, a small handheld glass, a folded fabric envelope, a clean and folded pocket handkerchief also embroidered with flowers, a small metal box with an odd latticed grill on one side, a closed metal box that rattled when she set it down, and a half a dozen gold hairpins. Her eyes flicked across her dining companion with a faint blush of embarrassment; he simply waved his hand in silent permission.

She looked herself over quickly in the mirror. She fiddled with one of the long hairpins for a moment, but appeared to have some difficulty with her right hand, even after she strove to flex her fingers a bit. So with her left leading the way, and small assistance from her strangely lame one, she ordered her rather wild and untamed hair back into suitable containment with the few precious pins. MacDougall found it remarkable that so small a change could make such a marked difference; she went from wild street creature to almost genteel within the span of a few minutes.

Her eyes fell upon her coin purse, and she fumbled with the strings until it was opened, and she pulled free a few shillings and shakily extended them across the table.

His brow shot up at the offer and eyed the money, glanced back to her face, and with a wry quirk of his lips, reached out and lightly pushed her hand back toward her. "I never let a lady pay for food."

Delicate eyebrows furrowed, and he bit back a chuckle. At least she was showing the slightest bit of spirit. "I'll not budge, lass. Keep yer coin."

Having lost the argument, she began replacing her items, beginning with the money, back into the pouch, but she paused over the handkerchief, unfolding it absently, taking a moment to stare at it as if it were some new specimen. The tips of her fingers traced over the floral pattern embroidered along the edges, and her gaze narrowed at something stitched in one corner.

"Can ye tell me, or show me, anything that would help? Anything in that bag of yourn?" he interrupted quietly, his arms folded upon the table, his posture leaning toward her in interest.

Her eyes came up again and searched his, her mouth opening and closing with uncertainty. By way of answer, she silently handed him the handkerchief, pointing to the corner.

Taking it gingerly between his fingers, he studied the elegantly embroidered initials. "M.E.," he read aloud, then flipped the handkerchief back to show her. "Your initials are M.E."

He quietly regarded the young woman sitting across from him more carefully. He peered at her facial expression, the somewhat confused, pleading aspect to her gaze. Was it possible? Given his profession, he'd seen ample examples of what a sharp blow to the head could do, although this was new even to him. Was she so injured that somehow she'd become unable to recall even the simplest of words?

"M.E. Does that sound familiar to ye?" he asked, struggling to keep his frustration out of his tone of voice.

"R-Rose," she shook her head, a frown on her lips. "No. Erm… brick. Water."

That was hardly helpful, but for her sake, he schooled his features to reflect only mild interest rather than the discouragement and frustration he was beginning to feel. "M.E." he mused again aloud. "Well, as yer needing a name, yer to be Emmy for now, least til yer able to correct me," he teased gently, handing the handkerchief back to the addled woman. "Emmy Rose. Lovely name, that." She merely watched him. He supposed carrying the conversation would be up to him, if there was to be one at all. He'd never relished in shallow pleasantries; in fact, this was the longest he'd talked to the same person in months, and this one wasn't even saying anything! But then, how else was he meant to help her? His own moral compass wouldn't allow him to leave her until he was sure she was safe, though at the moment, he was ready to toss said moral compass out the nearest window.

Though the serving girl set their meal before them and he began to partake of it, his gaze never wavered from the woman seated across from him, watching her intently, searching for any sign of guile or deception in her.

Margaret, or 'Emmy' as he was calling her, threw her handkerchief to the table with a huff of frustration and disgust, her posture deflating in a slump against the booth's corner. What was the matter with her? Why did half of her body feel as if it were still asleep? Why couldn't she get her words to obey? Why couldn't she even speak her own name? She understood well enough why her head and eyes ached so abominably; it had become obvious that she'd injured herself when the stranger had begun poking about the left side of her head. But then how did that explain how she arrived in this out of the way hamlet of a village? Or why every attempt at communication ended with muddled nonsense? This man must think her entirely mad and would send her to Bedlam before long unless she could make him understand, make anyone understand!

Her gaze again lifted and sought his, and though he ate his supper with apparent relish, his own gaze hadn't wandered from her face. With every emotion she possessed, she besought him with her eyes and expression, praying he might interpret her helplessness and aid her, not abandon her. *Help me!* "Brr-rick." *I haven't any idea where I am!* "Brick waa-water." *I'm frightened!* "Brick. Water... rose." *Please, help me!*

The man, Mr. MacDougall he had called himself, paused mid-bite and lifted his brows in slight question. "Miss?"

Pity and kindness shone in his eyes, but she had no way to request his continued assistance. The full weight of what this meant slammed into her with almost crushing force. She was left completely alone and at the mercy of this man, this village, and she did not even have her own name. How was she ever to explain where her home was? How was she to even *return* home?

Her breathing hitched and the table's few contents swam before her eyes. She was alone. The colour leached from her face. *Alone.* Her breathing became shallow, unsteady, and her hands reached to grip the edge of the table as if it were a lifeline. *Alone.* Her vision began to tunnel and dark spots appeared around the periphery; she swayed where she sat. *Utterly, hopelessly alone.*

"Breathe, lass."

She had been so lost to Oblivion that the warmth from his hand upon hers had not immediately registered. With a flutter of eyelids as if waking from a dream, she inhaled sharply, fairly gasping for regular breath, and the shadows gradually receded from the edges of her vision. His hand remained where it was, clasping hers with gentle, steady pressure, and she clung desperately to it, a tether to some small measure of stability.

Only after several moments had passed, once the fear and hopelessness had receded from her expression, did the man withdraw his hand. She instantly felt the loss of it.

"There. Roses back in yer cheeks, where they belong," he replied with a small grin, "if ye'll forgive the pun, lass."

She huffed a soft laugh in response, closing her eyes against the brightness of the room as much as against the rising desolations of her circumstance.

"I heard a riddle once: How do ye eat an elephant?" he asked suddenly, lifting his fork with a piece of chicken skewered to it.

She started, and her gaze snapped to his face in utter stupefaction. Why in heaven was he speaking of eating elephants?

"One bite at a time," he answered, his teeth sliding the morsel from the tines to chew thoughtfully.

Margaret continued to stare at him, lashes fluttering in bewilderment; the man had lost his senses.

He chuckled. "Ye've a big problem. Small steps can lead to big solutions. Ye've need of a place to sit and think. A safe haven, as it were. The good news is that yer not without means. Ye can take a room anywhere for as long as ye have need and give yerself a quiet place to rest, sort things out. I've seen injuries the likes of yourn before."

She quirked a dubious brow. *The likes of mine, says he.* As if he had ever met with another who could not string together two logical words.

Mr. MacDougall chuckled again. "All right, not exactly like yourn, but ye ken my meaning. Once yer settled, once yer head knows yer well and safe, things'll return to ye. Just ye wait."

Her expression remained skeptical.

For a moment he appeared as if he would let the one-sided conversation drop, but he finally continued after chewing through another bite of his meal. "I'm a fighter, a pugilist if ye want specifics. I fight other men for money, and as such, seen my share of knocks to the head and the effects. Some recover as if nothing were wrong; others've lost a few hours of memory, sometimes more than. At least it seems ye ken what I'm saying." His eyes narrowed and he leaned forward on his forearms. "Ye *can* understand me, can ye not?"

More or less. She had never before heard such a deep Scots brogue, and it warmed her through. Her head tipped this way and that with a teasing sparkle in her eye as if to mock him for his strong accent and missing parts of words.

"If it would please the lady, I could speak in this manner instead." He slipped easily into the most genteel of dialects that would have had him fitting in at any ballroom in Town during the height of the Season, and her brows shot upward in pleased surprise. "So you do prefer an uppercrust gentleman."

She rolled her eyes a little, and he chuckled, returning to his native accent, one that she preferred if she were to be honest with herself. "Least ye ken a wee bit."

She rather missed that one, and she stared.

Mr. MacDougall grinned. "Ken's our Scottish way of saying understanding a thing."

Her expression eased with his explanation, though her face was a study of puzzlement and concentration, along with a squint of pain that was becoming more permanent in her face.

"Ye've not had a sip of tea; can ye try?" He pushed the cup closer toward her, and she reached for it clumsily with her usual hand, focus and determination setting her features.

"Tis a start. Can ye lift it?"

She bobbled the cup when it left the table, and he caught it before anything spilled. "Try yer left, lass."

With a scowl of displeasure, she switched hands and was more successful in lifting it to her lips for a slow drink. Her stomach turned over with sickness and she quickly set the cup back upon the table, nudging it away.

"Yer head pains ye, aye? And yer belly's a mite ill?" he guessed. There was only one time in his career that he'd been hit so hard as to suffer for days after, and he still recalled the headache that accompanied him that week. "I ken well the last thing ye want is to put something in yer belly, but try." He tore one of the thick slices of brown, velvety bread in half and offered it across the table, this time extending it toward her left hand first.

After a moment, she capitulated and accepted the bread, nibbling at it slowly. Mr. MacDougall pushed the cup of tea closer once more, having noticed she had a little trouble controlling her right. When she glanced at him, he nodded at it. "Finish what yer able, and I'll take ye along, make sure yer safely settled."

She gave a slight glance around the room.

"This is merely a pub," he offered, guessing at her thoughts. "No rooms hereabouts. But we'll find a carriage house for the night. Should be at least one. We're some distance from the railroad, if my memory serves me, but it shouldna take overly long to walk, small hamlet like this. Ye'll be far safer in a carriage house, as well; little chance of being robbed of yer coin like before."

She started in fear. What was he saying about her coin?

"Caught a young flimp trying to pinch yer coin when I came upon ye in the street. Dressed in those riches, yer lucky he didn't beat ye to get at yer purse, or worse."

What little colour she regained quickly drained from her face and a hand fluttered up by her throat in distress. He grimaced and scrubbed a hand over his face. "Forgive me. I'm not used to keeping company with a lady so refined as yerself. I just meant to say that this is a far cry from a safe spot for ye, and I'll take ye somewhere that's decent enough for ye to stay the night."

Between the nausea already settled in her stomach and the fear of what she'd evidently escaped, the unfinished bit of bread was set on the side of the man's now emptied plate. Her gaze slid over the table and, with delight, she noticed she hadn't put away the vinaigrette that had materialised from her purse. She grasped at it and brought it eagerly to her face, inhaling deeply. The aromas of mint and lavender filled her nose, and the grip that headache and nausea had upon her eased for the moment.

Mr. MacDougall left money on the table and stood beside the bench, his hand extended to her. "Can ye walk?" he asked quietly.

She looked at his hand and unconsciously bit at her lower lip. What would her family think if they bore witness to this? With a small sigh, she slipped the dainty metal box back into the reticule, then replaced the torn and soiled gloves upon her hands, one at a time, fumbling so greatly with her right hand that the man finally knelt down at her side and finished the task for her. How mortifying! She could not even draw on her own gloves without assistance.

If the man minded, he didn't show it. Instead, those impossibly dark eyes smiled into her as he stood and again extended his hand, palm up. "Come, lass. Ye should be tucked away to rest."

Chapter Three

It had been twilight when they'd entered the pub, but full dark had fallen now, the oily tendrils of smoke from the gas lamps snaking their way into the air. MacDougall was on high alert. The woman by his side would have stuck out even if she were dressed in the same style as the village's occupants, but in her finery of silk and velvet, bedraggled though it was, she made a tempting target. He kept her safely between himself and the walls of buildings that lined the thoroughfare, letting her set their pace to whatever was manageable for her.

He stole a quick glance down at Emmy.

Miss Emmy, cannae forget the 'Miss,' his brain corrected him. Despite the name being a fabrication based on a pair of embroidered initials, he felt that it was important to think of her in formal terms. All this was but a detour. He would spirit her to safety then return to his life and plans.

He watched her from the corner of his eye for a moment and could not help but be impressed. Her head was high, her back straight. Despite her soiled fine attire, the woman still managed to look elegant, almost regal. She did not walk as other people did, she glided, practically floated, graceful in her gait despite the pain he knew she was feeling and the tiniest limp that he only noticed because he had searched for it. Her struggle became more evident as her pace slowed, though she maintained her fluid stride all the while, and he began scanning the wood signs hanging overhead for another inn that would not be so far a walk, lest he might end up having to carry her through town.

A stone's throw ahead advertised a place to stay by a sign which simply read *Inn*. With the feel of eyes upon them, the need to quickly get her off the street urged at him. So much for making it to a proper carriage house. His strides lengthened, and though he knew she struggled to keep up, he kept propelling them forward until he was able to tug the inn's door open and usher her inside with his hand flat between her shoulder blades.

She hesitated and peered in confusion up at him, but he nudged her further within. "Go inside and wait for me," he commanded softly in a low, even tone. He pulled the door closed before she had a further chance to pause, and he turned to face the threat he'd known to be closing in on them.

A pack of four young men sauntered towards them. One of these was the sneak thief that he had put a boot to earlier that evening. The other three were members of the street gang that the pickpocket belonged to. When asked by the others why he hadn't brought anything of value to the gang's coffers, the pickpocket told them what had happened to him. To the minds of the gang, this was an affront not to be tolerated: their effectiveness was enhanced by the fear that they generated. One of their own being pushed about was a bad sign as it hinted at weakness in a group that couldn't protect one of their own. The pickpocket had given the others a description of the man who had kicked him on the backside, and they had set out to find him and rectify things.

And now, here he was, right in front of them.

"Oi! Wanker!" one of the four yelled as he pointed at MacDougall and drew nearer. "Are you the daft bastard who put the boot to my lad Marty?'

He offered no verbal response, only stood still as a statue as the group drew nearer.

The pickpocket who'd been rifling through her clothes, Marty, pointed at the big man. "Aye, that's him!"

"Well, it appears an anointin' is in ord—"

Before the lead could finish his threat, MacDougall's fist crashed squarely into his face. The force of the blow spun the tough violently to one side, and he landed half in, half out of a puddle of dirty water. He was unconscious, completely out cold.

MacDougall didn't stop with that. The now unconscious leader of the gang was right: a beating *was* in order. While the other three stared in slack-jawed surprise at their prone leader, MacDougall kicked the next closest one in the chest. It was a loud, heavy, thudding blow that threw the recipient into the street. This one crashed to the ground, his sternum cracked, several ribs broken. He wheezed like ill-played bagpipes as he tried to breathe, and hovered precariously about consciousness. MacDougall snatched the next closest by the collar and slammed him against the front of the inn hard enough to render him unconscious.

Dropping this one to the ground, he turned to pin Marty the less-than-tough with a menacing stare. "Ye've a bone to pick?" he asked. His tone was calm and even, but there was a definite element of menace to it.

"N–no…" Marty stammered as he turned white as chalk.

MacDougall took a step towards him, who immediately threw both hands up, as if in surrender.

"I dinnae think as much. Go home and change yer sit-upons; ye've wet yerself."

Without another glance at any of the four, MacDougall turned about and returned to where his pretty charge now cowered in the doorway. Her hand was covering her mouth, her eyes wide as saucers as she beheld in stunned silence the brutal handling of the group of young thugs. By the time he returned to her side, she was trembling from head to toe, her breath sawing in and out in uneven little gasps, eyes dewy with unshed tears as she stared unblinkingly at the three discarded men strewn about the ground.

Her mouth opened and closed with soft whimpers, and he set gentle hands to her shoulders, turned her around, and walked her back into the tiny reception room of the inn. "I'm sorry ye had to see that," he murmured to her as they crossed the room to the attendant seated behind a worn wooden counter.

"We've need of a pair of rooms for myself and the lady."

The man behind the table snatched the only remaining key from the wall behind him and tossed it to MacDougall. "The room's all yours, but that's all there is. We're full up. There's a bout in town tomorrow."

One room.

For the both of them.

He bit back a groan. *Bloody hell.* As if the lady hadn't been traumatised enough already.

With Miss Emmy still in shock from what she'd witnessed, he fished the money to cover the cost of the room out of his pocket and laid it on the counter, then accorded the desk clerk a nod.

"Number six, upstairs," the desk clerk announced as he collected the room fee and handed him an already lit candlestick.

Taking her gently by the arm, MacDougall shepherded her to the stairwell and eased her up the steps. She allowed him to guide her mechanically, absently, as though her feet and legs were moving of their own accord. Once they arrived at the correct floor, he walked them down the hall to the room. Unlocking the door, he gently ushered her inside.

In she went and he followed on her heels, a sweep of the room taking in the simple furnishings of a narrow cot of a bed, tiny nightstand with pitcher and bowl, small writing table and matching chair, a closet, a foggy looking glass hanging on one wall, and a single sconce. No hearth. He was muttering under his breath as he closed the door behind him and locked it, pocketing the key. He guided her to sit in the only chair then paced away to light the other candle. That done, the candlestick was set down beside the bowl and pitcher and his hands were set to his hips, his brain turning over their circumstances and what ought to be done.

"B-brick… red brick… red… red…"

The timid voice behind him had him glancing back over a shoulder, and his features softened a little at the sight of her obvious distress. Running a hand down the length of his face, he bit back a sigh. "They're not dead; just… uhm… sleeping." Her haunted eyes tracked his movements, not warily, but not entirely trusting either. He sighed again. "They'd have done far worse to ye if they'd've gotten past me somehow," he admitted. "Most folks hereabouts are not the respectable types yer used to."

She looked so vulnerable, so lost. An unpleasant ache settled deep in his chest and he scowled. He cleared his throat and took stock of the room while Miss Emmy sat still as a statue, and just as expressionless.

"Uhm, ye take the bed, of course; I'll sleep in the hall, just outside the door. Oughtta be extra blankets in the closet," he offered in a genial, conversational tone, and then he went to verify the contents. Opening the closet door, he did find two spare blankets that he'd supposed would be there. One was tossed on the end of the bed for her use, and the other slung over his arm on his way to the door.

"Ow. Maaa… ow."

He stopped with his hand on the knob and twisted to glance at her. She'd moved to the bed but had yet to sit, her gaze fixed instead on the window as if she could see the bodies of the men below.

He scrubbed a hand down his face. "I'm sorry, lass. I wanted ye to go inside so ye'd not witness all that. Those lads were part of a street gang; one of them was searching through yer effects when I came upon ye." He paused, then continued. "These types only ken one thing: force. I had to convince them that going after ye again would be folly, and rather... dangerous to their continued health. But I'm sorry to have caused ye more distress; 'tis the last thing ye needed."

As if considering his words, she stood quietly for a long moment, biting at her lower lip before finally giving a small jerking nod of her head, as if she hadn't full control over herself just then.

He supposed that was as good as he was going to get. "Ye need rest, Miss Emmy. Sleep. None'll get through me." With that, he stuck the key in the lock on her side then walked through to the hall, firmly pulling the door closed behind him.

It took some time to drift into the restless sleep that finally claimed her, hours perhaps. She was incredibly uncomfortable, having no way to remove her day clothing and all the layers beneath it. She was also highly aware of the man that had access to her just on the other side of the door, a stranger she had not known even three hours earlier, and yet the sole person in the whole world she could call a friend just now. She wondered if he had been able to find sleep any easier than herself. Both candles had been extinguished, but ambient light from a street lamp streamed upward through a part in the nearly threadbare curtains, providing just enough illumination to outline the unfamiliar surroundings of the room. Finally, at long last, her mind dropped into numb slumber.

A faceless giant in an impeccable suit of clothes chased her through a shadowy labyrinth. She tore around a corner, coming to an abrupt halt when she came upon a plain-faced nurse dressed all in white, holding a silver tray, upon which stood a floral teapot and matching cup of steaming tea. "You should drink, little miss. I know how exhausted you must be. Really, a cup of tea will refresh you." She shook her head, eying the cup warily. The nurse advanced. "But your medicine. It's imperative that you take your medicine." I do not need medicine! *she wanted to shout, but her voice had been stolen away. Her feet remained rooted to the spot as the nurse came ever closer, the face contorting until it was nothing but a dark void. "Drink it. You must drink it," the nurse hissed. She twisted round to see if there was safety behind her, and instead found the suited behemoth bearing down upon where she stood. Though her mind shouted at her to run, she couldn't move, frozen in place as if she were made of stone. She was lifted up into impossibly strong arms and hurled into the void where she plummeted down, down, down. "No one will find you, my dove," echoed a man's voice around her, and his laughter followed her as darkness swallowed her.*

A gasping breath tore from her throat as she thrashed in a tangle of sheets and blankets, trying to free herself from whatever kept her fettered. Her gaze flew wildly about the sparse room, seeing nothing through the midnight dimness. Her mind remained locked away in the chains of her nightmare, and her lips parted in terrified scream.

The scream from the room at his back pierced MacDougall's slumber and he sat bolt upright from his place on the floor in the hall. It took him a moment to sort things out, and within a few seconds he was on his feet and quietly entering, surprised that she had neglected to lock the door behind him when she had gone to bed. He took quick stock of the small bedroom. The window was closed, the curtains undisturbed. Aside from that, they were two stories above street level, out of reach of any common thief in the area. Since he could quickly determine that no one had broken into the room, that left one other possibility: she must have been having a nightmare. Plucking his boots, coat, and blanket from the hall, he dropped them just inside the room before closing the door and padding quietly across the floor. He was bare of foot, but still had on his trousers with shirt untucked and collar unbuttoned.

"Miss?" he called gently aloud as he neared the bed. "Yer safe, lass. There's none here but us."

He dropped to perch on the edge of the bed, and he gently laid his hand upon one of her forearms. "Miss Emmy. Lass. Yer dreaming."

She gasped the moment his hand touched her arm and shot away from him, scrabbling backwards as if she wanted to climb the wall. But at last, her eyes finally focused on the figure perched on the bed a few feet away, his palms forward and arms slightly out in the universal sign of peace-keeping, and the breath she'd been holding came out in a rush. She tumbled forward into him, curling against him and clutching his shirt while burying her face into the fabric. Her body trembled against him as she fought to get as close to his warmth and comfort as possible, so closely, in fact, that he could feel her heart hammering against his own chest.

"Uhm, easy there. It, uhm, 'twas only a bad dream," he offered stiffly, his entire body wooden and unyielding. He gave her back an awkward pat to assuage her anxiety, but as her body began to tremble with the aftereffects of her nightmare, he gradually folded his arms around her, stroking her upper arms in a slow, soothing rhythm. "Yer safe. Dinnae fash yerself, lassie. None'll hurt ye while I'm here," he murmured, his accent thicker, his voice huskier.

A harsh pound on the door had his gaze swinging around, and he disentangled himself from her arms and went to see who he assumed was a concerned innkeeper.

Sure enough, there stood the man who had been downstairs, his feet bared and a candlestick in hand. "You planning to keep yer misses screaming all night?" the keeper muttered.

His ire stoked red hot at the dirty implication, but he mashed his lips together to fight back the threat he wanted to let fly. "Nae. Just a nightmare. We'll be quiet as church mice." Without letting the man speak further, MacDougall slammed the door and returned to where the girl was huddled, eyes almost too wide in her face, her arms locked around her knees. With a sigh, he took a seat at the foot of the bed, as far away as possible from where she sat in a tight ball of fear. She was already terrified; he had no desire to make it worse. "I promise yer safe. I'll even sit up and keep watch. Try to sleep again."

But she, evidently, had other ideas. Crawling frantically to him, she wrapped her arms firmly about his chest and burrowed closer, hot tears streaming from her eyes. Her shoulders shook with silent sobs, which soon gave way to soft hiccoughs as she attempted to pull herself back together. He lightly draped his arms about her, unsure about what else he ought to do, and waited for her to calm enough to return to her pillow. However, her form gradually relaxed and went still, then limp as sleep claimed her right where she was.

Clearing his throat gently, MacDougall craned his head down at an almost impossible angle to try and see her face. Though he was unable to catch sight of it, it was clear she'd fallen asleep against him, and biting back a growl, he tried to puzzle out what to do next. He didn't need much sleep to begin with, but he did require at least a little, particularly since he had a much anticipated match the very next evening. *No, this evening.*

After a light attempt to rouse her, he finally decided to prop himself up in a sitting position, with his back to the headboard. It took a bit of careful shifting and wriggling, but he finally managed the desired position on the bed without rousing the sleeping woman. She was still pressed against his side, with her head pillowed on his chest and shoulder.

His position upon her bed wasn't the most pressing issue in his mind at the moment. Rather, it was that he could easily make out the rounded swell of a small but well-formed mound beneath the front of the gown, and worse, he could feel it against his own chest. *Keep yer eyes up, ye eejit*, he scolded himself. It was not the gentlemanly thing to do! Even if he was not one in name, he was determined to behave as such with her. She deserved it of him. But she was pressed so closely to him. He was far from a prude, and it had been so long…

He grunted and forcefully averted his gaze in self-contempt.

Miss Emmy slumbered on; for MacDougall, sleep was a bit more evasive. Not only was he unaccustomed to sleeping literally wrapped up by another person, but what felt like small sticks continued to poke and prod him through his shirt from where her head rested. Fighting down an annoyed growl, his hand finally lifted to search through the curled tresses for the offenders, and his finger and thumb came up with a pin. That's all it was: a hair pin. In the dark he stared at the small object. How did this slight, bent piece of metal keep everything in place? Of course he'd watched her put it all back up, but still! Another poke revealed that there was more than one, and he absently began to pluck each feminine torture device free until all the wealth of hair was let loose to cascade down her back and over his arm. He stared at it. Did all women's hair look like a river of spun silk the way hers did? In wonder, his fingers sifted through the soft ribbons of hair before he targeted a singular lock and rubbed it back and forth between his thumb and fingertips, relishing in its impossible softness. A tantalizing aroma wafted up from her waves now fully unbound.

In spite of himself, he bent his head to inhale the scent of her.

And he immediately regretted it.

She trusted him to keep her safe, and he felt like a reprobate for the liberties he was taking. True enough, there was no way she would know, but he knew better, and she deserved the utmost respect. He simply had to keep himself in line. She was in distress and he only existed in her world to help her find her way back to her friends, nothing more. As soon as she was safe, he would pass out of her sphere and return to his own. That was that.

Tugging the blanket up over her sleeping form, he finally drifted off himself, the scent of her hair haunting his dreams while his arms tightened unconsciously about her.

Chapter Four

A hazy plume of blue smoke snaked upward from a pipe, creating a sinister halo about the oiled golden hair of a handsome, well-dressed gentleman seated against one window of the first car. The young man was feeling quite cocksure of his little scheme, and this had been no short-sighted, simple feat, either.

From a young age, he developed a taste and desire for the finer things in life, and they had always seemed just out of reach. Being the fourth son of a baron, there was little chance of any inheritance passing to him unless a wealthy relative suddenly materialised from the proverbial woodwork, and then of course said relative would first have to die before any money passed to him. But as of yet, there were no wealthy relatives to give him a fortune. His elder brother, twelve years his senior, would inherit house and title from their father; the second brother had made the military his career, the third pursued law. He was not so inclined to work as hard as his siblings; it was much easier to demand that which he wanted and be utterly churlish and disruptive until the house relented for the sake of peace. Even his father gave way before his bully of a younger son.

But tyrannising one's own household could only go so far in regards to any sort of inheritance, thus he decided, as quite a young teenager, to pin his hopes of wealth to a woman who would bring such to a marriage.

Having set his sights upon Miss Margaret Everleigh, the comely young girl who came with a dowry which would keep him in exquisite comfort for decades, he dogged the activities of the Saxon family who had taken in the orphaned cousin. He spent season after season ingratiating himself to London's cherished beauty that he might find favour in her eyes. He had been quietly laying plans for months within the circle of their social acquaintances, dropping small hints in their ears regarding his concern over Margaret's health, spinning stories of regular headaches, flagging memory, and sudden fits of irrational pique that dissipated just as quickly. Once those seeds had been sown, he quietly made it known to their circle that he sought to take her north to a country retreat outside Newcastle, a retreat that was an utterly fabricated location. There, he claimed, she could rest well away from the bustle of London's dizzying social schedule, and once she had time to rest, he planned to propose. They had, after all, been courting for months and he finally decided to press his suit and make it official, joining their families at last as her parents surely would have wanted. Their friends had been ecstatic for them and eagerly promised to keep his secret about it all, as he had wanted to surprise his lady love.

To Margaret, herself, he spun yet another story about a poor, elderly aunt who relied upon him to make her final days pleasant. With the dear aunt's health steadily declining, this might be his last chance to see her. Would not Margaret please join him? She was so lovely and diverting that his beloved aunt could not help but improve and, with any luck, her days with them might be prolonged. Confused and irritated, but with a heart that longed to help and bring comfort to anyone who needed it, and given that she was perfectly amenable to dodging part of the Season in Town, Margaret had assented.

Hattie Stewart, his actual lover of nearly a year, had been employed to go along as companion. With Margaret's notoriously soft heart, playing up to her sympathy had been a cinch. A fable was expertly recounted of how Hattie had lost her previous position and how her invalid mother relied heavily upon Hattie's meagre income… if only the girl could but find temporary employment until a more permanent position was secured. Margaret had not wanted an unknown companion for such a lengthy excursion, but she figured it was as easy as not to hire this girl on for a month or so. Besides, she promised her regular companion, Cossett, time to return home, and a chaperone was indeed needed. So, rather than taking one of the undermaids from her townhouse, Margaret had conceded to take on this Miss Stewart instead. Just as he'd planned.

The man allowed a private sneer to curl his upper lip; Margaret had been as easy to mould as clay in a potter's skilful hands.

Patience had paid off at long last, and the finish line was just ahead. Even now, with Margaret resting in a private berth with a headache of their own devising, Hattie was steeping a special tea for her new mistress, the brew laced with a potent sedative he provided. It would make controlling her that much easier. Only he and his Hattie knew their real destination: a private asylum across the Solway Firth in Scotland by way of Whitehaven in Cumberland. He had already agreed by contract to continue sending sums of money to fund Dr. Mortimer Cross's experiments as long as Miss Everleigh was kept in a pliant stupor. The good doctor had only been too happy to comply with the promise of such wealthy patronage. Besides which, it certainly wasn't the first time a woman had been shut away by put-upon relatives. No less than a dozen of his patients hadn't a single ailment when they first came to him, and legitimate madness was only a few months down the road once locked behind the doors of Moorsgate Lunatic Asylum.

He exhaled again, sending another cloud into the already thick air of the car. Hattie had been pestering him for months regarding marriage, but with the Everleigh fortune at his ready disposal, he could fly far higher than the ruined daughter of a country gentleman. Of course she need not know that; let her believe he would marry her and help return her respectability. Perhaps he would keep her on after all, at least until he was quite ready to sever their ties permanently.

At that moment, the very creature of his thoughts appeared in the doorway to the car, her brows pinched and face panicked. Extinguishing his cigar, he unfolded his length from the velvet upholstered seat and walked briskly to join her in the interim between the cars.

"She's gone!" Hattie blurted before he had even fully closed the door behind him.

"Quiet! Keep your voice down!" he hissed as he snagged her by the elbow and steered her to a corner.

"I went to take her the tea, just as you instructed, but the bed was empty! Her boots, her coat, her bonnet; there's no sign of her!"

"She is most likely walking about to stretch her legs, or went in search of a cup of tea for herself," he assured.

"No, I already checked with the porter onboard. Indeed, she is nowhere to be found!" Hattie cried, wringing her hands together fretfully. "Do you think she could have overheard us?"

"Impossible! She would never stoop to eavesdropping," but even with that assurance, the seed of doubt had been planted within his brain.

"But if she heard!" mewled the girl pathetically. "What if she went to the authorities? Oh, Phillip!"

Biting back a growl, he gathered the puling woman in his arms and swallowed down his irritation, smoothing his voice to the silky, reassuring cadence that always charmed unsuspecting women. "Now now, my dove. Worry not. Did I not promise I would take care of you, come what may? Why do you not go lie down in Miss Margaret's berth, and I will come to you with a fresh cup of hyson, prepared with honey just the way you like. Then we will calmly discuss what ought to be done." He tipped her face up with a firm touch beneath her chin and pressed his lips against her forehead, brushing a lock of strawberry gold away from her face and waiting until the trust returned to her eyes before he deigned to bestow a smile upon her. "There's a good girl. I'll be with you in ten minutes."

Hattie returned the smile and dabbed her tears away with her fingertips before she nodded resolutely and left to do his bidding. His grin vanished behind a snarl of annoyance as he went to find the porter, one hand slipping into his pocket to finger the vial of arsenic stoppered and awaiting further use. There were benefits to having toyed with medical school, after all, and it would not be the first time he'd sullied his hands to get what he wanted.

Chapter Five

MacDougall was an early riser out of habit. Every day at five o'clock, regardless of season, special occasion, or weather, with his mind wound like a clock, he would climb out of bed, dress, go for a two hour run, then eat a quick breakfast. Every. Single. Day. As it was a bit after five now, and the lady did not appear as though she would wake any time soon, today would be an exception to the previously unbroken rule. He was trapped, held captive by the soft chains of Emmy's hair and slumbering form.

Miss Emmy, blast it all. Keeping the formality prominent in his mind felt most important. They would part ways soon.

He was restless, and for more than one reason. First, his body and mind were already in gear. It was time to get up and go; he had never been the type to laze away the morning when he could be up and about being productive, and his routine had never been interrupted before. Second, he hadn't been this intimately close to a woman for quite some time. Unlike many of his counterparts, MacDougall was not a promiscuous man, nor was he prudish. He enjoyed carnal intimacy, of course, but it was not the end-all-be-all of his existence, as seemed to be the case with so many others. He had regularly passed on offers of a non-committal exchange from some very attractive women. As a result, he had not shared a bed with anyone, intimately or innocently, in, well, years, now he thought of it. Truly, it had never been an experience that he could honestly say he missed enough to pursue, no matter how much his few casual chums railed at him for needing a woman.

Third, while he had lain with some truly beautiful and desirable women, not one of them could have held a candle flame to the slumbering one cradled against him just now. To say that she was beautiful was an understatement of a monumental sort. She was far from just lovely; such a word did not do her justice. No, she was elegant and resplendent, what he considered almost ethereal in her physical splendour. Her hair smelled soft and sweet; her skin, where he could see it, was flawless. When her eyes were open, they were wide and brilliant, and a most peculiar colour, like a melding of wine brown and dark amber. Her entire form seemed to be slight and willowy, slight of waist with slender limbs. Her chest didn't strain at the front of her dress the way a doxie's did, but he had the feeling that they were as pretty and well-formed as was her face.

Not that he was thinking of her breasts!

He grumbled under his breath even as he remained still so as not to disturb her. He couldn't go for his customary run. He couldn't get the scent of her hair out of his nose and mind. He couldn't help but imagine what she might look like without all of the layers of the bulky dress and coat. And the fact that he was so uncontrolled in this moment irked him to no end. He was *always* in control of himself... until now.

What was it about this slip of a woman that upset every increment of restraint and forbearance? Maybe he did need a woman, after all.

He had unconsciously begun to comb his hand through her silken, unbound hair, and it produced a soft moan of sleepy contentment from the woman that startled him into halting his every movement. That had to be the most sensuous sound he had ever before heard in his life, and he felt his body tighten in response to her. She stirred a bit, tensing and relaxing muscles that had remained dormant throughout the night, snuggling nearer to him and her hand, which previously had been pillowed beneath her head, slid across his stomach to curl around the side of his waist. His neck tensed as he swallowed, watching her with rapt attention and willing his body's morning alertness to soften and relax before she woke and noticed it.

MacDougall continued to watch her, still as a statue, willing her back to sleep, and as proof of God's existence, she stilled against him once more and her breathing evened out as deep sleep overcame her again. Her body fully relaxed against him, and gradually, he relaxed as well. Unable to help himself, his fingertips coasted up and down her spine, and eventually he fell back to sleep, one hand curled possessively around her waist.

It was hours later when he awoke again. The sun was streaming brightly through the window, creating a patch of light on the floor which indicated the lateness of the hour. The angel in his arms still slept, and he bent his head to draw her scent into his nose as he had the night before, his conscience blissfully silent this time as he did so.

After a few more sleepy moments, her arm gradually came to life and stiffened enough to lever herself up and off from his chest, and he immediately missed the weight of her against him. Her eyes blinked open, gaze lazily drifting upward until they landed upon his very alert, very awake face. Her gaze tripped into his dark-as-coal eyes and they two stayed frozen there for a long moment while a gentle smile played at her lips. And damned if his gaze didn't skip down to her mouth. That luscious, kissable mouth. If he were to lean just slightly forward…

The sleepy peace didn't last.

Reality evidently crashed into her all at once. With a yip that sounded comically like a startled puppy, she scrambled away and off the bed. A string of nonsensical words and sounds spilled forth, each stumbling over the other in a rush to be vocalised while she hid her burning face in both hands, and she finally crumpled onto the chair in mortification.

While she panicked, he fought to remain calmly situated, at least outwardly. Propping one foot flat on the mattress and casually folding his arms across his chest, he regarded her with a bemused sparkle in his eyes and a gentle, albeit rakish, grin. "Nae harm to me. Ye needed the sleep, and I believe my virtue's still intact," he teased with a wink. "Dinnae fash." Once he was certain he wouldn't embarrass himself, he rose from the bed and padded over to the pile of blankets he had left deserted on the floor by the door when he'd abruptly come in during her nightmare. "Are ye hungry?" he asked as he plucked up a blanket and folded it.

Her hands slowly lowered from her face, though her cheeks were still heavily coloured in humility. She felt dizzy and disjointed; the headache that had seemed to ebb during the night crept forward to settle once more behind her eyes, and her stomach felt sick with emptiness. When she lifted her eyes and saw the man making the bed in which she'd lain, she blinked and stared.

He shot her a boyish grin. "What? Never saw a lad clean up after hisself?"

She actually laughed, a soft merry sound that lit her eyes, and he resolved to try and make that expression appear on her face as often as possible.

"How do ye feel this morn? Any change?" When she didn't respond, he tried another tactic. "Can ye point to where it ails ye?"

Her nose wrinkled and she slowly lifted a timid hand toward the left side of her head, then her throat, and finally down to her belly. "Point, no…" Her features pinched with frustration and she finally dropped her forehead into her hand.

His expression softened. She'd added a few more words to her vocabulary and they almost made sense; that had to be a good sign, didn't it? He crouched before her. "Will ye let me take a look if I promise not to touch it?"

Pursing her lips together, she leaned forward in silent acquiescence.

"I'll be gentle as I can," he vowed as he stood upright only to stoop over her head, fingers parting her hair gingerly to seek out the actual point of injury. The feel of her nerves twitching beneath his fingers was the only indication that he'd located it, and turning her slightly toward the sun's rays streaming through the window, he carefully parted the strands to peer at the wound. He released a breath upon seeing a lack of angry red swelling around the injury, and no signs of yellowed discharge either; just a regular new scab with an understandable amount of swelling.

"Looks better than I could've hoped. I'm thinking ye'll have need to breakfast afore long." He stepped away long enough to swing into his coat, then noticed the handful of hairpins on the tiny nightstand table. With a wry smirk that was only slightly apologetic, he scooped them up and held them out to her. "And, uhm, right sorry am I about yer hair."

She blinked rapidly at him, then her gaze skipped around the room until it fell upon the modest pile of pins. Her face flushed hotly and her hands flew up to her head, palms smoothing over her hair she evidently only just now realised had been let down completely.

"Yer pins were trying to stab me in the night," he explained. "Sorry if such was a liberty against ye." His hand remained extended to her, and he again watched in absolute wonder as she worked rapidly put back into proper order the mass of hair that had cascaded down her back. "Shame ye've need to put it back up."

Her eyes shot to his face and, if possible, her cheeks burned brighter. Her posture straightened as she put her back to him and deftly tamed the wild locks of tawny brown.

More akin to roasted chestnuts.

He cleared his throat with a stifled growl; one evening with her and he was turning into a bloody poet. "I dinnae mean that how it sounded. Only that– what I mean to say is—" He tossed the remaining pins on the writing desk by which she sat and paced away, pushing his hands frustratedly through his hair. "Never ye mind," he muttered. This was why he kept to himself and avoided the society of the perfectly proper. Life was just simpler when left by himself. Introduce one pretty face into his life and he was stumbling over himself like a lad that had his first peek at a lady's bared calf.

"Uhm, we need to get ye some other clyse," he offered abruptly to change the subject.

She had just finished placing the final pin, and she froze, her eyes fluttering in bewilderment as she slowly twisted around to stare at him.

"Clyse," he repeated, then with a rather droll expression, he switched to what he called his toff speech. "*Clothes*, my lady. You do rather draw attention to yourself in our present locale, such as you are."

Her brows furrowed as she glanced down at herself, then she lifted a troubled gaze back to his face.

"We'll get some food in yer belly, then we'll see about some different *clothes*," he emphasised. With a slight jerk of his head in the direction of the door in silent indication, he marched himself through it and yanked it closed behind him.

In the hall he paced the floorboards, shoving his hands through his hair in irritation. What was he doing? This wasn't like him! He had always kept to himself, gone about his life with nothing to tie him to one place or another; he followed the wind, as it were. If he wanted to stay in a town, he stayed; if he wanted to move on, he did so. He preferred his life of solitude, guarded it fiercely, and though he had already planned on staying in this small hamlet for the day and evening, he was already itching to move on.

The reason for it was obvious, and he slung a pointed glare at the closed door, beyond which lay his confounding burden with her glorious wealth of hair and wide sparkling eyes.

Cursing under his breath, he took himself below stairs to relieve himself, and locate the coldest water he could find.

Margaret—*No, Emmy*, she corrected herself; perhaps it would be easier to think of herself with the name this Mr. MacDougall gentleman created— remembered her precious pouch of belongings and eagerly pulled it out from her coat. First, she examined her hair in the glass to ensure it was as neat and orderly as she was able to make it, and added her folded kerchief in a witching way to act as a head-covering. It was no simple feat with only half a dozen pins and a hand that still was not quite obeying the way it should have been.

Odd, that. It rather felt like the prickling sensation that came after one slept upon one's limb for too many hours. It did not ache as if bruised, yet as she stared down at the offending hand, she could not force it to do exactly as she wished, particularly not small, precise movements, such as sliding a hairpin into place.

She glanced around the room and spied a bowl with a cracked pitcher; that would do as well as anything, she supposed. With her left hand, over which she had far more control than her right, she carefully poured cool water into the bowl, then bowed low over it and gently passed handful after handful over her face, scrubbing away the dirt of the street she was certain still streaked her face. There were no towels, so with a wrinkled nose, she used her other handkerchief instead. Seeing the faint streaks of grey upon its white surface created a pang in her heart, and she reminded herself that she just needed to get home and she would have every dainty and clean article at her fingertips

Home. Why did that word cause her stomach to clench with anxiety and her heart to flutter unpleasantly? Slowly sinking to the edge of the bed, she tried to force her mind to recount the events of the previous day. But after several minutes, nothing appeared in her memory before seeing Mr. MacDougall inside the public house. Before that... before that...

Her brows furrowed and her lips tugged downward in a frown. She vaguely remembered packing, although it was entirely possible that memory belonged to a different trip altogether, but the circumstance surrounding whatever had brought her outside her normal sphere of living was nothing but a blank void. Even the name of this village was unknown to her.

How long she sat there, grasping at cobwebs, she didn't know. At the tap at the door, her heart slammed briefly against her chest before a familiar voice called to her from the other side.

"Miss? May I enter?"

Mr. MacDougall. Just the sound of his deep brogue stirred a comfort and assurance in her, even as her heart skipped a little. "Eeee-oh." She huffed in annoyance; being unable to vocalise her thoughts was maddening.

"That's Mr. 'Eee-oh' to ye, lass," he teased as he came in, and he laughed softly when she scowled at him. "Ye needn't call me anything at all, if it vexes ye. Though yer far and away the most fetching lass I've seen when yer annoyed with me."

Her face burned even as she turned her face away.

She heard his footsteps carry him nearer, but he stopped before he reached her side. "Forgive me. As I mentioned, I'm not used to being around society that's as highborn as ye obviously are. I mean no disrespect." When she peered back at him, his hand was on the back of his neck, looking almost sheepish. "We're in a strange situation, me and thee. If I knew without a doubt that I could deliver ye into the hands of yer friends, sure and I would do so. But—" He sighed and went to her, knelt at her side and looked honestly into her face. "Yer injured, yer vulnerable, and yer alone. I'd be a rotten excuse of a man for certs if I left ye to yer own devices. Do ye think ye can trust me enough to get ye back to where ye belong?"

She could not help the smile that curled her lips, and she gave her head a jerky little nod; even her larger movements didn't entirely do what she told them to.

He nodded, then snagged her gloves and helped her wiggle her fingers and hands into them. "Let us find ye some food and good strong tea. I'm famished, and ye ate little yerself yesternight."

He led her down the stairs and out onto the street, and one of her hands shot up to shield her eyes as a bright ray of sun greeted her. The air was crisp and clear, having had a reprieve from the smokestacks sleeping through the night, and a light snow dusted the streets, making the town look far cleaner than it really was. His companion seemed to take in the surroundings with something akin to awe, and he finally took her hand and threaded it through his arm to urge her along.

She was kept safely between himself and whatever buildings they walked alongside. Anytime she stole a peek at him, his eyes were ever on the lookout for trouble, scanning every nook and cranny, it seemed. The security she felt at his side melted the remaining fright of the previous evening, and the township was bright and friendly now. The women of sin had since slunk away from the doorways and open windows. Drunkards were likely still sleeping off their stupors.

73

The smell of baked bread wafted toward her, and she was obliged to place a hand over her midsection as her stomach gave an interested rumble.

He suddenly leaned down to whisper, "Once we eat, we'll see about purchasing some clean garments for ye."

She peered down at herself and gave a soft huff. As they continued along, she fumbled with her reticule and finally withdrew the embroidered fabric envelope. When she managed to unfold it, she tapped MacDougall's arm and showed him the contents of what was a travelling sewing kit: pins, needles, several colours of thread, a pair of confoundingly small scissors, and a few other dainty items.

"I think yer gown is a bit beyond the help of a simple needle and thread. The gown is badly soiled in spots, and if you continue to wear garments once fine now tattered, townsfolk will think yer, well, offering something yer not."

Her steps pulled up abruptly and the colour from her face blanched while one hand fluttered like a panicked bird about her throat. Her companion halted beside her. "What is it, Miss Emmy?" he asked, his voice pitched low.

She stared at him helplessly, fearfully. Her gaze darted about the street as if the very monster she feared might suddenly appear, and she took a step closer to the wall, seeking its protection.

Mr. MacDougall leaned a shoulder against the brick near where she stood, towering over her slight stature, largely shielding her from view to aid in hiding her from sight. "I dinnae ken what's going on in that head of yourn, but I promise ye, if anyone tries to harm ye, they'll have to get past me first. And I'm a professional boxer, mind."

Large eyes blinked up at him, and as she took in the fierceness of his expression, the determination in his eyes and the set of his jaw, she believed him.

"Now, as to clothes, Miss Emmy... Not to pry into yer affairs, but ye should be able to purchase anything ye need on account if ye dinnae have the funds with ye. All ye need is to—" He stopped short and sighed, gazing down at her in sympathetic concern. "All ye'd need to do is tell them yer name."

My name. My name which I cannot even speak. Her face fell momentarily, then suddenly lit up as a thought struck her she hadn't yet considered. Her calling cards! Another frantic rummage through her bag yielded the beautiful ivory card case her cousin had gifted her earlier that week, and she flipped open the lid in elated expectation... which deflated the moment she saw the emptiness within. She then recalled her mistake: new cards had been printed for her and replaced within her old case before she left for the north. She'd been so eager to depart that she hadn't switched the cards, themselves, to her new case.

"What about writing it down for them? Sure and ye could manage that," he prompted.

Emmy shook her head sadly, lifting her right hand and showing just how little control she had over it. Even if she was able to write legibly enough, no one would believe that to be her natural hand, and thus discount her credibility. She felt the tell-tale sting of oncoming tears and she quickly averted her gaze, blinking the moisture back until she was certain she had her emotions in hand again.

If Mr. MacDougall was frustrated with her, he didn't show it. Instead, with his hands on his hips, he glanced around until he seemed to spy something in particular, then steered her in that direction.

What he'd seen turned out to be a tearoom. While neither were dressed in their finest, it was clear they were respectable enough. As she still struggled to communicate, Mr. MacDougall ordered for them both: a dish of shirred eggs, thick slices of ham, rolls with butter and honey, a pot of tea for her and a stout cup of chicory coffee for himself. He ate with relish every bit that was placed before them, as well as whatever she left untouched. For her part, Emmy only managed a cup of tea and a few nibbles of bread.

"Are ye not feeling well, lass?" he murmured quietly.

She offered a wan smile, hoping it was enough to satisfy his curiosity.

It wasn't. His forehead wrinkled in evident concern, and she pushed a bit more cheer into her smile, at which he merely quirked an eyebrow. "Ye think ye fool me?"

Her expression shifted to sweet innocence, and he chuckled under his breath as he rose to his feet and offered his arm. "Come along. One new gown for ye, then we'll get ye back to rest yerself."

She sighed and her shoulders drooped as she accepted his hand to stand.

"There now, lass; yer not allowed to surrender just yet. 'Tis only been a day. Sure and things will be better on the morrow."

Chapter Six

At least, MacDougall *hoped* things would be better on the morrow. It had been ages since he'd been responsible for any person other than himself, and while he knew he was capable of shouldering the burden, it wasn't ideal, not for his lifestyle and certainly not for hers. Everything about her belied her station; she was a true lady in every sense of the word. Even when she struggled with her movements, there was an innate grace that showcased her delicate and petted upbringing in society.

A society leagues above his own, and he had no business keeping company with her, even if it was as a helpful service.

With that dour thought came an idea which should have been his first impulse. "Once we find a suitable dress for ye, we'll stop by the station and check the schedules for the next train bound for London. Ye should be able to find yer way to friends once yer again in London." He assumed she came from London; did not all the wealthy originate in London at some point or another?

Her hand immediately fell from his arm and he pulled up short, looking back at where the woman was frozen to the spot. "Miss Emmy? What happened?" He stepped back to her and wrapped her hands in his own, chafing the ice away from her fingers as his eyes scanned the street. Nothing looked out of place or suspicious. Satisfied that she was at least physically safe, his gaze returned to her face. She'd gone pale and her eyes had taken on an almost haunted appearance.

No, not just haunted. Hunted.

Glancing around, he ushered her away from the street to a quiet alcove out of the way, then continued to rub her hands between his own.

"What frightens ye, lass? Did ye see someone?"

She gave her head a jerky little shake.

His brain scrambled back over what he had said and done before this sudden change. "Do ye fear having to… to find a new dress for yerself?" He doubted that was it, but he was grasping at straws.

Another shake of her head and she gripped his sleeve. "Riv-river. No. Brick, brick cinders… rose water." She grunted in frustration and tore her hands away, balling them into tight fists of what he could only suppose was exasperation.

"All right, not dresses," he confirmed, palms up and forward in surrender. *What else could it be?* He grappled for other subjects he'd mentioned. "London? Train?"

She suddenly clamped both her hands around one of his wrists, clinging desperately to him in utter terror.

"Yer afraid of something on the train?" he questioned. "Can ye nod yer head that's what ye fear? The train?" She finally nodded clumsily as if she'd never made the movement before, fear now mixed with uncertainty.

He tried to think about what he knew regarding her sphere of society. "Did ye come from London?" He paused, then prompted her again to nod if it was so, which she did. He could work with that, except that meant... *Damn it all.*

He turned various options over in his mind. "I dinnae suppose travelling to London in yer company would ease yer fear, would it?"

Miss Emmy stared hopefully into his face.

He pushed his hand through his hair and tipped his head back, staring at the sky, beseeching heaven for help, or mercy, or both. He didn't need this, and he quickly decided that Fate had a very poor sense of humour.

"Verra well, then," he relented with a sigh. "I'll take ye to London myself. But if we've need to avoid the train, it will take some time to travel."

When he glanced down at her, he found her eyes wide with mollification, her hands clasped against her heart, and a smile on her lips. Suddenly, the trek south didn't seem so unappealing.

"Yer travelling without a chaperone; I'll not be responsible for your reputation. Unless ye've a better idea?"

She chewed thoughtfully on her lower lip and looked about as if the answer might be written in the sky overhead. MacDougall waited for a half a minute before taking her gently by the elbow, then slipping her hand into his arm. "Let's ponder that as we find a shop where ye can buy a cleaner gown. Have ye money in that bag of yourn?"

In answer, she rummaged through the pouch again, and with a hand, he stilled her search. "Not out on the streets, lass. We'll find a store, then ye can rifle through yer effects."

They continued their stroll in silence, with MacDougall quickly slowing and shortening his stride to match her diminishing one. By the time they arrived at a third-hand shop, her expression was listless and her skin pallid, and she leaned heavily upon his arm. He stopped her before they entered the shop. "We can return later when ye've more strength."

In response, the woman's back straightened and her eyes glinted with fresh determination.

"Very well then; in ye go. I'll stay out here, if 'tis all the same to ye."

Her brows pinched in concern. "Water rose. No. Cinders." She huffed in annoyance.

MacDougall bit back the frustrated oath that threatened to spill out and rolled his eyes upward, asking heaven for strength. "Fine. I'll be yer translator, but dinnae get used to this. Soon as yer speaking, yer on yer own with making nice with the townsfolk." Tugging the door open, he ushered her inside.

The shopkeeper eyed the pair curiously; between MacDougall's unusually tall height and Miss Emmy's once-fine clothes, MacDougall well knew they made an odd couple. He forestalled any questions from the shopkeeper, however. "The lass is in need of some new togs. Have ye anything that will fit?"

The grizzled man swiped a hand over the top of his balding head and gestured to a table where coarse wool skirts and petticoats lay folded haphazardly with another table near at hand which held well-used half boots and woollen stockings. Against a wall there hung half a dozen drab-coloured dresses and some aprons which seemed to still have enough life in them to be practical. Shawls hung on hooks against another wall, and still another table held old-fashioned bonnets and various lengths of knitted gloves.

She bit down into the pout of her lower lip, gaze taking in what was available with a dismayed light in her eyes. A dainty hand snuck out to finger the material of a few garments, and she promptly dropped each.

Steady footsteps came up behind her, loud enough not to surprise her when he appeared at her side. "I ken this isn't what yer used to wearing. I'd be happy to take ye to another, finer shop of ready-made gowns, but I'm afraid we'd stick out sorely as a pair as we travel. For certs I'm no fit companion for ye. I'm not fit to even be a personal driver, even if I had access to a rig." He glanced back at the shopkeeper, who had since shuffled back to his stool behind the counter to polish his spectacles. "I'll do what I'm able to get ye back to yer folks safely, but we're a mite limited in resources without yer proper name."

She heaved a deep sigh, and he felt her frustration. This was hardly how he wanted to spend his time, either, fetching as she was. True enough, beyond tonight's match he didn't have any other fights lined up; he'd been planning on taking a break and finding work as a field labourer, or a dock hand, or even in a factory… anything that didn't involve shattering a man's jaw. But to play nursemaid and groomsman to a genuine lady who's hands had never done an ounce of work wasn't on his agenda of preferred pastimes.

He watched in astonishment as her posture and entire demeanour changed before his eyes. She threw her shoulders back, lifted her chin and set her jaw in what he could only imagine was determination, then quite resolutely plucked up two petticoats, a pair of stockings and boots with almost new laces from the table beside, then around to choose a deep, hunter green gown from a hook after seeming to size each one with her eyes. Then she turned to the old man behind the counter, opened her mouth to speak, then closed it and looked around the small shop once more.

"What's that?" the owner asked, raising bushy brows and glancing to MacDougall for interpretation.

"I believe she wants to change into these pieces. Do ye have a changing room she can use?"

"Payment first," he stated, holding out a grizzled hand.

Without pausing, Miss Emmy fished out the appropriate money and dropped it in his hand without ceremony.

The man counted the coins carefully then thumbed at a curtain hanging on one wall. Casting a somewhat worried glance at her protector, she took her newly acquired disguise and disappeared behind the curtain to change.

While MacDougall waited for her to dress, he perused the merchandise himself. However, a few short minutes later, Miss Emmy poked her head out through the curtain with a whine of protest.

"Aye, lass? What ails ye?"

She scowled and plucked at the sleeve of her gown, then turned and made as if to try and unlace the dress herself. MacDougall set his hands to his hips, dropped his head forward, and bit back a groan. "Is there a woman hereabouts that can help her change?"

The owner eyed him then held out a grizzled hand. "For a price I'll fetch my woman."

MacDougall dropped a coin into the man's hand with annoyance writ across his face.

The owner waddled away with a grin, yelling for his wife as he went. It wasn't long before both he and a clearly overworked and exhausted woman returned, and the woman went straight to the curtained changing closet and let herself in. MacDougall heard a surprised squeak and bit back a chuckle as he continued to look through the wares. Thinking over what he'd seen Miss Emmy grab, he added a fleece-lined hooded wool cloak, knit gloves, and a scarf. If they were to avoid the trains to instead travel entirely by coach, he wanted to make sure she would be warm enough. He was used to roughing it; he was absolutely certain she was not.

Several minutes later, after MacDougall paid the clerk for the additional gear, Miss Emmy reappeared in her new working class attire, her expression unsure but her posture as erect and stately as ever, her eyes bright and cheeks flushed. He couldn't help but smile out of pride in her. He could only imagine what a strange and alien situation this was for her, yet she seemed to be largely taking it all in stride, conforming as needed.

He nodded his approval as he crossed the floor to where she stood, and gently draped the cloak about her shoulders, then handed her the scarf and gloves. "Ye look verra nice," he complimented quietly, the Scottish burr thick upon his tongue. She smiled softly, and his heart gave an odd sort of kick in his chest.

He offered his arm to her, which she took without hesitation, and he guided her out and along the thoroughfares, his steps slowing more and more to match the woman's flagging energy.

By the time they reached the inn, it felt as if the woman at his side were barely awake, so heavily she leaned upon his arm for support. He ushered her inside and instantly sought out the innkeeper with his gaze.

"Have any rooms opened?"

"Not a one," answered the innkeeper. "Will you be wanting your same room for tonight?"

For answer, he paid the man then guided his charge to the stairs. When her foot clumsily missed the first step, he swept her up and into his arms, bearing her across his chest, and hurried up to the room. Once within, he set her gingerly to sit upon the sole chair in the room, bracketing her between his arms until he was sure she wouldn't topple off the seat. While she remained upright, she swayed slightly and her eyes were closed against the pain.

"With yer permission," he mumbled as he pressed the backs of his fingers to her forehead, then against one cheek. "Ye've a fever, I think. Look me in the eye, lass?"

She did as she was bidden, lifting eyes that were too bright and didn't seem to entirely focus upon his face, almost as if she were looking beyond him. He took sturdy hold of the front legs of the chair and dragged it about so the sun streaming in through the window would shine into her face. She cringed and pinched her eyes tightly shut with a moan. His hand reached for her face, cupping the uninjured side of her face, his thumb grazing the top of her cheekbone. Her skin was hot beneath his hand and he noticed a fine sheen of perspiration about her hairline. He frowned. "Just for a moment, lass. Let me see those lovely eyes of yourn one more time."

Squinting into the light as she obeyed, MacDougall leaned forward and stared, a slow frown forming. The black circles in the centre of her eyes didn't respond the way he expected them to when turned to the bright sunlight, and he struggled to remember what the doctor had said upon looking in on himself and the other bruisers after a particularly violent hit to the head. All he could recall was that opium or laudanum was often given if the pain was too extreme, and then instructions to stay abed until any sickness and dizziness passed.

"How feels yer head? Nod if it pains ye."

She managed to nod a little, continuing to squint her eyes.

He rose to standing and pulled the curtains closed, then with a glance and a thought, tossed his coat over the rod in effort to block more of the light from brightening the room. "Back into bed with ye, and I'll see about finding some powders or aught for ye." Her brows furrowed with protest, and he simply scooped her from the chair and up into his arms, despite the squeak of surprise that leapt from her lips. "Will ye stay here?" he asked as he settled her slowly and gently upon the bed.

The scowl of stubbornness that met him elicited a low chuckle.

"I'll take that as an aye. I've need to attend to a few things, but for certs I'll return soon as I'm able. Try to rest." And with those parting words, he left.

As he went downstairs, he passed the chambermaid working her way through the floor below. He pressed a few pennies into the girl's palm. The girl was hardly a teenager if he were to judge by appearance alone, but she must be trustworthy enough to be employed at an inn, he supposed. "The lady in room six is ill with a head injury; there's nae need to clean the room. I hope to be back shortly, but please look in on her, see if she needs anything. I know 'tis not yer usual job, but I'll pay ye whatever extra ye think is appropriate."

"Of course, Sir. I'll go right up soon as I finish these few rooms, nice an' quiet-like. Treat her as if she was me own flesh an' blood. Thank yeh, Sir."

With another nod, he hastened down the stairs and off to locate a chemist.

True to her word, the girl, Molly by name, peeked in on Emmy within half an hour, rapping lightly on the door before letting herself in. "Ah'm Molly, Miss. Yer husband ast if Ah could please look in on yeh, said as ya wasn't feeling well," she offered quietly. "Can Ah fetch yeh anythin'? Cuppa tea? Cool cloth fer your head?"

Emmy peered at the girl and tried to smile. The accent was thick; she had to go over the girl's words in her head once more before she dissected the girl's meaning. Even then, she couldn't remember how to tell her what it was she wanted.

"Ah'll just knick this 'ere pitcher right quick an' be back 'fore yeh can blink," and off the girl went.

Emmy must have drifted for a bit, for when she opened her eyes again Molly was letting herself into the room again with a fresh pitcher in one hand and a steaming cup of tea, sans its saucer, in the other. She used her foot to gently push the door closed and carried the vessels to the bedside table. The teacup was set down first and the bowl filled with cold water. A clean square of linen from the girl's own apron pocket was pulled forth, doused and wrung out, and tenderly applied to Emmy's forehead.

"There yeh are, Miss. Now yeh just lie still an' Ah'll play nursemaid. Me own sister ain't well an' Ah've 'elped her lotsa times." Molly began on Emmy's boots, unlacing and removing them. "Yer feet're like ice, Miss! Inta bed with yeh!"

With the efficiency of a well-trained lady's maid, Molly helped divest Emmy of her cloak and even went so far as to help her out of her overdress and corset. Emmy was then tucked into bed, with Molly swaddling her patient's feet and legs with the spare blanket before tugging the bedclothes up to her chin. Emmy stretched a trembling hand toward the teacup, but Molly took notice and held the cup to her lips, letting her take small sips before a wrinkle of her nose declared she wanted no more. When Molly noticed that Emmy's face suddenly paled, then flushed, water from the bowl was promptly dumped back into the pitcher and the now-empty basin was held beneath Emmy's chin as she heaved.

"Shh. There now. It'll be a'right," Molly crooned softly as she took a seat beside Emmy. The cloth that had dropped from Emmy's forehead was taken up, wetted, and replaced across the back of Emmy's neck before a strong, comforting arm wrapped behind her shoulders to support the young woman's weight. After several minutes, Emmy curled feebly into Molly's side and sank into sleep.

When she finally drifted to the surface once more, the room was empty. The chair had been pulled up to the side of the bed near the side table, the bowl now perched on the seat within reach should she need it. The cloth was neatly folded upon her brow but was now unpleasantly warm, and she swiped it from her face, tossing it away from her without a care where it landed.

Her stomach lurched and she twisted, reaching for the bowl as her insides convulsed though her stomach was long since empty. Sweat poured from her face;

every inch of her skin felt like it was on fire. As her gut calmed, she collapsed onto her side. Ice settled into her bones and she groped blindly for the blanket.

How long she lay there, she knew not. Her head pained her terribly, and the room around her was blurred as if it had been painted with too much water. After several minutes, Emmy gradually sat up, her body and mind unsure of the new position. Once things settled within her, she glanced slowly around, blinking hard to try and focus her eyes but to no avail. She had not come here by herself, surely; someone had helped her. A woman? No, that did not seem quite right. A man, then. Yes, she was fairly certain it had been a man, one who made her feel safe, protected. Who was he? *Where* was he? Perhaps he left and meant for her to search for him. If she could only find him again…

Cold vaguely registered with her as she stood to her feet, so a blanket was wrapped about her shoulders before she shuffled to the door. Unaware of all else except the need to locate the man for which her mind groped, she left the room, padded shakily down the stairs, and out the door onto the street.

Chapter Seven

MacDougall went to the neighbourhood apothecary, where he procured a tonic, the chemist assured him would ease the maladies of head and stomach. He was on his way back to the hotel when he decided to make another stop.

After some deliberation, he bought some basic food supplies to keep in the room. He wasn't certain as to how long he and Emmy would be keeping company, but given the fact that she was likely still suffering from the effects of her injury, she wasn't on stable ground, physically or mentally. That meant that he would likely be looking after her for at least a few more days. He also had to consider her plight beyond the space of those few days. He suspected she might be on the run, either from something or someone. If that was so, she was remarkably ill-equipped to keep ahead of whomever or whatever the supposed threat was.

On his way back to the inn, he popped into a tiny bookshop and, after perusing the shelves, purchased a copy of the play *Much Ado About Nothing*. She might grow restless and bored locked up in the room while he was away that night, and women of her quality and station were all supposed to be fond of the Bard's works, weren't they?

After procuring the book, he made his way back to the inn. He was just around the corner when he stopped dead in his tracks.

Emmy?

She was perhaps twenty paces away, bare-headed, hair slipping down from its pins, clad in a blanket and stockinged feet. She looked confused and distraught, as if unsure as to which way to go, or what to do. Was she trying to sneak away from him? Did she think she would be better served on her own? Well, that certainly wouldn't do, particularly wandering around in her unmentionables with no shoes and a blanket as a cloak. She was more likely to end up as some fiend's snack than anything else. With a shake of his head, and before he could examine why he refused to let her make her own way, he stole up quietly behind her.

"Going somewhere?" MacDougall murmured over her shoulder.

She yelped with a start and whirled about, her hand pressed flat against her heart, eyes wide, then slowly her expression melted into one of puzzlement.

He stood there, one brow quirked, with a dry, sardonic expression on his face. "Trying to give me the slip, lass?" he asked dryly.

"I— I'm—"

His brows rose sky high. "Aye? Keep trying."

"I'm— head. No— I—" Her energy seemed to drain from her then and with a heavy sigh she leaned against the wall, tipping her head against it as if it were suddenly too heavy to efficiently support.

MacDougall meant to tease her for leaving, but with her quickly diminishing strength, he changed course. "Come on then. Back upstairs with you, Magellen," he quipped, offering his arm to her.

Her eyes popped open and she stared at him with surprise. He smirked. "Aye, I've read a history book. Try not to faint with surprise." He tugged her along with him, muttering to himself as they went. "Not even gone an hour, take all this trouble to keep ye safe and off ye go on yer own, without shoes on yer feet even in this cold. Some gratitude that is. Thought ye posh types learned how to be thankful." One of her hands palmed her forehead and she wobbled when she walked. He frowned; she was getting worse.

Only after they returned behind the door of room six did he dare speak, feeling he had just enough hold on his fear-based temper to keep it controlled. "What were ye thinking, lass? If someone without kind intentions came upon ye—" He sighed and scrubbed a hand down his face before fisting one hand and pressing it to the doorframe, his back to the erstwhile runaway. "I'm only asking ye to stay here to protect ye. Yer not a prisoner. If ye want to be left to yer own cleverness, I'll leave the noo and ye'll never set eyes on me again." MacDougall stopped. He mashed his lips together in thought, caught between wanting to run for the hills and his desire to remain with this vulnerable, mysterious young woman. "I— I only want to keep ye safe."

Silence answered him, and when he turned to face the room, he found her curled on her side upon the bed, both hands over her forehead, stockinged feet peeking out from beneath her shift.

He sighed again. Kneeling beside the pack, he rummaged through it until he pulled free the bottle of laudanum he procured, and he carried it to where she lay. Eyeing the chair and bowl that had been moved beside the bed, he frowned. "Were ye ill?"

Emmy lowered her hands and peered at him helplessly, giving the tiniest shrug.

"Cay ye not even remember that?"

She shook her head minutely.

"Do ye remember *me*?" That was a frightening thought, that somehow he'd been erased from her memory. The thought unsettled him, and he didn't want to examine the reason why.

To his alleviation, her expression melted into a soft smile of recognition. "Mmm... Maaaac... Maac..."

He grinned like a fool then. She remembered him! "Aye, lass. Mac." *Yer a bloody eejit, man.*

Spying her cup of leftover tea, he unstoppered the bottle and added some of the drug to the liquid. "Just a tiny bit to help with yer pain."

Once Emmy levered herself up on an elbow, she took the cup uneasily in her left and forced herself to drink. She coughed twice, her face contorting in displeasure at the bitterness, but she obediently finished it and handed it back to him empty.

"I've need to check in soon at the mill for my fight tonight, Em– Miss Emmy."

Her eyebrows soared and she struggled to sit upright in frightened panic.

He set gentle hands to her shoulders and held her down. "Easy, lass. Remember, I'm a boxer; 'tis what I do. I'll make sure the lass from earlier comes back to check on ye. Perhaps she can be persuaded to bring ye a bite for supper." At her wrinkled nose, he smiled sympathetically. "Ye should try to take something. Ye need to keep your strength to heal." He eyed her for a moment longer. "Can I trust ye to stay put ye this time?" he asked, a teasing light in his eyes despite the firm intonation lacing his words.

She nodded, relaxing into the pillows at her back as he lit the candle that stood on the bedside table.

He got to his feet and fetched his sack from the corner of the room, slinging it over one shoulder. "Try to sleep. I'll be back afore ye know I'm gone." With a grin and a wink he let himself out, reminding himself to seek out the cleaning girl first.

It was a difficult task not to worry about the man who had assigned himself to her protection. If something happened to him, what would become of her? What would happen if he injured his head so badly that *he* experienced the same symptoms as herself? Or worse, forgot who she was, or who he was? Emmy somehow recalled that such things were possible, and she shuddered.

She settled deeper into bed and closed her eyes, allowing scenes of her life to dance behind her eyes, those from before her present condition. There were trips to Bath and to the shore, sea bathing with her friends, balls and parties with the ladies and gentlemen of court, hours spent at the theatre, laughter, and dancing…

One thing puzzled her suddenly—a memory from that very morning of great heaps of snow shovelled against the buildings they passed as they walked to breakfast. The last event she could recall before meeting Mr. MacDougall was a card party at her townhouse in London. It had been in the beginning of March.

It was common practice for herself and her friends to winter in and around Town, frequently vacillating between London and her cousin's country estate of Brookshire, which had served as her home after her parents died. The small cluster of friends had little reason to leave the area entirely until July or August when the weather turned too hot. But what had brought her away from Town at such an odd time as this, right in the middle of the Season? And why a place as cold as this? She wished she could ask what month it was. If she could not even remember packing to leave London, or Brookshire, in the first place, how much time had passed since that card party?

There was a concerning void where she knew additional information ought to be, and being unable to clearly communicate simply added to her frustration. Why could she not remember why she was here?

Whether she truly slept or not, she could not tell. But some time later a gentle knock sounded at the door, and Molly's thickly accented voice came drifting through the wood. "Miss? Are yeh awake, Miss?"

I'm awake, Emmy thought while her mouth answered, "Teeee." And inwardly, Emmy rolled her eyes in annoyance. *Ridiculous problem. Will I forever be trapped inside my own head?*

The door opened and Molly appeared with a heavily-laden tray between her hands. She carefully bumped the door closed with her hip before setting the legged tray over Emmy's lap. "Yer husband says yeh oughtta eat much as yer able. Ah know yeh've been ill, but it's best ta eat so yeh don't waste away ta nothin' but a breath. Yer already naught but a wee sprig, Miss. That is— Oh, Ah'm awful sorry, Miss! Ah always talk too much. They always tell me ta hold me tongue but—"

Emmy set a reassuring hand on the girl's wrist to still her apologies. She didn't want to show how nonsensical her speech was, but she offered a warm, kind smile to the working girl and shook her head gently.

"Thank yeh, Miss. But, Miss, if yeh don't mind me askin', don't yeh speak a'tall? Yer husband said as yeh couldn't say much."

Of course he would. Thinking quickly, Emmy patted her throat and frowned. She didn't like to lie, even in action, but there was little other way to explain what ailed her, especially as she wasn't entirely certain, herself.

"Oh, a sore throat. Ah see. Ah'm most sorry, Miss. How miserable fer yeh, that it hurts yeh such that yeh can't even say a word."

Emmy only smiled and took up the spoon, eying the bowl of lumpy brown gravy that, oddly, sent tempting aromas to her nose. It looked unlike anything she'd ever had, and her expression must have communicated her thoughts because Molly chuckled.

"Have yeh never had stew, Miss?"

Was this what common folk ate? Emmy curiously stirred the bowl then slanted a dubious look at the girl, which brought forth a merry ripple of a laugh. "It can't bite yeh, Miss. Try it. Ah'm sure yeh'll like it."

Casting Molly a dubious look, Emmy dipped the edge of the spoon into the gravy and tasted it. While it looked frightful, it tasted as good as it smelled, and Emmy took dainty spoonful after spoonful, chewing each bite carefully and allowing the flavours to mix upon her tongue. She even tore into the hard slice of bread to dip it into the savoury broth.

Molly busied herself around the room, occasionally casting curious glances back to the young woman in bed. "I wish yeh could talk, Miss. Yer ever so lovely, an' Ah'm just sure yeh're from a lovely home. Yer husband looks as if he would move th' world fer yeh."

Her face burned as she picked at the meal. Despite what the girl thought she saw, it was more likely that MacDougall was eager to get her off his hands. What trouble she must be causing him, upsetting the order of his life like this!

She made it through half the bowl of stew and a few bites of the bread. Once she finished the tea laced with the chemist's tonic, Molly tucked Emmy into bed with the care of a mother to a small child, and Emmy was asleep in minutes.

The sole candle had burned down when she next awoke, but with a smile she saw that another stood beside it, ready to take its place. A gift from Molly, she imagined. She was thankful for the dim light, for her head felt as if a mallet continually attempted to split it in half. Sitting up gingerly, she cast a look around her humble surroundings to find that nothing had changed. MacDougall's sack was still missing. Molly had removed the tray. There was no way of knowing what time it was. Easing herself out of bed, and pausing to ensure no nausea overcame her, Emmy padded slowly to the window and peered through the slit in the curtains to the roads below. They weren't entirely empty but it was clear the hour was late enough that many had already found their beds.

Where was Mr. MacDougall?

Wrapped in his coat, MacDougall sat on a bench apart from the actual ring waiting for his call to fight, dully watching the fire flicker from the ends of the various torches which lit the area for boxers and spectators alike. He hated waiting for his turn when there were several pairs matched up before his fight. He would much prefer arriving, fighting, and leaving in quick succession. Fortunately, as he was not the main draw for the crowd tonight, he was not the last bout. His cut might not be as large, but he didn't care.

Not anymore.

All manner of headaches came with being a top draw. Managers, backers, and handlers all wanted a piece if you were a main event level boxer. Once they had their hooks in a boxer, it was exceedingly difficult to shake them loose. Moreover, there was the criminal element to it which he detested. Heads of organised crime groups loved to fix big fights and wager on the predetermined outcome. By sticking to the smaller, lesser known mills in the countryside, MacDougall didn't draw as much attention as the bigger names, and he preferred it that way.

Coercing him into taking part in a fixed bout would not have been an easy feat to begin with. He had no wife nor family for any interested parties to threaten in order to secure his cooperation. At one point, a low-level bully had threatened MacDougall's person if he didn't throw a fight. The man had spent the following four weeks in a bed. When he did leave, he was missing seven teeth, had both arms wrapped in splints, and he would never again have full use of his fingers.

"Highlander! You're up!" someone barked.

He hopped down from the table and plucked up a heavy towel. He had on the usual togs: snug-fitting buff pantaloons that stopped mid-calf, stockings, and a pair of soft leather shoes that came to just the ankle. With the towel over one shoulder, he headed for the ring.

MacDougall heard none of the crowd's noise as he stalked towards the area roped off for their use. He absently nodded at his second and his bottle man as he climbed through the ropes, and then waited for the introductions to be made. Again, he paid little attention to the goings on surrounding him. He kept thinking back to the lady he left behind.

When he first happened upon her, was it purely coincidental or was there more to it than that? He had a feeling deep in his gut that it wasn't simple happenstance. Had Divine Providence laid her in his path? If that were so, far be it from him to deny fate. Besides, what sort of heartless cad would he be to desert her when she was in such a helpless state? He could never live with himself if he abandoned her now. And what if the unthinkable occurred this very night and he was injured to the point of uselessness, himself? Who would care for her then?

Both fighters were called to the centre and he shook himself back into the present to approach the young up-and-comer from somewhere across the water, New York per his introduction by the referee. The Yankee was reported to be slick, shifty, and swift, the likes of which hadn't been seen since Gentleman Jack. The rules of the bout were listed but he scarcely listened—MacDougall knew them like the back of his own hand.

His mind and thoughts kept returning to Emmy. *Miss Emmy, blast it all; remember the 'Miss'.* Even when the call came for the commencement of the first round, he didn't seem to hear it. It took the sudden cacophony of the crowd to throw his brain back into his body. MacDougall blinked as he watched the New Yorker dance and gambol about, putting his dazzling footwork on display. He feinted a few punches MacDougall's way, but never connected. As the Yankee danced about, he noticed that his opponent dropped his right hand whenever he danced to his left.

MacDougall followed the American about until the opportune moment presented itself.

The Yankee repeated his flawed pattern, and when he did, MacDougall sidestepped and launched a left hook over the Yank's lowered right hand. The punch caught his target flush on the jaw, and the New Yorker dropped on the spot.

Inwardly, MacDougall cringed. He had wanted the bout to be over quickly so he could return to Emmy, but he had meant to pull his punch at least a little. With his natural strength already more than any man he'd met, he was always careful in the ring. He was a fighter, indeed, but he never intended to cause irreparable harm to any of his opponents. MacDougall swiped a hand across his jaw as he observed the Yankee. The man lay motionless on the ground, blood trickling from his mouth and his right ear. The entire right side of his face began to swell immediately and rather grotesquely. He was carried off to his corner and his men slapped at the uninjured side of his face, sponged him off, even plied his mouth with brandy, trying to urge him back enough to fight.

Thirty seconds passed, then the additional eight, and it was all over. The Highlander was declared the winner, and one again had displayed how he earned the moniker.

The crowd was fairly wild in amazement, but MacDougall ignored it all, quickly leaving the ring, snagging his opponent's colours as he went. He took no time to change, and instead shoved his clothes in his pack, swung into his coat, and eagerly wove his way through the pressing crowd to collect his winnings. Good-natured slaps to the back were received affably enough, but he ignored all attempts to engage him in conversation.

It was late by the time he finally left the mill, and he jogged the final few blocks to the inn. The manager who had been backing the New Yorker had waylaid MacDougall, keen on signing him to a contract and bringing him to the Americas to go on tour. He promised MacDougall the sun, the moon, and the stars. If he performed as well as the manager supposed he would, MacDougall even had a shot at being named champion over both countries.

With Emmy forefront in his mind, he stunned the manager and the owner of that particular mill by promptly announcing his retirement from fighting regularly. He may dip in and out, but as for making it his career and making his way to the larger fights outside London, he was done.

When he arrived back at the hotel, he was still dressed in his fighting togs.

"Sorry to be so late," he apologised cheerfully as he entered the room and peeled his coat off. His duffel bag was dropped onto the floor by the door, the coat draped over it, and he tossed the pouch containing his earnings from the gate onto the table.

The woman went from listless to alert in a trice, and her expression was one of clear relief. She began to get up, but stopped abruptly and set her hand to the wall, apparently to steady herself. But her eyes hungrily roved over his face and form, searching for signs of injury that needed tending. Her lips moved to form words that simply wouldn't come.

MacDougall took pity on her, guessing at her line of thinking. "I'm hale as ever; he never touched me. It was all over in the matter of a minute or so. I was late because my opponent's manager tried to talk me into signing a contract with him. He wanted to take me to America and put me on tour. That's the problem with the fight game, ye ken. His fighter was out cold, and he's courting me as his replacement. Not a loyal soul to be had from the lot."

He'd been so worked up with disgust over the American manager that he'd overlooked one very important detail about himself: he was essentially half-naked. Bared from the waist up, clad in nothing but his fighting pantaloons and a pair of boots, he was used to trodding the ring as he was before a crowd, but here in this room, alone with a young vulnerable woman, his blunder was painfully obvious.

Given the sudden flush that rose into her cheeks, she had come to the same sudden realisation. Her focus was blatantly below his face, her gaze skipping across the expanse of his sculpted bared chest, his broad shoulders, the pair of muscular arms which tapered to thick wrists. Her lips were parted as she stared openly at him.

His throat felt like sandpaper and swallowing was almost painful. "I should clean up. Put myself into more... suitable attire," he said quickly. Stooping over, he snapped up his pack and practically sprinted out the door and into the hall.

As Mr. MacDougall took his abrupt leave to wash up, Emmy dropped her face into her hands, pressing cold fingers to her burning cheeks. What was the matter with her? Ogling him like some common hoyden! She was utterly ashamed of herself.

She calmed her racing heart with several deep breaths, and only when she felt that she had herself well in hand did she slowly look about to see what needed to be done. Molly was under the impression they were husband and wife, and it was just as well that Emmy was unable to correct the sweet, unassuming maid. It simply would not do to set tongues wagging. The scandal would destroy her reputation and, oh!, how her mother and father would have felt it if they were living! No, it was best to hide and continue to play the role assumed of them.

But in pretending to be husband and wife, how could she force him to sleep in the hall as he had the night before? Now that Molly had cared for her, she was more likely to check on them again first thing in the morning perhaps, and then what? It would be left up to Mr. MacDougall to tell a falsehood on her behalf, and not for the world did she want to put him in a position to have to lie.

Slowly surveying the room, her gaze landed upon the folded extra blanket at the end of the bed, and then to the mound of pillows against the head of the bed. With furrowed brows, she rose gingerly to her feet. Her right hand snagged a pillow while her left took hold of the folded edge of the wool blanket. Careful, measured steps carried her across the floor to the wall by the door, and there she knelt.

When the door reopened, MacDougall was dressed again in the clothes she'd seen him in before he left. Was that the only set of clothing he owned? Was that how other people lived, with only one or perhaps two sets of clothes and that was all? Mr. MacDougall had yet to mention anything about his place of birth, or even a permanent home. Was he a wanderer perhaps?

"Lass, what are you doing upon the floor? You'll catch a chill and then we'll really be in a spot." He knelt beside her and looked as if he were prepared to lift her off the floor when he stopped and took in what she'd done. It was a crude attempt at a bed on the floor, the sheet folded in half once, covered by a blanket, one corner of it turned back. There was even a pillow at one end. "Ye made a bed for me?" he asked huskily. "Cannae remember the last time anyone turned down my covers."

She smiled a little, and though her pain was evident, her eyes sparkled just a little.

Clearing his throat, he scooped her gently into his arms and carried her back across the room, settled her on the mattress, and tugged the blanket up to her chin. As he did so, the backs of his fingers just barely brushed against her jaw, and his hand drifted up to her cheek, then to her forehead. "Yer still a mite too warm. Nod yer head if ye've taken yer medicine."

Emmy nodded, her brows pinched. Her suffering was evident in every detail of her face, and he wished there was a way to carry the burden for her.

He cast about for some form of assistance and his gaze landed on the bowl and pitcher and the cloth square folded beside it. Pouring water into the bowl, the fabric was dipped, squeezed, and settled over her forehead. "Close yer eyes, lass. Rest the noo. We'll each of us get a good night of sleep, and come the morn we'll start our way to Manchester, then on to London." He hesitated and she wondered if there was more, but he instead returned to the small bedroll she'd created for him.

She listened to his steps leave the bedside, and she lifted one side of the handkerchief to watch him. He stood over the bed she'd prepared for him, hands on his hips, and he shook his head. Then he locked the door, set the key on the writing desk beside the envelope he'd first brought in, then pulled the end of the sheet and blanket along the floor until it lay directly in front of the door. He toed off his boots, hunkered down, punched the pillow twice, and settled beneath the blankets without any further preparations.

He was protecting her, and her heart warmed as she dropped the deliciously cool cloth back across her eyes. Anyone else might take his position across the door for trapping her within, but she knew better. He was an honourable man, a natural defender. Odd that he would choose to put himself in harm's way again and again as a boxer, making his living with his fists and causing harm, yet she never, even for a moment, feared him. Being alone in this room felt like the most natural thing in the world, and the realisation of it stunned her. What could it all mean?

Her thoughts turned toward her friend, Mr. Wainwright, a prominent man in her circle of intimates, truly one of the few constants in her realm of existence besides her cousin. He had shown interest in her romantically, but it seemed it was more in jest than anything. Even so, it was impossible not to compare him with Mr. MacDougall as far as she understood him. They were both men she would consider as gentlemen, one most obviously born to the title and the other one who decided to behave as one. She could not even imagine Mr. Wainwright lending his assistance to a stranger, not in any way beyond opening a door or holding a chair, and even then it would only extend to ladies he admired. She had heard him on more than one occasion offer snide comments regarding others in their set who perhaps weren't as handsome as others. Such hadn't ever bothered her before, indeed she hadn't even noticed and in fact had laughed along with her friends at the expense of others. Now that she had spent time with Mr. MacDougall, little though it was, she was quite sure he would never do such a thing. He brought to mind a knight of old, who might slay a dragon ravaging a village one day and bring money to a poor family the next. If he had something disparaging to say about a person, he would say it to their face, and never for the purpose of simply being cruel. It seemed impossible of him. He was simply too noble a man for such a petty action, and more and more, Mr. Wainwright, of whom she used to think so highly, continued to pale in comparison when judged beside the Scotsman.

With a lingering memory of the Scotsman's gentle touch whenever he aided her, she slept.

Chapter Eight

The next morning came, and like clockwork, MacDougall was up, dressed, and ready for his run before the sun had even begun peeking over the rooftops. His beautiful roommate was still sound asleep, though her features were pinched as if pained or in the throes of an awful dream. He carefully peered at the source of her injury and before he could stop himself, the backs of his fingers brushed lightly across her forehead. He snapped his hand back, angry that he'd allowed himself to act so familiarly while she slept. Surveying her wound was one thing; taking such an intimate liberty while she slept was quite another. He should hold himself in tighter control than that. But she looked so unsettled, the urge to comfort her in some small way was overpowering. At least that was what he would tell himself was his reason for behaving thus.

He forced himself to step back and dragged his hands down either side of his face. A good long run in the cold was what he needed, so after pocketing the room key, he slipped out for his usual ten miles.

When he returned, she still slept on.

And on.

And on.

He folded his bedroll and stacked it in the corner. He slipped out and found a simple breakfast. He thumbed through the book he'd purchased for her. Even after hours, she continued to sleep. After much pacing, he went back and sat at the room's small writing desk to puzzle out what he ought to do next. It appeared she had suffered a more significant injury to her head than he previously supposed, and that would require a visit from a doctor. It wasn't the most modern or respectable village but surely there had to be someone who might have a better knowledge of this than what he'd gleaned during his earlier years as a boxer.

He sat forward, forearms braced atop his thighs, fingers loosely entwined, and he studied her. The redness on her face where she was struck was angrier and more defined, and when his eyes drifted to the slender column of her neck, where more bruises told the tale of her abuse, his blood boiled. How he longed for just five minutes with the black-hearted monster who had put his hand to this young woman in such a vile way. There would be little more than a pulped mass by the time MacDougall finished with him, and he noticed his hands fisting as he imagined it.

He wished she was able to speak to him like any rational lady, then everything would be untangled and logical. As it was, it was impossible to know how much she knew, if she even really understood her situation and remembered all that had happened. What if there was memory loss in addition to her other hindrances? It wasn't unheard of in the ring; perhaps she suffered that as well. There was no denying her intelligence, of course, and it was clear that she was to the manor born, but he was stuck in a maddening dilemma. What was he to do?

He counted his winnings from the previous night's match, something he had neglected the night before... something he had never neglected to do straight away during the span of his entire career! This woman was turning his world upside down. It was all there, and if he'd had any reservations regarding her character, they were dispelled at once. It would have been the easiest thing in the world to steal the money from the desk; it had been in plain sight all the night through. But she hadn't. Likely, such a thing hadn't even occurred to her. Not surprising; she was a true gentlewoman through and through, and genuine in her injury he was certain.

Up until then, he had always assumed ladies of the highest rungs of society to be uppity, superior creatures with no thought or concern of anything besides the latest fashion or ball. This mystery woman was leagues from his previous supposition. She had shown only momentary hesitation when they'd purchased the clothing, but had resigned herself to it almost immediately. She hadn't appeared to complain about her situation save for an occasional huff of frustration, and who wouldn't be exasperated by her current crisis? In fact, he reflected that he, himself, behaved more aggravated by this sudden turn of events than she did.

She had slept long enough, he decided. Moving to the side of the bed, he hesitated for a moment before sinking to perch on the very edge of where she lay, and his hand covered her shoulder to lightly shake her. "Miss Emmy? Time to open yer eyes." He waited and watched, and though she stirred, she didn't wake. "Come now, ye'll sleep the day away, lass," he said louder, giving her another gentle nudge. "Miss Emmy."

He sighed when those beautiful eyes of hers finally opened. He'd had doctors in the past warn of the danger when a head injury patient couldn't be woken. "There ye are, lass," he crooned. "How feels yer head?"

She blinked slowly, staring at him as one solving a mystery. His heart gave a painful lurch. "Do ye ken who I am? Recognize my face?" he asked quietly, holding his breath in fear. "Nod if ye know me."

She bobbed her head just enough to answer and he smiled to himself. At least she knew him; he wouldn't frighten her as some strange man in her bedroom.

"We'll mend ye yet. Can ye take any tea?"

Her face drained of its remaining colour, and she slowly turned her head back and forth on the pillow. Her eyes glistened, and to his horror a tear slipped free and trickled down her cheek into her hair. Why did his entire body feel as if he'd just been laid out on the ring floor? Another tear escaped from her eyes and it almost killed him. Without thinking, he reached for her and lightly brushed the traces of moisture from her face.

"Och, dinnae cry," he bit out, his voice husky, his accent thicker with emotion. "I'll not leave ye to yer own devices 'til yer reunited with yer friends. Just… dinnae cry. Please, lass. I cannae stand it."

Her lips turned down in a frown of defeat and her eyes drifted closed, muscles going lax and face slowly drifting to the side. His heart seized in his chest.

He was known in the boxing world for being calm and in control at all times, never letting emotion get the better of him, in the ring or out of it. But he was near frantic now inwardly, and outwardly he clenched his teeth together so hard that his jaw ached. His fingertips desperately glided along her wrist until he felt the steady thump of her heartbeat, and relief nearly levelled him.

After a moment, clarity returned. First, he took up the small bottle the chemist had given him and pressed the opening to her lips, letting the smallest bit trickle into her mouth before stoppering it again. Then he took hasty leave of the room to seek out Molly.

He found her on the first floor after asking the main innkeeper for her whereabouts. "The lady ye cared for yesterday is ill, and is growing worse. Have ye a break to fetch a doctor? I'm a stranger here and dinnae ken where to find one," and he offered her a shilling.

"Ah'd like ta help, but Ah can't leave 'til after supper, Sir. Ah live just 'round the corner if yeh wantta go ask me little brother, Freddie. He's home ta help with our sister who's bedridden. You can say Ah sent yeh an' he'll bring the doctor 'ere." She explained where he could find the old tenement where her family lived as she continued to bustle around the room, changing out the sheets and blankets and sprucing up while the current resident was out.

At that moment, the innkeeper called down the hall for Molly, and she hurried away, leaving MacDougall to wonder if he dared leave Emmy alone, even for so short an errand.

It didn't take long for resolve to spur him into motion, and long strides ate up the street between the inn and the row house Molly had described. When he located the correct door, he had to keep himself from pounding on the wood. When a tiny boy tugged it open and peered around, MacDougall immediately crouched down to his level. "G'morning there, lad. Are ye Freddie by name? Yer sister sent me."

The boy's eyes flew wide with alarm. "Is Molly hurt?"

"Nae! Nae, lad, she's hale and safe at work. But she sent me to ask a favour of ye." He held out the coin he'd previously offered to the boy's sister. "I can pay ye for yer time."

He didn't think it possible, but the boy's eyes widened even more as he took the coin in his small hand and stared at it. "A whole shilling, Sir?" he squeaked.

"To be sure. And an extra penny all for yerself if ye do yer job quickly. Are ye game?"

The little boy stared longingly at the coin, then peeked over his shoulder in concern.

"Ye'll be back afore too long. Miss Molly told me of yer other sister; I think she'll be all right. I just need ye to fetch the doctor. Ye know where to find him?"

"Oh, aye!" the boy exclaimed, his face brightening a little. "Ah can do that! Ah've had ta get 'im plenty of times." His expression clouded. "He comes over ta see Anne when we can pay him."

Well didn't that just pluck at his heartstrings? MacDougall fished out another shilling and handed it across. "To pay for the next visit. Tell the doctor to come to the inn where Miss Molly works, and when yer done, come find me at room six for yer penny. Can ye do that for me, lad?"

"Aye, Sir!" The boy scampered back into the tiny apartment, leaving the door open, and after another moment, he reappeared with a cap on his head and shoes on his feet. "I'll bring th' doctor right quick!" And without further explanation, the child sprinted down the lane and vanished around the corner. With the lad on his way, he took his hurried way back to the inn, stopping at a pub to snag a London newspaper on his way.

Upon entering the room, he found she hadn't moved so much as an inch, and while he hoped it meant she hadn't awoken in a panic to find him gone, it concerned him that she hadn't roused even the slightest bit. He thought back over his boxing career as he spread the papers out on the room's desk and didn't recall ever having injured his head as badly as what seemed to ail her now. He hoped that quiet rest would do the most to aid in her recovery. He knew of nothing else to try, and cast a prayer heavenward that the doctor would be proficient in his knowledge.

While he awaited the doctor's arrival, he took the time to idly peruse the paper for no other reason than to pass the time. He sat back and slowly read each page in turn, though it was only when he hit the third page that his interest piqued. The page contained numerous headlines, none that would have given him pause but a week before. But circumstances had changed for him.

BEAUTIFUL ADVENTURESS ROBS HOUSE OF THOUSANDS IN PRECIOUS JEWELLERY!

And further down, another headline:

TITLED LADY ELOPES TO GRETNA GREEN!

And yet another:

YOUNG WORKING WOMAN FOUND DEAD ON LIVERPOOL MANCHESTER LINE! POSSIBLE FOUL PLAY!

His face grew pinched in a scowl and, angry as he was, he read every word of the gossip page twice through. He never realized how harmful such articles could be; he'd never paid them any mind before. Now, however, it seemed that every article had the potential to describe his Emmy, and with a growl, he surged to his feet, pitched the offending paper out the window, and yanked the casement shut with a dull thunk.

The sudden noise from the otherwise silent room had her gasping in surprise from the bed, and with a wince he stepped to her side and sat. "Sorry, lass. I dinnae mean to startle ye. 'Tis nothing."

After studying his face for a long moment, she settled back against the pillows, though she kept her eyes locked with his.

"How fare ye?" he asked tenderly. Her mouth opened to speak, her expression a study in intense concentration. He held her gaze pityingly. "Words still escaping ye?" There was no answer, so he continued, "I've sent for a doctor, lass. He should be here ere long."

Her brows furrowed at that, and when her lips clearly wouldn't obey, she made a circle shape with her thumb and forefinger.

That was new, and he leaned forward in interest, gaze flicking between the round shape with her fingers and her face as she struggled to sift through her brain for the correct words. "Circle, lass?"

She nodded, then pressed the 'circle' against her palm.

"Circle... in yer hand," he mused to himself. His gaze skipped away as he searched for the connecting thought she was unable to voice. "Circle... In yer hand... circle... doctor... Coins?" He glanced at her. "Do ye mean coins to pay for the doctor?"

Her eyes sparkled with accomplishment.

"Nae, lass." When it looked as if she wanted to argue, he gave her hand a pat. "Allow me to do this small thing for ye. I've money put by for emergencies; and if for some reason we need more between here and there, I'll figure it out. Let me play knight to yer damsel in distress for a wee time."

She shot him an indulging smile with the smallest flick of her eyes upward as if she were rolling them at him.

"Thank ye for protecting my fragile masculine ego, my lady." Clasping her hand in both his, he bowed gallantly over it and pressed a kiss to the back, and was delighted to see her cheeks softly flush pink at his over exaggeration of gallantry.

A knock at the door surprised them both, and MacDougall was across the room in a second to see who had arrived.

Not the doctor as he had hoped, but little Freddie, his cheeks red and eyes bright from his exertion of running across town and back. "Doctor's wife said t'would be some hours yet, Sir," he piped. "Ah told her it was terrible important." The boy shifted from foot to foot, hands fiddling with the buttons of his tattered waistcoat. "Ah'm awful sorry Ah couldn't get 'im ta come with me."

He tugged the promised penny from his pocket and flipped it to the boy. "I'm right thankful ye told the doctor to come, lad. That is for anything ye wish to use it on, dinnae need to share it with yer family if ye dinnae wish to."

The boy looked at it in wonder. "All fer me, Sir?"

He grinned and ruffled the lad's toe-blonde hair. "All for ye. Ye did yer job well, and with yer help, we'll make this lady here feel better." He stepped aside and allowed the boy a view of Emmy in bed, still awake and watching the exchange with an alert gaze.

The boy leaned to the side and peered into the dim room, his eyes immediately going to the bed where Emmy lay. He approached the bed respectfully, his expression too understanding for one so young. "Me sister Anne's dreadful ill, too. Doctor says he can't fix her, that she needs better air. But Ah hope he can fix *you*, Miss."

Emmy's eyes filled with tears almost instantly, their depths shimmering in the low candlelight. Moving slowly, she pulled free her purse from beneath her pillows, fished in it, and eventually came up with three gold sovereigns.

MacDougall had come up behind Freddie and settled a large, comforting hand on his small shoulder. Watching Emmy hold the coins out with a trembling right hand, he slid his hand down the boy's arm and moved his hand open so she could drop the coins into his palm. He couldn't help but share a smile with her over the lad's head. Were all the puffs of fashion and society as kind and generous as she? Somehow, he doubted it. "That's three pounds there, lad. Sixty shillings."

The boy stared at the coins, then at the lady, too stunned to speak.

She inhaled slowly, deeply. "Water—no... wat—no. Red?" She sighed and her eyes sought out MacDougall, pleading with him.

He patted Freddie's shoulder. "She was greatly injured and has trouble with her words. I believe the money is for yer family. Is that right? Nod if 'tis right, lass."

She nodded her head and turned her smile to the boy, her hand out to drag the side of her forefinger along the rounded, freckled cheek, a gesture which made MacDougall's heart turn over in his chest for a reason he didn't want to examine.

"By saints," the boy whispered. "All fer us? Thank yeh, Miss. Molly'll be so surprised. Maybe we can get somethin' extra good ta eat this week an' Anne'll be all better."

Emmy gave a watery smile.

He steered the boy toward the door then. "She needs to mostly lay still and quiet. Ye tell yer sister our prayers are with her, with all of ye." At the door, he extended his hand, man to man. "I thank ye for yer help, lad. Couldna have done it without ye."

Freddie grinned a classic little boy grin. "T'weren't nothing, Sir!" and he scampered off down the hall and was gone.

With the door closed, he rejoined Emmy, this time snagging the sole chair by its back and setting it beside the bed. "Ye made their month, if not their year," he remarked as he sat. "Doubt if that family has had a decent meal in their lives."

Her lips tugged downward in a deep frown.

He sighed. "Tis the way of things for most. Everyone has to work to put food on the table, even bairns his age sometimes."

Tears welled again, and when one escaped, he reached impulsively forward and caught it on his thumb as it slid down her cheek. The contact stilled them both, and his heart stuttered. He cleared his throat and forced his hand away from her face. "Cannae stand to see yer tears, Emmy lass," he replied gruffly as he retreated to the chair.

When had he stopped calling her Miss altogether? *Bollocks.*

For the remainder of the day while they awaited the appearance of the doctor, MacDougall read quietly from the Shakespeare comedy he'd purchased. She drifted in and out of sleep, and he wasn't sure how much she heard. Besides passing the time with the book, he also sought to anticipate her every need. At some point, tea, bread, and a good strong broth had been delivered, likely by their angel, Molly, and he thanked heaven for the kind-hearted girl.

It had been dark for hours when the doctor finally announced his arrival by a firm, solid rapping on the door, and MacDougall was already letting the man in by the time Emmy dragged her eyes open.

"Thank ye for coming, doctor," he welcomed as he stepped back and out of the way.

The grey-haired doctor shuffled straight to the bed and took a seat in the chair MacDougall had vacated. "Tell me what's happened."

The brevity with which MacDougall detailed Emmy's injuries was akin to a soldier reporting to his captain. Each piece of information was to the point with nothing embellished; simple and straight-forward.

As the doctor listened he proceeded through his usual routine: checking her eyes, glancing over the darkening bruises upon cheek and throat, monitoring her pulse with a well-trained touch, and gently prodding the young woman's head around the injury site. Though Emmy's brow furrowed against it, she made no sound or move of protest against the ministrations. MacDougall had to consciously root himself to the spot to restrain from taking action against the man who caused her further pain, doctor though he may be.

"How is your vision, my dear?" asked the wizened old doctor.

Her eyes flicked in MacDougall's direction before they settled upon the wrinkled face of the doctor. "See… brick, no. Brick—"

"Tis another effect, doctor," MacDougall interrupted. "Words seem to escape her; she cannae find the right thing to say. As to her vision, her eyes follow me all right, though as ye can see for yerself, she's rather heavy-lidded. She has been given laudanum with her tea, just the least bit to help her rest."

"Fascinating," the doctor murmured, likely in response to her condition regarding her lack of verbal ability.

After a few other pointed questions regarding what had been done for her comfort, the doctor stood. "There is some cranial swelling, though I see no evidence of abscess. Her inability to speak I find intriguing and would greatly enjoy studying her further. For now, I recommend a trepanning to relieve the pressure, which will in turn alleviate more of her symptoms, I believe."

"What is trepanning?"

"It is a professional medical procedure in which a trained physician, such as myself, takes a trephine drill to bore a hole into the skull."

MacDougall was proficient at controlling his expressions regardless of the situation, but even he found it difficult to school his features in that moment. "I think perhaps 'tis wise to allow her to make such a decision for herself."

"As her husband, it is well within your right to make such decisions for her," the doctor protested. "It would be best to commence with the procedure as soon as possible. There is no telling how much worse the pressure will become if something is not done."

"A delicate procedure such as that cannae be safe to perform outside a hospital," argued the Scotsman, seeking a way to block such an invasive procedure without the woman's express permission.

"On the contrary, it is quite safe. I have performed a dozen at least, both in the home and in a surgery. I assure you, the lady will be perfectly well, and better than once the procedure is complete. We ought to move forward with all haste, truly."

MacDougall had heard enough, and with a large hand settled upon the doctor's shoulder, the man was steered in the direction of the door. "Even so, I think we'll take our chances and let the lass keep her head in tact."

"Indeed, you are making a grave mistake, Sir," blustered the doctor as he was ushered out into the hall.

"Mayhap. I'll see my way to live with it, though," and the door was succinctly shut in the well-meaning doctor's face. As an afterthought, MacDougall threw the lock, then turned to find Emmy fretting and restless in the bed, her face pinched with anxiety. He crossed to her and sat, gathering both her hands in his. "Dinnae fash. I'll not let anyone get to ye." Her eyes continued to skip warily about the room as if she expected the doctor to re-materialize at any moment in their midst, medical instrument in hand. "I'll protect ye. Yer safe," he assured again, rubbing the backs of her hands with his thumbs.

It suddenly came to him that he was still a virtual stranger to the young woman; how was she to know he would keep her safe, that in neither anger nor harm would he ever lift a hand against her? For some reason, gaining her trust was suddenly of the utmost importance. "Ye ken that I'll never hurt ye, aye?" She stayed where she was, her gaze worriedly scanning the room. "Look at me, lass. Please." With his hand beneath her chin, he gently guided her face, and he instantly fell into the depths of her eyes that peered up at him. True enough, the lass trusted him if her expression was the smallest indication. Words failed; awareness crackled between them while the silence stretched until, finally, he bowed his head and pressed a gentle kiss to her forehead, a vow of protection, of steadfastness.

"I'll return shortly. Dinnae fash; I'll lock the door behind me," he murmured against her hairline, then was gone.

Emmy stared at the door, breathless, her cheeks flushed and eyes bright in a way that had naught to do with the laudanum drifting through her. Her belly was full of butterflies twisting and turning; her heart felt as if it were trying to escape from the cage of her lungs, so quickly it raced! Slowly, she lowered herself back to the pillows, her body still but her mind spinning with pleasure.

To say she trusted him was an understatement. Even as often as Mr. Wainwright passed in and out of her day-to-day life, she held herself aloof from him according to expected propriety and had no inclination for more. Becoming familiar and intimate with Wainwright had simply not occurred to her. She knew in the recesses of her mind that he wished to press his suit, but somehow she felt as if he would demand formality and deference from her at all times, even when alone in one another's company as husband and wife. For that reason, she could not imagine herself marrying him. He was too... Oh, what was the word? Wainwright was too much like the rest of her circle, and she wanted something else. Something different, something that, until that moment, had been indescribable.

She wanted a husband that would care for her, of course, but also someone she could laugh with, someone with whom she could enjoy life. So many of her set were so stuffy and self-absorbed, almost to the point that they didn't carry themselves as fellow humans. At times it seemed as if some of her fellow companions believed they were superior simply because of their money and stature in society. But that was all luck of birth; none of them had any control over such a thing. Perhaps there was much more to a person than their fine clothes and massive holdings, after all.

This Mr. MacDougall was a *man,* not just a gentleman. True, she knew nothing of his family or his origins, but he was true and steadfast. She felt the truth to the depths of her being, that this Scottish boxer was more of a man than almost every other gentleman she had ever met, excepting perhaps her dear cousin.

She smiled then.

Michael.

Her cousin was seven years her senior and as dear to her as any person could be. Her parents died when she was still a small child, and her beloved older cousin had begged and pleaded with his own father and mother to take her in rather than sending her to her godparents, whom she scarcely knew. Her godparents lived nearly permanently abroad and everything she knew was in and around London, Michael had argued. In addition, their estate was essentially a second home to her while her parents had lived, so close in heart were the two families. Thus a governess, a Miss Grant by name, was brought into the family just for her and Brookshire was made her official home.

Emmy's smile broadened as one memory followed another. Miss Grant was no longer Miss Grant, but Mrs. Southerly. The woman had married the year prior, and Emmy graduated from having a governess to being waited upon by a proper lady's maid.

At that moment, a thought suddenly struck her, one which had her brows lowering in concern and confusion: where was her lady?

Emmy could remember nothing regarding her coming away from Town; there seemed to be a few days missing from her memory. But having left London, surely Emmy would have brought Cossett along. She could hardly travel alone! And if something happened to her, then her maid would naturally be the first to call attention to her disappearance! Would there perhaps be something in a newspaper? Would her maid think to do such a thing? It would not do to be so conspicuous, but what else could be done? Oh, where was Cossett? How could she have neglected to think of her until just now? She ought to communicate this new possibility with Mr. MacDougall, but how?

With a frustrated huff, she curled up beneath the bed's comforts and willed herself to sleep, hoping things would miraculously sort themselves out by morning.

Chapter Nine

Emmy was miserable. The next several days passed in a fog of agonising sluggishness and missing stretches of time and awareness. She slept more than she thought possible for any human, eating little despite how often Mr. MacDougall urged this or that dainty upon her. Molly frequently stopped by to check on the lady's progress, as well, slipping small packages of cakes or biscuits as Mr. MacDougall ordered them, given his hesitation to leave the injured and fevered woman by herself. He took on a few more boxing matches, but only if Molly or one of her siblings were able to come and sit with Emmy. When alert, Emmy attempted to pay for all the additional trouble she was causing for the people in her small sphere, but of course, Mr. MacDougall would hear none of it.

Emmy, for her part, was only awake for short snatches, the days and nights running together until she had no understanding of the passage of time. Her head ached from unrelenting pounding and acute pressure, and she often suffered a sour stomach. Not that she was able to explain either ailment to her temporary guardian. She felt guilty for disrupting his life so entirely, but what else could she do? Whenever she tried to leave, she found herself dizzy and out of breath before she even made it to the door. Thank goodness for Molly's help; Emmy did not relish having to relieve herself in front of Mr. MacDougall, though she had already embarrassed herself thrice as she experienced sickness in the second chamber pot Molly brought for that express purpose. As far as she could ascertain, Mr. MacDougall took the inconvenience of her illness in stride and with gallantry. He acted as if it were all the most natural thing in the world, and never once made her feel guilty about such normal functions.

By now it was clear to her that, low born the Scotsman may have been, he was a true, sterling gentleman to his core. He took as much care of her as she'd seen in mothers with their own children, always tender and understanding, and never did she observe even a flicker of annoyance in his expression. If anything, he seemed to grow ever gentler with her as time passed. He read to her for hours on end, had gone so far as to additionally purchase a few other books to read once he'd read through the Shakespeare comedy twice. If he was in the room, he was always near at hand, seated in a chair toward the foot of the bed, ready to pop to his feet each time she stirred back to consciousness.

Molly and her family read little, but they were encouraged by Mr. MacDougall to practise as often as they chose while they watched over the invalid.

Though the words were halting and coarse, the sound of someone reading reassured Emmy that she wasn't alone as she remained abed and allowed her head to mend.

Many several days later. Mr. MacDougall strode into the room with an eager, almost boyish smile upon his face. She was already awake, and her brows lifted in gentle curiosity.

"I've a surprise for ye, lass," he proclaimed as he strode across the room. "If ye'll permit me..." He turned the covers back and tenderly scooped her into his arms, bearing her across his chest. She had little choice but to allow him to take her where he wished; she could protest and he would oblige, but she felt weaker than a new kitten with as much fight as a wet towel. She was surprised to find Molly in the hall with a grin much like the one Mr. MacDougall wore. What were they planning?

"Where?" Emmy quietly asked. It was one of the words she'd regained over the weeks of rest and recovery, although any word over which she had intentional possession came haltingly after a pause of determination and focus.

With the care of one watching over something treasured, Mr. MacDougall bore down the hall to a different room... a bathing room. It was a small area, with the outer wall of the room boasting a modest hearth with an iron crane on either side, each holding a large kettle of what she assumed was water. A bucket sat steaming on the wood floor beside a well-used rag rug, which was spread before a decent-sized copper tub, with a wood stepping stool standing alongside. A grey linen sheet, which she was sure began its life as a pristine white colour, lined half the bathtub, and a washcloth was draped over the side for her use. Deliciously scented steam wafted from the tub; between that and the fire crackling in the hearth, the room was delightfully warm and cosy.

Turning sideways to shuffle them both through the door, he then set her carefully upon her feet, his hands upon her shoulders until he was certain she was steady. Molly came to her side and slid one arm behind her lower back while the other braced her elbow. "Ah'll care fer her; don't yeh worry, Sir."

He stepped back and even bowed. "Enjoy, lass," and with that, he departed, shutting the door behind him.

Molly turned to her and smiled. "He wanted ta do somethin' nice fer yeh, Miss, with yeh being stuck in bed fer s'long. Yer lucky ta have a husband dote on yeh the way he does. Would that I'd be s'lucky some day."

Emmy blushed. She was, of course, unable to correct Molly's assumption, and it was better for her own reputation to let the impression stand as it was. She was utterly safe, really; no one knew she was in this tiny hamlet of a village, and no one knew her real name. It was rather freeing, now she thought of it. Living anonymously, without all the constraints her place in society put upon her, gave her a taste of the simpler life. The manners and expectations weren't as rigid, and she felt more at ease, more at peace with herself. She had not realised how utterly exhausting it was to be shuffled from one engagement to the next, pressured to be perfectly charming yet docile at every turn. Of course, she was more docile now than she ever had been, but something told her Mr. MacDougall would not be the type of man possessed of such outlandish masculine conceit that he would rage at her the moment she expressed an opinion, if such a time ever came.

She blinked against the momentary reverie and came back to the present as Molly good-naturedly helped her disrobe. The girl was so kind and natural, she was rather amazed that Molly hadn't been snapped up by a wealthy family as a lady's maid, or at least for a better position than working at a second rate inn. Then again, Molly had a family relying upon her; with a sick sister, it was doubtful she would want to live in another county, thereby rarely seeing her family. Molly had the sort of family Emmy had always longed for, one where they delighted in each other's company through pleasantries and hardships.

Molly had procured a soft flannel bathing gown and slipped it over Emmy's head once she'd been divested of her other clothing. That done, it was with deliberate care that Molly aided Emmy in stepping over the edge of the tub and settling into the warm confines of the water. "I've found some soft soap for you," the girl offered as she hoisted the bucket up and slowly poured it into the tub at Emmy's feet. "Ah don't wantta hover, Miss, but Ah'll stay if ya need me to."

Emmy smiled in gratitude and slowly shook her head.

Molly then tugged free a small brass bell from her apron's pocket and set it on the stool. "Ring out if ya need me. Ah'll be cleanin' on this floor but Ah'll listen for ya." With a quick little curtsey, the chambermaid took her leave and closed Emmy into the wonderful heat of the room.

Normally, she preferred the bracing nature of brisk baths with cool water, even an occasional shower—her cousin had procured one the year before and it was a great relief on hot days. However with the chill seeping into the room more each day, the hot water was delicious and relaxing and she felt she would like to stay cocooned in it forever.

She could not, of course. When the water began to cool, she gave her hair a brisk scrubbing, then the rest of her body. There was no more clean water in the bucket, so she contented herself in sliding down until she fully submerged her head to rid her hair of the soap. Once she felt she was as rinsed as possible, she reached over the edge for the bell.

She had only just shaken it when there was a knock on the other side of the door, and Molly's cheerful giggle tinkled out. "Ah s'pose that means yer finished, Miss?" The girl peeked her head in, then fully entered and closed the door behind her.

It was something of an involved process: getting out of the tub, freed from the dripping bathing shift, rubbed dry. She was unable to lounge about in a dressing gown as she might have done at home. Molly laced her into the corset she had blissfully been without for weeks, and helped her redress in the common clothing she'd purchased that first day. By the time Emmy had completed all that, she panted for breath and her face was flushed. "Down," she whimpered. "Down… chair."

Molly frowned and guided her to sit on the stepping stool. "Oh, Miss! Ah've made yeh work too hard! Ah even promised yer husband Ah'd care for yeh," she fretted as she fled from the room. Emmy was utterly unable to stop her before she was gone.

Mr. MacDougall appeared a minute later with Molly on his heels. "Ah'm so very sorry, Sir. I was just dressing her. Ah didn't know she'd weaken so very much from it."

"Ye did just fine, Molly, better than I could have," he assured her even as he plucked Emmy from the stool to carry her back. "Thank ye for yer kindness and aid. We would be lost without ye."

Emmy offered a glimmer of a smile, then settled her head against the man's strong, supporting shoulder. He hadn't far to walk, but between her exertion and the gentle rocking motion of his gait, she was asleep by the time he tucked her back into bed.

One morning some days later, as MacDougall folded his bedding as he did every day, Emmy reached out and knocked lightly upon the table to get his attention, something she'd taken to doing earlier in the week.

He glanced over his shoulder and smiled gently at her. "Morning, lass. Are ye better'n ye've been?"

She slowly nodded her head. The ache and dizziness in her brain had yet to abate, so every movement she made was still done with the utmost care. "Eeeeee— ink. Ink... story, no—ink."

MacDougall's brows soared and he quickly came to the bedside, dragging the chair close enough to sit and take a hand of hers. "That is a new one. I hear ye, lass. Story. Ink."

She nodded again. "Ink… rrr-write… ink."

"Ye wish to write something? A letter?" When she scowled in response, MacDougall bit back a chuckle. "All right, not a letter, then. Keep trying. I'm listening."

She looked into his face for a long moment, drank in his steadiness, and peace slowly overtook her features as she did so. Finally, she sighed and a flicker of a smile curved her lips. Then, with a fortifying breath, she started again. "Write… ink… story."

"A book? Ye want the book I bought ye?"

She shook her head and bit at her lower lip. "Ink… paa-page? Page. Page. Pape." A glimmer lit up her eyes and she continued. "Pape. Pape." She turned her focus upon MacDougall and stared at him intently, as if she were willing him to understand and translate for her. "Pape. Pape!"

"Pape? Pape…" He blinked. "Paper?" The joyful sunshine that broke through her expression fairly blinded him. "Paper! Yer saying paper. Do ye mean paper to write on?" He left her to hurry to the writing desk, lifting up loose leaves of blank pages in example.

She shook her head. "Pape. Pape," she insisted.

"Aye, paper. I hear ye, lass." He stood with his hands on his hips, mind untangling the knots her train of thought created. "Paper… Do ye mean a newspaper?"

Emmy squealed softly in excitement. "Pape!"

He slapped his hands together. "Newspaper! Aye! I'll go and fetch a newspaper! Every newspaper I can find!" And without attempting to collect further information, MacDougall was out the door, leaving her to collapse in exhaustion against the pillows.

Emmy sighed and closed her eyes as she relaxed against the pillows. What relief she felt in being able to speak something else, and something that actually made sense, at last! With Mr. MacDougall on his way to find a newspaper, there was more of a chance of her finally making her way home. She intended to search the papers for mention of herself, or an accident nearby, or even something about Cossett. She dimly recalled having had such a thought before that awful stretch of darkness and illness from the previous week. Now that her mind felt clearer and her body stronger, she was determined to do all she could to relieve Mr. MacDougall of his duty.

Why did her heart ache at the thought of being separated from him? He was still very much a stranger, albeit a generous and noble one. But she was not his responsibility, although he had taken such upon himself most kindly. No, she ought to return to London as soon as may be, to move on with her life and allow Mr. MacDougall to return to his, even if such a thought brought a sharp pang to her insides.

Emmy pushed herself upright the moment she heard the key in the lock, and her eyes were fixed on the stack of newspapers in the man's arms. He kicked the door closed, pocketed the key, and crossed the room to drop the pile at the foot of the bed. He quickly sorted through and separated each individual paper from the others until at least a dozen various papers littered the bed.

"Cannae understand why yer needing this many papers, but here ye are. A few are local, few from the northerner regions, two as far south as London. Course the news 'tis several days old by now," he mused aloud.

Emmy reached for the nearest paper, unfolding it and taking her time to look over the contents. Sensing movement, her gaze lifted to see Mr. MacDougall with his arms crossed and his eyes fixed intently upon her. The man fairly vibrated with energy and she fought back a smile. Did the man know how to sit still? Allowing a small grin of amusement to curl her lips, she gestured to the chair he always occupied, then went back to her reading. The squawk of the chair legs on the wood floor declared that he'd finally seated himself, and a rustle of paper indicated he was reading now, as well.

"If only ye could tell me what we're searching for," he commented as he turned a page. Emmy's attention snagged upon the word 'we' and her insides warmed at his obvious alliance with her, further proof that he meant what he had said when he declared his intentions of staying with her until she was reunited with her people.

Forcing that line of thinking from her focus, she stared at the words printed on the pages in her hands, and squinted. The words were there but she was unsure if it was her eyes or her mind that struggled with bringing the print into focus. She had thought and hoped that this would miraculously solve her dilemma; instead, it created another hurdle to overcome. Her eyes stung with the onslaught of tears and she pinched her eyes closed to keep them in control.

"Miss Emmy, lass?"

She sighed; of course he would notice. His care of her broke the tenuous hold she had on her emotions and tears escaped from the corners of her eyes, dripping silently down her cheeks. The mattress dipped and she knew he'd come to sit beside her. The newspaper that had been on her lap was dragged away, and she felt the warmth of his hands envelope hers.

"Here was I thinking we spoke about those tears of yourn," he teased lightly as his thumbs swiped at the damp streaks upon her face. "Cannae bear to see yer tears, lass, especially since I cannae fix what ails ye."

Emmy glanced at the papers helplessly, her grand idea of helping her situation dissolving. Why could she not read and understand the words? She had always been a fine reader and enjoyed novels and poetry alike as a pastime. Never in memory could she recall any difficulty in reading or comprehending; what was wrong with her?

Mr. MacDougall followed her gaze to the papers and picked up what she'd been perusing. "Did ye find something in here?"

She shook her head.

"But something upset ye," he assumed as he glanced over the first page as if expecting the answer to leap at him.

She nodded glumly. She had no way to even describe what disturbed her! "Not. Not… page. Story, no. Page…" What sort of life would she live if she could not communicate with anyone? What if the rest of her life was like this, locked in her own mind, proper speech escaping her? Would Michael perhaps send her away to an asylum?

"Shh, Dinnae fash yerself. I'll put it right somehow," he assured, interrupting her rather morose way of thinking. Emmy slowly shook her head again, and his dark brows lowered over his eyes in concentration. "What could have upset ye about the paper if 'tis not *in* the paper, itself?"

Emmy reached out and traced the lines of print, then pressed her open hand to the page with a frown, and she prayed he would correctly interpret her meaning. "Page… eyes… no."

It was a full minute of silence before the light of understanding flared in his expression. "With the troubles ye have speaking, can ye not read?"

Her lips still tugged downward in a frown.

"Well, that certainly makes it difficult for ye."

With a whine and a moan, Emmy dropped her face into her palms and doubled over her lap.

Mr. MacDougall chuckled. "Surely 'tis not as bad as all that. Yer taken care of, ye've enough food, yer warm and protected. Everything else will work itself out, lass. Remember, I'm not leaving ye until yer home where ye belong. Dinnae give way now." He paused, then continued, "Ye understand all I say to ye, aye?"

Emmy straightened slowly and nodded.

"Then I'll read aloud to ye. If something strikes as odd, ye inform me, and we'll puzzle it out together, me and thee." He moved back to the chair, took up the paper she'd discarded, and began to scan the columns of printed text as he settled into the chair.

To MacDougall's disgust, there were more of the same sorts of headlines mentioned in these papers as he had found the weeks before, scintillating phrases meant to lure readers to dive into whatever gossip had been scraped together. He'd spend the past hour reading the headlines to Emmy in hopes that something would trigger a memory, and he would read through the article itself if it appeared it might help, but so far, nothing had caused much more than a furrow of her brow.

"Here's one: Deceased Woman on Liverpool–Manchester Railway Identified as Harriet Stewart," he recited from the headline before flicking his gaze at Emmy to gauge her reaction. She had perked up some, her eyes alight with intelligence as her memory struggled to grab hold of something just out of reach. "Do ye recognize the name, lass?"

Emmy chewed upon her lower lip thoughtfully before finally, slowly, nodding her head.

"Let us see, then… Says she was from St. Giles. Worked as an undermaid for a family in Woodbridge." He was silent as he scanned the article for pertinent information. It detailed how long she worked in Woodbridge, a small bit about her family, her age. "She recently left her position in favour of accompanying a lady being transferred to an insane asylum in Scotland, then planned to marry." He paused, scowling. "Does any of that sound familiar to ye?"

Her face was a study in desperation for recollection; her eyes skipped unseeing around the room as if wildly trying to snatch information flying through the air like dragonflies. Her jaw was set, her lips were pursed together in a tight line, and a deep V had settled between her brows. Even her hands were in fists in the blankets at her side.

"Lass, dinnae force it to come. I'm sure what needs to be remembered will be in time. Yer still healing."

Her face cleared of its concentration and she shot a scowl in his direction, which surprised a laugh out of him. How quickly her emotions shifted! "I say it for yer benefit; dinnae kill me over it."

Her eyes narrowed afresh, and he bit back a second chuckle that threatened to spill forth. He wasn't sure he wanted to face her ire. "All right, lass. I concede."

She looked almost pleased and smug, and he shook his head. "Back to the papers, then."

The next piece that truly caught his attention was the offer of a reward. His eyes drifted lazily over it, thinking it would lead to nothing given that it was a small local paper and Emmy was clearly from the upper crust London set. But as he read through it, it was clear there was a connection. "Lass, I think I've found something: 'Reward for information regarding missing heiress. A well-dressed young woman from London went missing from the train en route to

Liverpool. May be confused with possible paranoia. Brown hair, hazel eyes, average height. Last seen wearing a pink gown and yellow long coat. Contact Mr. Wainwright—'" He set the paper down to gauge Emmy's reaction; confusion held place as the primary emotion in her expression. "That was what ye were wearing when I came upon ye. Can ye recall a man with that name?"

She nodded without hesitation but did not appear alarmed or frightened by the name.

"You must have been travelling in his company for him to be the person of contact if anyone finds ye."

Emmy started at that, her back straightening and a small frown tugging her lips downward.

"Do ye remember travelling with him?"

She shook her head slowly. "...no."

He glanced briefly at the paper again, thoughts turning over and over. "I'll contact him at once if ye wish it, but I'm not sure ye can trust him."

She blinked rapidly and started again.

"Hear me first. He describes ye as confused with possible paranoia. Aye, yer confused enough now from yer injury, but unless he left ye on the street injured, yer confusion happened from hitting yer head, and he's describing ye as addled *before* that. Since ye cannae answer me in words, I ask ye: have ye reason to believe yerself even a wee bit mad?" His expression showed he already knew the answer.

He watched as understanding dawned in her face. Emmy shook her head and slowly sank at back against the pillows.

Setting the papers aside, he dragged the chair just a little closer and braced his forearms atop his thighs as he sat forward. "If ye'd feel most comfortable with yer own folk, I'll contact local authorities and have them put ye in touch with yer Mr. Wainwright at once. I'm sure he'll return ye to yer friends and family." It was a fight to keep his expression blank as he made the offer, but his hands, out of her sight as they hung between his knees, fisted as his entire being rebelled at the thought of her care being handed over to another man.

He had no claim on her, he had to remind himself. Yet for the first time in his life, he wanted the settled down type of future most everyone around him seemed to desire. And impossible as it was, he only wanted it with this beguiling woman before him.

"Is that what ye wish for me to do, Miss Emmy?" he asked, struggling to replace emotional distance and formality between them.

Emmy's breath stalled within her lungs as she held Mr. MacDougall's focus, that darker than dark gaze which could easily be frightening and foreboding yet was nothing but warm and kind and patient with her. They had been in one other's company almost exclusively for over a fortnight, yet it felt like months. She had been entirely vulnerable and at his mercy, unable to protect herself if he had wished her harm, and not even once had she ever feared being in his presence without a chaperone. It would be the largest scandal of the Season, possibly beyond, and would follow her the rest of her life should any of this become known to the papers; her family name would be dragged through the mud of society. Her fate would be sealed and no one would come within five miles of her. Her cousin, Michael, could care for himself, but surely he had the desire to marry and have a family one day, and likely sooner rather than later. Her reputation would be in irretrievable ruins should anyone learn that she had been living with this man alone, and it would of course affect Michael's ability to make a good match for himself. And Molly, sweet girl that she was, hardly counted as a suitable chaperone, nor was she present at all times as was proper.

As she thought over it, not only did it not bother her as much as it ought, but she found the idea of another imposing upon them rather distasteful. And gracious, what did that say about her? She *should* want to return to her old life as soon as may be! Yet...

"Miss Emmy?"

His deep voice pulled her back into the present moment, and she blinked.

"Do ye wish to reunite with Mr. Wainwright and have him accompany ye back to London?"

She sighed. Wainwright would never understand what complications she now faced; rather, she knew he would be annoyed with her for not being able to communicate efficiently. To be sure, he was kind enough, and it was more than clear that he wished to press his suit, but she'd never been interested in him in that way. Fortunately for her, a marriage of convenience was not something her situation in life would require; she need not marry at all unless she wished to, and she had no desire whatsoever to join herself with Wainwright. His few pleasantries paled in comparison to the Scotsman who had taken it upon himself to protect her. Uncurling herself, she reached for MacDougall and set a timid hand upon his forearm. "Heeere. Here."

His expression softened instantly, the warm light returning to his eyes. Keeping his eyes locked with her own, he took her hand in both his, bowed low over it, and kissed the backs of her fingers.

An unspoken vow was exchanged between them at that moment; she felt it in the deepest recesses of her heart and soul. An invisible tether wove its way into existence between them, strong enough that her chest ached from keeping herself anchored where she was instead of pressing herself into his arms. As he worked diligently to remain a gentleman and handle her with respect and propriety, she would respond in kind.

Mr. MacDougall came to himself first, standing and stepping away until he stood in the centre of the small room with his arms akimbo. "Yer an unfair temptation, *Miss* Emmy," he growled, dark eyes flashing in a way that made her entire body heat from the inside out. Clearing his throat, he headed for the door, and Emmy gave a little exclamation of wordless protest at his leaving.

He stopped with his hand on the doorknob. "That article gave me a way to find a clue we've been missing: yer name."

Chapter Ten

The cold bite in the air did much to clear the haze from his brain and the fire that raced through his blood. MacDougall had always been possessed of a fine mind and memory, so as his desire cooled, the details of what he'd read over the course of the morning in the newspapers returned to him, and as he walked, his thoughts began to connect and rearrange the various bits and pieces he'd gleaned.

There had been more in the paper than he had revealed to the injured woman. In addition to proclaiming possible paranoia, it also stated that she had escaped from the train bound for an asylum, and that she was mildly insane. It didn't give him her name in print, but it was a sure thing that the local constabulary would have it, as it was a local paper that had printed the advert for the reward. He would go and feign interest in the reward and fish for whatever additional information was available to him. If they had been closer to Liverpool, he would have applied himself to the police there, as it was a larger force and would likely know more than even this small collection of village watchmen. As it was, he didn't anticipate there being much to be learned. Whoever this Wainwright character was, he had a plot against Emmy; MacDougall could feel it. He just had to protect her.

Not for the first time did he wish she could communicate freely.

It was a fruitless enterprise, wishing for her brain to be miraculously healed, so he continued on his way toward the constabulary.

He had not made a habit to frequent either constabularies nor any sort of police headquarters, as were available in the London area, but he expected more than a small cottage occupied by a man with his feet on a table and his cap pulled down over his eyes. With a huff and a roll of his eyes, he rapped solidly upon the wall just inside the door, and the watchman jerked awake, dazed eyes rapidly scanning the parlour before settling upon MacDougall's frame.

"Oi! Scared me to death," breathed the watchman as he scrubbed a hand down his face and rolled to his feet. "Right sorry about sleeping. Baby's teeth are coming in; wife says we need to get his gums lanced."

Having nothing to say nor add to that piece of unsolicited information, MacDougall pretended the man said nothing at all. Rather than speaking with his native Scottish brogue, he disguised it with the hopes of confusing anyone that might try to follow their trail. Something in him felt a trap tightening around Emmy, and a need to protect her anew surged to the forefront. "I've a question to put to you. I read in the newspaper there's a reward for information about a mad woman some dandy thinks is around the village. Do you know more about it?" He forced himself to grin, though doing so made him feel as if he were somehow betraying Emmy's trust. "I've an eye on that prize."

The watchman yawned, setting his hands to his lower back in a stretch backwards, as he sleepily answered, "I haven't much more information than that. Course if you grease my fist a bit…"

Figuring something along those lines would be the response, MacDougall fished a coin from his pocket and slid it quietly onto the table, brows raised. "I'll split the winnings with ye."

Without blinking, the man slipped the money into his waistcoat pocket. "The pink said the woman's name was Everleigh. He wanted to keep it quiet on account of her being from some well-to-do family in Town. I don't know nothing else."

MacDougall slowly nodded, wondering what other hooks he could drop into the water. "Strange that a tulip would be up this way, and in a small village like this."

"Said he was taking her north to a hospital or asylum or some such; guess the woman's a bit dicked in the nob."

Pieces clicked together in MacDougall's head, and he flipped another coin to the officer. "Keep it under yer cap, if ye would, give a lad a fighting chance for that purse." Without another word, he strode out the door, leaving the sleepy constable to return to his nap.

So not only had Wainwright placed the advert, he had been in this very hamlet within the past couple days. If MacDougall passed him on the road, he'd never know it. He was newly thankful that Emmy was safe at the inn and unable to leave the bed. Until he was absolutely certain this Wainwright had her best interest in mind, which he now doubted, he wouldn't surrender her to any but her own family, and even then he would withhold her if he thought for a moment they meant her harm. Until then, he'd be suspicious of any well-dressed dandy.

On his way back to the inn, he detoured into the used clothes shop where he and Emmy purchased her 'disguise' weeks before. He decided she may have use of clothing that would be an even better disguise if she, in fact, was in danger of being found by someone who meant her harm, thinking it more appropriate for her reputation if she had the appearance of a boy rather than the lady she was while she travelled in his company.

To his disappointment, the shopkeeper recognized him, and for the first time he rather resented standing out from a crowd with his height. If the clerk remembered him, there was a chance the man also remembered her, and that could prove problematic. It wasn't a very large town and she'd been seen wearing the very clothing described in the reward advert. While he didn't fear anything from Molly and her brother, surely there were plenty who would be only too delighted to report they'd seen her in hopes of collecting the promised reward.

He quickly collected a pair of trousers, a flannel shirt, a coarse waistcoat missing its buttons, and two pairs of good thick socks, all in a size he hoped would fit her slender form. He also purchased a plain brown canvas coat, much like his own, a cap, and a canvas pack to stuff it all in.

"Left the chit at home this time, did yeh?" the shopkeeper jeered, and MacDougall groaned inwardly. So the man did, indeed, remember them both, and that could prove dangerous.

"Careful with how ye speak about my sister," MacDougall growled, letting his genuine irritation flare even while he sought to cover her identity. Paying the man, he stuffed his purchases into the pack and stomped toward the door.

"Yer 'sister' left her mighty fine gown and coat when she left."

That pulled MacDougall up rather abruptly, and he pivoted to stare down the old man behind the counter.

"I've still got 'em if you want 'em back, for a price," the shopkeeper prodded with a grin.

"Keep them," MacDougall mumbled, then strode resolutely out the door.

So not only did the man recognize and remember them, but he even had in his possession her old clothing. Buying them back would do nothing to safeguard her; too many had already witnessed her in the village wearing the clothing described in the reward advert: not just the shopkeeper, but the lad who had rifled through her clothing, the gang MacDougall had thrashed later that same evening, everyone at the public house and again at breakfast that first morning, as well as anyone else who may have taken note of her presence around the town before his path crossed with hers. Their wisest course of action would be to leave first thing in the morning, perhaps a little before daylight while the town still slept. He was used to living much of his life on the road, so while it wouldn't be arduous for him, it was sure to be difficult upon his more tender-footed companion. With people watching out for a young woman dressed a certain way, there was little chance of her being recognized. Indeed, how many people in the country and outer villages regularly read the newspaper? Even so, it was wise to be cautious. He detoured toward the town centre where he purchased some necessities for the road: food and drink of course, and also a lantern, three wool blankets, a swath of thick canvas, and a large tarpaulin, along with a good length of sturdy rope. While he did not plan on returning to London solely by wagon, he desired to move a few days' worth away from where they had been staying before arranging a stage for himself and Emmy.

As he walked briskly back to the inn with his arms heavily laden with items, his brain fitted together one piece after another in rapid fire. There had been that article about a dead woman found on the train, which was likely the same woman mentioned by name in the paper he'd read that very morning, Harriet Stewart it had said. And it had mentioned that she was taking a madwoman to an asylum. Then the watchman had said Wainwright was taking Emmy—for he had no doubt in his mind it was she whom the advert referenced—to an asylum, and that she was mildly insane. Was it possible that the insane woman Miss Stewart had been travelling with was the very same for whom this Wainwright searched?

But then Miss Stewart's poor body had been discovered on the train weeks ago; the first headline he'd noticed suddenly came to mind, about potential foul play, disclosed before her identity had been uncovered. Was it possible the two events were connected? And if so, was Wainwright a desperate enough character to kill someone in the way of his plot? Emmy could be in even greater danger than he had supposed, and the sooner he removed her from this village, the better.

"We've got ta leave, lass," MacDougall announced upon re-entering their room as the daylight waned.

Emmy pushed herself upright from her reclining position against the pillows, alarm in her face.

"Seems as yer Mr. Wainwright is pretty intent on findin' ye, an' havin' ye in his power," he continued, his Scottish burr thick with his urgency, and her expression pinched in concerned bewilderment. "Do ye feel oop ta th' journey?"

With her lips set in determination, she nodded, swinging her legs over the side of the bed. Bless her for trusting him without question, for not delaying when time was of the essence. With careful, measured steps, Emmy padded across the room to fetch the second-hand boots that she had yet to place upon her feet. With clumsy hands she managed to stuff her feet into the boots, but tying the laces proved beyond her ability.

MacDougall took a knee before her. "Allow me, Miss Everleigh," he murmured as he tied bows in each boot's laces by turn.

Her head snapped up, her eyes wide and mouth agape.

He chuckled. "Aye, I know yer true name, the family name at least. Still dinnae ken yer Christian name, but 'tis more proper this way, I suppose. I ken yer not fully recovered, but I fear there's too much danger here to stay," he explained as he stood, then helped her to her feet. She teetered a little. He reflexively steadied her with his hands cupping her elbows, and her palms settled against his chest.

He froze.

He took a moment to study her with new eyes. Her colour was what he would assume was normal, a complexion that was naturally fair but with the glow of a healthy blush in her cheeks. She didn't appear to be squinting as she had been toward the beginning of their acquaintanceship, and her eyes glimmered in the lamplight with awareness and intelligence, as if the cobwebs of the previous weeks had finally been swept away from her mind.

He stumbled into her gaze and his heart clenched, halting for a moment before racing double time. The flecks of gold ignited within her eyes and set the depths flashing and sparkling like sunshine on rippling water. Impulse overtook him, and a work-roughened hand skimmed up her arm until he cupped one side of her face in his palm. He dipped his head slowly, his eyes searching her face and expression for any sign of aversion or the slightest bit of hesitation.

Instead, she tipped her face up and leaned toward him.

The first brush of his lips against hers was pure heaven. It wasn't just the softness of her mouth and how eagerly she yielded to him, nor was it the feel of her silken hair between his fingers as he cradled the back of her head; it wasn't the taste of her—a taste that was fully unique to just her, one he would dream of every night for the rest of his life. It was everything about her, like an angel deigning to grace him with her presence, and yet she stood willingly in the circle of his arms, returning the kiss with equal ardour, her hands curling into his shirt. Possession roared through him, and he wanted nothing better than to crush her to him and plunder her mouth. Each touch remained measured and gentle, however, with his entire focus finely attuned to every nuance of the woman against him.

After long minutes, or perhaps hours, of indulging himself in her, he finally, and quite reluctantly, leaned back enough that their lips parted from one another. Her breathing was ragged, and he couldn't help but feel rather pleased that her eyes were unfocused and her cheeks were flushed, proof that he affected her at least as much as she affected him. Setting his forehead to hers, he simply breathed, allowing his galloping heart to slow to a more normal pace. "Sorry, lass. I fear I got a mite carried away."

In answer, she rose to her tiptoes and kissed his cheek, then lightly, briefly, kissed his lips before she settled against his chest, ear directly over his heart, and with a grin he couldn't stop if he'd tried, he wrapped both arms about her and held her close.

"Yer dangerous to my heart, Miss Everleigh," he rumbled.

She leaned back in his arms, and when he peered down at her, he found her scowling at him. He had to chuckle, she tried so very hard to appear fearsome. "What's got yer ire now?"

She huffed, brows pinched, and she pointed at herself.

"Aye? Yer Miss Everleigh."

She shook her head. "Mmm… me. Em… Em."

His brows rose and he cupped her face. "Ye… what?"

Again, she shook her head. "Em… mee."

He watched her for a long moment, listening to her repeat the odd phrase thrice more before understanding ignited in his brain. "Emmy? Not Miss Everleigh. Emmy is it to be?"

The smile that spread across her face was blinding, and she turned her head to kiss his palm.

He shivered and his throat thickened. "Verra well. When 'tis just me an' thee, Emmy ye'll stay." Her declaration of wanting to remain on familiar, intimate terms with him set a fire blazing in his belly, and he closed the gap to give her one more kiss before he stepped back, even taking his hands away from her and linking them behind his back. "We need to go, and if we dinnae leave the noo, ye may never see the outside of this room again," he threatened, his voice low. With heat and promise in his eyes, he swept about the room, hurriedly gathering their few belongings.

Emmy insisted upon leaving something for Molly, the girl who had been so kind and generous over the previous weeks. While MacDougall prepared for their flight, Emmy made a crude attempt at penmanship. Given that her right had refused to obey her orders the way it ought, it took far longer than MacDougall wanted if his agitated pacing was any indication, but at last she scrawled out, "Thank you. Emmy." A few more coins were folded securely in the paper and Molly's name written on the outside for her to find the next morning.

"I've a thought," MacDougall replied as Emmy concluded her note. "To be sure 'tis likely an unnecessary precaution, but what would ye say to wearing the togs of a boy?"

That arrested Emmy's attention rather suddenly, and she stared at him openly as he held up what he'd purchased earlier that day.

"If anyone is looking for a beautiful young woman of wealth and status, what better way to disguise yerself than to appear as a lad?"

He could see in her eyes that she understood his point, but it was evident that she was more than a little reluctant to don the trousers and waistcoat. She relented, however, and moved across the floor to take the clothes in her hands.

He smiled. "I'm only thinking of yer safety, Emmy. If aught were to happen to ye…" The sentence was left unfinished, but there was a hint of fear and torment in his eyes. "Can ye dress yerself?"

She nodded in determination.

"I'll take things down to the wagon I've secured and will be back for ye shortly. Keep the door locked." With that, he was gone.

It took longer than he had hoped to ready everything for their flight, but finally, MacDougall hurried back up the stairs, taking them two at a time. He rapped gently at the door before letting himself in. "The wagon is all ready for—" He pulled up short and stared, mouth agape, fire sluicing through his veins.

When he'd purchased the apparel for her earlier, he hadn't realised just how form-fitting a pair of trousers were; he was suddenly, painfully, aware of it now. The legs of the garment Emmy wore now were a little loose, but they displayed the slender curve of her calf and then rose all the way to the juncture of her legs. His mouth went bone dry and his throat worked several times in an attempt to swallow. He inwardly cursed his idea of having Emmy go about like a lad, and he had a feeling this vision would torture him for long weeks afterward.

"We should go," he rasped, finally recovering his voice. "Do ye need my help with anything else?"

The oversized canvas coat was still draped on the bed, and she slipped into it quickly; MacDougall thanked heaven that the coat's bottom hem fell well below her hips. He made quick work of balling up her discarded dress and petticoats and stuffed them in the bag he'd left in the room for that purpose. With one hand gripping the sack and the other slipping around Emmy's palm he led the way out into the hall and down the back stairs.

Darkness always fell early in December, and the hour felt much later than the reality. With fresh snow drifting down from the heavens, only lamplight lit the avenues and reflected upon the snow both on the ground and in the air. It wasn't as dark as he would have hoped, but there was nothing to be done about it now. MacDougall paused Emmy's forward motion when she would have followed him out into the night. Leaning out, he peered this way and that before taking her elbow and ushering her to the wagon. Without warning, he plucked her off her feet and set her onto the seat, then circled the vehicle and jumped up beside her. He spared a moment to toss a heavy wool blanket around her shoulders and another around her legs and feet, then gave the horse a brief lash with the reins to propel the beast into motion. With the blanket up over her head like a hood to further shield her face, they began their flight from the village and into the unfamiliar countryside.

Chapter Eleven

It was several hours before MacDougall finally pulled
the dray horse over to rest. He had set a slow, easy
pace for the equine, thinking not only to spare the
animal but also hoping that the nonchalant speed
would garner less attention than a wagon flying down
the road at such a late hour, adding to the ruse by
affecting a bored slouch in the seat. It so happened
that he'd had to pull over so a rushing stage could
pass by, and he decided it was as good a time as any
to give the horse a chance to nose about the ground
for snow-covered grass and snack upon a few
handfuls of grain.

Emmy had fallen asleep about an hour in, her
weight growing heavier against his side, and he had
been obliged to wrap an arm about her back to ensure
she would not topple from the seat. Her close
proximity aided in keeping him warmer, as well. But
now, the hand holding the reins was growing numb
with cold, and with the horse stopped and the wagon
pulled off the road, he sought to carefully settle

Emmy along the seat upon her side. Once he was certain she was balanced and would not fall, he chafed his hands together several times as he hopped down to tend to the horse.

There was only one lantern with which to light their way, and again he was thankful they didn't set a break-necked pace for themselves, otherwise they surely would have crashed, so dark was the oppressive cloud cover. It was fortunate that he was a man who could function on little sleep; it would be well to travel through much of the night and perhaps stop for a couple hours before dawn broke. Pulling a sack from one of the crates of supplies, he tromped through the ice-crusted grasses to where the horse stood, eagerly bobbing its head up and down. MacDougall chuckled in amusement as he fished out a handful of dried corn and held it near the animal's mouth.

Once the horse had finished a few handfuls of feed, it continued to munch and chuff at the grass underfoot, and MacDougall stomped around to push sensation back into his frozen feet. Being cold while travelling was a hardship he was well accustomed to; if his sacrifice kept Emmy warm and comfortable, it was worth the discomfort. All that to say, he fished out the oiled tarpaulin meant for creating a shelter and tossed it about his shoulders.

The horse continued to graze and rest its legs, and he climbed onto the bench seat once more, careful to perch on the very edge so as not to rouse the sleeping maiden. Even dressed as a boy, the beauty of her face gave her away and he hoped to avoid most people as they continued on, otherwise the charade would be next to useless. Gazing down at her, he tugged one hand free of its glove and lovingly stroked the curve of her cheek. The honour he felt at being in such close and intimate proximity to this angel given form, the trust she'd put in him as her protector and champion, made his heart swell in a manner entirely new. He had simply desired her before, but now he felt his emotions shift to something much deeper, much more tender, ones that brought to mind longings of hearth and home.

As much as he wanted to allow her to sleep, knowing she was still recovering, they needed to get moving again. Being only a handful of hours outside the village wasn't nearly enough. He was unfamiliar with this area of the country, but there was no telling how close, or distant, the next village was. He slid his arms beneath Emmy's torso and gently positioned her upright again, then draped his arm about her, urging her to settle against his side as she'd been before. The reins were taken up again, given a snap, and off they went again with Emmy barely stirring.

She was trapped in a maze of clawing branches and thorns that tore at her sleeves and whipped against her face as she raced through endless streets filled with eerily lit mist and red lanterns.

"But I love you. I love you!" came a voice that echoed on all sides of her as she ran.

No! No! Leave me alone! her mind screamed. She did everything she could to shout in protest, but she felt as if her mouth had been sewn shut, and not even the tiniest sound could escape.

After running for ages, she at last ran head-long into a brick wall, covered with creeping vines which immediately encircled her until she could not move a muscle.

"Oh, my dove, you should have submitted to me. Now no one will find you."

The squeal of train brakes surrounded her as the ground vanished beneath her feet, and she plunged down... down... down...

The hellish screech of a night bird pierced the otherwise peaceful night, and Emmy jerked awake, flailing against what she was sure were ropes detaining her.

"Whoa there! Easy!" He yanked back on the reins, jerking the horse to a halt.

Emmy continued to fight against the layers of blankets that were cocooned around her, her dream-addled mind certain of danger.

"Yer safe, lass. Yer with me, MacDougall. Remember?" he urged, his hands palms out, making no move to touch her in this state.

Her breaths came in shallow gasps, her eyes flying wildly about the darkness until the remnants of the nightmare melted away and Mr. MacDougall's face gradually came into focus. "Mmm... Mac?" She heaved a sigh of relief and stilled her panicked thrashing, her hands grasping at the sleeves of her shirt as if to pull it around her.

Seeing her intention, he slowly leaned down and retrieved the fallen blankets, then tenderly wrapped it back around her shoulders. "Twas just an owl, Emmy my lass. Yer safe."

She nodded in agreement, inhaling a steadying breath and releasing it slowly. "Tha— tha— thank— thank—"

He grinned and lightly swept away the lock of hair that had fallen across her forehead when the cap flew from her head.

"Yer improving. More words every day."

She sighed heavily, relieved, and cast her gaze about the darkness. "T...ow— tow— town? Town?"

"We've passed through three other villages and I've not seen another for a few hours. 'Twas too dark to read the last sign."

"Stay?" The lack of hesitation surprised even herself, and she smiled proudly.

"I'd planned on pushing onward, but we can make camp for the remainder of the night if ye wish," Mr. MacDougall offered.

With a soft, caring light in her expression, she timidly cupped the side of his face. "Stay. Close... close..." She couldn't remember what came next, so she trailed her fingertips down over his eyes.

He chuckled a little as he took her hand and kissed the back. "Aye, Emmy my lass. I'll stay and close my eyes for a bit." After tugging the blankets around her snugly, he made quick work of unloading what was needed to craft a quick shelter away from the road in the trees. She peered through the darkness, straining her eyes to watch him. A large piece of stiff fabric was shaken out and draped over a branch, rope added to the corners somehow and driven into the ground to make a triangular shape with half the tarpaulin draped over the end of the branch, thus creating a third wall and leaving just one side open. He returned and took a folded bit of canvas from the back, then returned to the shelter and spread it on the ground within it. He came back a third time, this time to snag their sacks of clothing with one hand, and with the other he helped her down from the wagon's seat. After unhooking the lantern and handing it to her, he led her over the uneven ground of frosted grass, tossed the sacks inside, and lent her a hand to help her within. She guessed at the purpose of the sacks and set them against the wall as pillows.

He vanished yet again, and after listening to the wheels creaking as the horse was led further off the road, he reappeared with three more blankets in his arms. Without a word, he settled her down, wrapped one of the doubled-over blankets around her feet and legs, then tucked two of them around the rest of her body until she felt as if she were rolled up in a rug. He kept the final blanket for himself and spread himself out as far away from her as he could.

She lay on her side, just able to make out his profile in the dim light of the lantern hanging at the opening of the tent. They had barely settled and already Mr. MacDougall's chest rose and fell in steady rhythm. How was he already asleep?

Emmy was tolerably warm for several minutes, however the cold was soon seeping through the fabric's weave. How wicked would it be for her to lay closer merely for the sake of additional warmth? She had slept in his arms once before after that first awful nightmare. She trusted him implicitly; he'd given her no reason to do otherwise, and honour fairly thrummed through him with every action. She was already compromised, utterly ruined if anyone were to discover what her life had entailed over the last countless days. With a shiver, she scooted closer and closer still until she was snuggled right against the man's side.

As if anticipating her, his arms opened and he turned to his side in one movement, drawing her to his chest and resting his cheek against her hair. "Is this all right?" his deep, husky voice rumbled in her ear.

She smiled and wiggled closer, delicious warmth washing over her while the sense of safety chased her anxiety away.

"Sleep the noo. I have ye."

That was all the assurance she needed, and within moments, they both drifted to sleep.

Early morning birdsong filled the air as the first pale streaks of light speared the darkness and chased away the night. MacDougall felt unnaturally warm, and it took less than a second to realise why.

Emmy lay snugly against him, facing his chest, and both his arms encircled her shoulders and waist. His body was turned slightly toward her and one of his knees had slipped its way between hers in the night. He swallowed down a lump large as a boulder and slowly swivelled his hips away from her. It took every ounce of self-control and restraint to stay where he was, to not press the woman onto her back and explore every inch of her. But, by God, he had never wanted anything more.

He was about to disentangle himself from her when she began to stir. Tipping her head back, she smiled up at him, and it hit him square in the chest. He pushed himself up on an elbow to hover over her, and he was about to cover her lips with his when he stopped himself, eyes pinched closed in a war with himself. "I dinnae want to take advantage of ye. Yer too precious for that."

In answer, Emmy lifted her head and initiated the kiss for him. Her display of permission and willingness broke the tenuous hold he had on himself. He palmed the back of her head, tangled his fingers in her hair, and took his time savouring the taste of her.

By the time he forced himself to raise his head, Emmy's arms were encircled about his neck and they were both struggling for full breaths. He set his forehead against hers, revelling in the sensation of her soft body conforming to the hard planes of his. "What ye do to me," he confessed.

She laughed softly and kissed the end of his nose.

He braced himself on his elbows to peer down into her face, fingers sweeping across her face. "God above, yer beautiful, lass." He dipped his head and kissed her again, masculine pride swelling when she moaned softly. Shifting his head more to the side until he found the perfect fit he sought, he fairly devoured her mouth, groaning as he settled his hips against the cradle of hers.

Then all at once, he froze.

What was he doing? Even if she did not belong to another, she for certs did not belong to him, nor did he not belong anywhere near her world. The realisation was as efficient as a bucket of freezing water. He abruptly leveraged himself up. "I cannae do this."

The light that had sparkled within her eyes went out like an extinguished flame.

Gritting his teeth and clenching his jaw until it hurt, he pushed himself back onto his knees and thence crawled from the tent. "I'll give ye some privacy to refresh yerself, Miss Everleigh, then we ought to be on the road again. We need to get to Manchester." He strode off and vanished from sight, the sound of his footsteps crunching through the icy terrain fading entirely.

Emmy sat up and stared at the opening of the tent in doleful confusion. Why had he suddenly rejected her? She had thought he enjoyed what they shared. It was monumental for her, though perhaps, if she examined it further, perhaps it meant less to him than to her. Her heart ached, the pain radiated from her chest all the way into her arms and legs until it was nearly unbearable. She was unsure if she had ever experienced pain like this before; her chest felt as if it were bound tightly with ropes, as if it would burst if not for the skin keeping it in place.

She slowly untangled herself from the blankets and left them wherever they fell, then crawled from the tent and wandered away into the trees to gather her dignity about her like a fortifying wall. She knew not where Mr. MacDougall was now; at this precise moment, she did not care. Stepping around to the back side of a trunk, she pressed back against it, sighed, drew in another breath, and sighed again. Tears burned her eyes, but she fought them back and refused to allow them to form.

It was several minutes before she made her way back toward where the tent had been, only now there was nothing but a melted patch of grass, and Mr. MacDougall sat straight-backed upon the wagon's seat, awaiting her return.

She felt odd carrying herself with her usual pride and aloofness dressed in the clothing of a working boy, but she held her chin high and marched back to the wagon. Without a word, he jumped down and made to help her up; she ignored him and climbed onto the wagon's seat herself. One of the blankets was folded on the bench between them, and she shook it out and threw it about her shoulders. Folding her hands primly in her lap and keeping her eyes fixed on the road ahead, she waited.

Neither moved, and Emmy forced her gaze to stay where it was and not even flick in his direction, no matter how badly the impulse may have been. The wagon shifted side to side as he pulled himself aboard again; with a snap of the reins, the wagon lurched into motion again.

The steadfast horse plodded along, and hour after hour crept by as they made their slow journey toward the next large town. MacDougall had offered her a portion of bread and an apple as they went, but she remained stoically silent and still. Rather than eat it himself, he tucked it back into the crate holding their food supplies. He also offered her the jug of cider, but as before, she ignored him and it was replaced with the rest of their rations.

It was a dreary, grey day, typical for the time of year, with clouds so thick it was impossible to tell what time of day it was. Despite the nip in the air, the snow was held at bay and, while a thin layer still dusted the road and fields, nothing new fell from the heavens. Silence enveloped the countryside. Even the birds ceased to sing and tucked themselves into the safety and warmth of their nests.

MacDougall finally pulled the wagon to the side and allowed the horse a deserved rest. He glanced in Emmy's direction and drew a breath as if to speak, then decided against it and let himself down. He headed off for the trees, and when Emmy stole a peek in the direction he walked, she saw nothing.

She twisted quickly round, snagged a large chunk of bread, tore a piece of meat, grabbed an apple, then scampered down and ran for the trees on the other side of the road, the opposite way she had seen MacDougall go. Once she was out of sight, she sat at the base of a large tree and ate ravenously, finishing all of the apple but stem and seeds. With a happy sigh, she leaned her head back and let her eyes drift closed.

MacDougall had watched from the tree line as Emmy made the dash from the wagon, ensuring she was safe and pleased to see she'd taken food. Taking note of where she'd vanished, he relieved himself and returned to the wagon. He ate some of their stores, himself, and bided his time, allowing Emmy her privacy.

As he finished his meal, a stage came roaring by, and he was thankful she was nowhere in sight for anyone to see from the windows or roof. He merely tugged his own hat further down over his eyes and ducked his head to keep his face hidden from view. Once it vanished around a distant curve in the road, he climbed down and stood at the roadside with his arms akimbo. "Lass? We ought to leave." He waited for her to reappear, but he and the horse remained the only living beings in sight. "Emmy, lass?" Still, no one appeared.

Giving the horse's neck a pat, he headed off to the trees where he'd seen Emmy run off half of an hour before. "The horse has had his rest; we should be going." He peered around one tree, then another, and another. "Emmy?"

A pinecone sailed at him and hit the side of his head with a crackling pop.

"Oi. Hey!" He whipped around to see an absolutely furious Emmy with her hands on her hips and her eyes flashing with fire. "Throwing things now, are we?"

In response, she scooped another pinecone up and hurled it at him. This one, he caught and tossed to the side. "Violence doesna become ye."

She huffed, and threw yet a third pinecone. This time, after batting it away, he advanced on her. "Stay in high dudgeon if ye want; we're going." He snagged her by her upper arm, gave a brief stoop, and over his shoulder she went with a shriek of protest. She pounded on his back with her fists, kicking and wriggling, but he easily contained her over his shoulder with one arm over her back and the other against the backs of her knees. "I told ye I'd get ye back to yer friends in London. Once I do that, ye can do whatever 'tis ye want."

"Stop! Down! Stop!"

"Sure and now ye gain more words," he muttered. He finally dumped her upon the wagon seat. When she would have jumped up, he firmly set a hand to her shoulder and pushed her back to the bench, then climbed up beside her. Before he was able to grab the reins, Emmy's hand reared back and flew forward, slapping him across the face.

The cold caused his face to sting, and it must have hurt her, as well, if her wince was any indication. But the fact that she'd struck him stung more than the physical blow. Even so, his face revealed nothing but bored apathy. "Feel better?"

Her arm arched back for a second, but a lightning fast reaction had his hand grasping her wrist, stilling her movement before her hand got halfway to his face. "Ye only get one free pass. Now, are ye finished?"

She wrenched her arm free with a furious cry and scooted to the far end of the bench, arms crossed irately, her jaw set and brows lowered.

Satisfied she wouldn't attempt to attack him again, he snapped the reins at the horse and they lurched forward, regaining their former pace.

They travelled a full mile before MacDougall ventured to begin conversation. "I ken I've set up yer bristles, Emmy, but—"

"Lee."

He blinked and glanced over at her. "Lee?"

"Lee. Lee— no. Lee. Ever. Ever… Lee." She punctuated her success with a nod. "Everleigh."

He felt as if she had stabbed him through with a knife. "Miss Everleigh," he assented bitterly. Her chin lifted a touch. His assessment of her ire was correct, then: he'd hurt her feelings and injured her pride. With that as the case, he would happily fall on his sword, as it were. "I owe ye an apology. I lost my control and– and——" His brain searched for something to say that would soothe her ruffled feathers. "And I treated ye with less respect than ye deserve. I imagined emotions and intimacy where none existed." The words stuck in his throat, and the pain was acute. "I dinnae deserve to even sit near ye, and I ken it well. I'm sorry, lass. Miss Everleigh."

And with that, they lapsed into heavy, prolonged silence.

The first thick, wet flakes of snow started to fall as the daylight began to fade. The cap and scarf had been enough for most of the afternoon, but as the flakes turned into large clumps and the wind began to swirl around them, she pulled part of the blanket up and over her head, creating a makeshift hood that shielded her ears and part of her face from the elements. Her posture grew more slouched in the seat in attempts to make herself as small against the wind as possible, and a glance at Mr. MacDougall showed he wasn't as unaffected by the weather as he would have wanted her to believe.

Within a half an hour a thick carpet of fluffy white covered the landscape and there was no way of discerning the difference between road and field. Mr. MacDougall muttered something unintelligible beneath his breath, then finally guided the horse off to the right, presumably off the thoroughfare, and as far in the direction of the treeline as he felt they could safely go. Leaving Emmy in the seat, he jumped down and quickly unharnessed the horse, leading the animal into the trees and tying the long reins to a thick branch protruding from a fallen tree. He tramped back to the wagon, grabbed an unused blanket, and carried it back to where the horse stood; it was tossed over the beast's back and smoothed out to give it some warmth. Mr. MacDougall pulled something out of his pocket, fed it to the horse, and gave it several loving pats and strokes against the neck.

Emmy, rather than waiting for him to come back for her and treat her like a useless child, climbed into the back of the wagon and tugged the crate of food toward the open back. She hopped to the ground then heaved the crate out; once she had her balance and a firm grip upon the box, she clumsily waddled in the direction of the copse of trees near where the horse was tethered. Looking at the ground, it seemed that it was largely sheltered from the snow and wind and was a most logical place to shelter for the night. It would be too dangerous to continue on the road when visibility was slight due to darkness and falling snow combined. She finally reached the place and fairly dropped the box to the ground; it was far heavier than she had anticipated and carrying it as far as she had was a strenuous task.

"I would have gotten that, lass," he argued, but instead of coming to where she stood in the grove, he went back to the wagon for their other supplies. Shaking out her arms, she followed and fell into step. "Ye needn't to help."

Her response was to glare and drag another crate into her arms. Even if it was too burdensome, she would never permit him to see it. Instead, she struggled her way to the copse, and Mr. MacDougall unloaded all their belongings by the time she made it with her second trip.

He was already creating a new shelter for them, hurriedly to beat the full fall of darkness, and what appeared to be larger than the one from the previous night. She knew not how else to assist, so she stood helplessly by and watched with rapt attention. He moved with practised familiarity, the ease that only came with long repeated movements and plans. It wasn't long before something of a crude little hovel made of tarpaulin, canvas, and rope, complete with walls staked to the ground and even a fabric door. She shook her head in disbelief and wonder.

"In ye go," he grumbled, holding the flap of the 'door' open for her, and once she was within, he went about grabbing the crates and bringing them further into the trees and away from the open treeline where snow could reach them.

It was dark within the shelter, and she had been about to call out when Mr. MacDougall's arm appeared through the slit in the flap holding the lantern. She took it from him and settled upon the ground to take stock of what they had.

"We've need of a fire; I'll return shortly." The snow swallowed the sound of his retreating footsteps and she was left in eerie silence.

She had never been expected to prepare any sort of meal, and she looked through the stores of food with curiosity. The bread and apples she had seen of course but what else had he secreted away for them? After investigation, she had come up with a small slab of pork wrapped in waxed cloth, a decent chunk of hard cheese, two bundles of watercress, more apples and bread, and a jug of what smelled like cider. There was also a black iron pan, a wood spoon, and a knife in a sheath.

Memories from her distant childhood drifted forward and took shape; one in particular was of her standing on a wood stool, an oversized apron tied over her afternoon dress, deliberately cutting some form of food under the watchful eye of the estate's cook. An idea formed, and turning the crate over, she unwrapped the meat, set it down, and very slowly sliced long strips of meat with the knife. What had the cook said all those years ago? *Mind your fingers, child. You only get ten.* Smiling at the recollection, she adjusted her hold on the cold slab of pork and continued, keenly aware of where the knife's blade was in relation to her hand.

Gradually she heard the sounds of rustling outside the tent, the snaps and knocks of twigs and branches coming together, and finally the crackling of flames igniting the timber. When he popped his head inside, Emmy had successfully sliced the meat as well as the watercress and had everything in the pan awaiting the fire.

Mr. MacDougall was utterly shocked if his expression was any indication, and she flushed softly with self-confidence. She was keenly aware at how truly useless she was in any way that truly mattered, and being able to provide the smallest bit of service was pleasing.

"Ye've— how did ye—," he stumbled, his astonished gaze flicking between her and the skillet.

She passed him the pan with a smug little grin. Once he took it from her hands, she cleaned the blade of the knife off using her shirt sleeve then sheathed it akin to the period of a statement.

He stared at her for a long minute, his jaw working as if he debated speaking, then he ultimately disappeared behind the flap.

Emmy couldn't help but be pleased that she had struck him rather speechless. There was more to do, so she continued creating a pleasant space within, spreading a handkerchief atop the box with the lantern in the centre so it could act as a table, and she set up two areas for sleeping with his clothing sack and hers for a pillow with a blanket for each.

The inside looked much homier by the time he re-entered the tent bearing the steaming pan of supper. He pulled up short when he saw the atmosphere she had created, and again, he looked as if words escaped him. The stupor did not last; he soon entered and cast about in search of a place to set the broiling skillet. "I dinnae wish to scorch yer fine handkerchief, but I appreciate the effort ye took to make things look nice. Thank ye."

Understanding, she moved the lantern and whisked her handkerchief off the surface, and he set the pan atop it as he sat.

"Eat. How?" Getting nowhere with words, she made as if she would pick up a piece of the meat with her bare fingers.

Mr. MacDougall gently caught her hand to stop her. "That will burn ye. I made these," and he produced a pair of narrow sticks that were sharpened to a point at one end. One was handed to her, and he used his own to spear a piece of cooked watercress then a slice of meat beneath it.

She watched in surprised fascination as he ate in this primitive way before doing likewise. One must make due with what one had available; if she wished to eat, it would be done this way or with her fingers. Indeed, this was much more preferable to eating with her hands. The pair ate accompanied by the sound of crackling branches set aflame outside the tent, neither wanting to be the first to attempt to speak regarding the events of earlier that morning. Even Emmy, who had little verbal communication at her disposal to begin with, made no effort.

The modest supper was polished off quickly, and after each partook of several drinks from the cider jug, Mr. MacDougall excused himself to clean up, and Emmy slipped out to relieve herself and scrub her hands with fresh snow. When she returned, the fire had been built up again and the flaps of the tent kept open to allow the heat to fill the interior. When she entered, she found a cloth wrapped bundle beside one of the bed rolls. Upon placing her hand on it, she found it radiated warmth and she gasped. Mr.

MacDougall poked his head around. "If ye keep a large stone near a fire and then wrap it up, ye can put it in yer bed or hold it against yerself as ye sleep. It will help to keep ye warm." Their eyes met and a tenderness passed from one to the other and back again, then he was gone and the moment was over.

To help ward off the cold of the elements further, Emmy slipped into all the clothes she had available. The exertions of changing into layer after layer had her quite warm throughout, but once she settled into the blankets for her bed and her body stilled, she felt the cold of winter night do its best to intrude on her comfort. She settled the warming stone to the bottoms of her stockinged feet and within moments, she was asleep.

Sleep typically came quickly and easily to MacDougall. He had spent more than half his life on his own as a hired hand, travelling from town to town, going wherever his heart desired, whenever he wanted. A life of hard labour and fighting in mills led to deep, restful sleep practically every night.

Tonight, slumber was evasive, and his mind wandered unbidden.

He was the sole child born to a Highland laird and his wife who, according to what he'd been told, were murdered just a few weeks after he was born. A rival clan sacked his family's home and MacDougall only survived due to the quick thinking of his wetnurse. When the massacre of the laird's household began, the nurse smuggled the baby out of the castle, and out of the village, in a basket like Moses of old. She had just enough time to flee with the infant to safety, leaving him on the doorstep of a cottage outside the township, before she was forced to return home to try and protect her own children. The village had ultimately been spared as long as the occupants pledged their loyalty to the new clan family. But word of the laird's demise had spread, and the family who discovered the baby at their door fled before there was any chance that they might meet a similar fate.

Young MacDougall was passed from family to family throughout the Highlands, their superstitions stronger than their desire to take the boy in on a more permanent basis. No matter how far he travelled, the sinister tale of his origin followed like a dark, forbidding shadow. Any mishap that occurred in his proximity was ultimately placed upon his small, innocent shoulders, and he was forced to move on. He was made to feel like a cursed child, somehow responsible for every death and illness. It did not matter that the boy was stronger than an average lad his size; that only added to the dark stories that wove themselves around him until they were practically part of who he was. It wasn't until his fourteenth year that he was finally taken in by a man distantly related to his own father, and for the first time, he was treated as a member of a family. Alongside the man's other sons, MacDougall was taught to hunt and fish, and how to forage off nature for what he needed to survive. He learned to build shelters when one had no tools at one's disposal, learned how to start a fire, and learned how to survive no matter the weather or circumstances. For three happy years, Arran

MacDougall belonged to someone. Then at seventeen, with the death of the family's patriarch and MacDougall's foster father, he was set adrift once again, this time closing his heart against all people for good.

Until now.

He turned his head and glanced at the young woman curled up a few feet away. He had never been as thankful for such upbringing as he was in this moment. If he had not been raised with such attention to survival in the wilds of the moors, what hope would he have had to keep Emmy safe during their flight to the safety of the south?

He sighed and tossed an arm over his eyes. He'd made an awful mess of things in his attempt to protect her from himself. She was already compromised enough, having been forced to keep solitary company with him. Her people would never forgive the offence, even if all that she had endured was explained. He'd heard that those of high society held grudges for perceived slights, and that a woman's reputation was tenuous as spun sugar. After all she had already borne, would she have more to suffer upon her arrival home?

And what an idiot he was to fall for a woman who was leagues above his own station. It was possible she could even be a titled lady. Anything that had developed between them must be severed for her own sake, and doing so would rip his heart out.

He blinked and sat up suddenly. *He was in love with her!* He groaned and fell back against the sack he'd been utilising as a pillow. He was an utter fool.

MacDougall cast another look at Emmy. She had been shivering more and more over the past hour. He tossed his blanket aside and stole furtive peeks beneath her own blankets until he located the now chilled stone she'd placed there when it had been warm. Tugging it free, he crawled from the small shelter to switch it out for a few of the others that ringed the still smouldering fire. They were brought inside and he set them against the bottoms of her feet, careful of their temperature so as not to burn her delicate skin, even sheathed in wool stockings as they were.

In her sleep, she hummed in pleasure as the warmth seeped through her, though her frame still trembled with cold.

The debate in his mind lasted less than a heartbeat; he snagged his blanket and spread himself out behind where Emmy was curled on her side. He threw the swath of wool over them both then proceeded to mould his body against hers, one arm sliding beneath her neck and the other circling her waist, adjusting himself until he was pressed against her back from shoulders to ankles. Her shivers instantly began to subside and she sighed with contentment.

"Let me hold ye, *mo chridhe*," he whispered in her ear, hoping it would penetrate her dreams somehow. "Just one last night before I have to let ye go." He pressed a kiss to her temple, and she made a soft sound like a purr as she sank deeper into peaceful slumber.

At least one of them could sleep.

Chapter Twelve

There was no birdsong to greet her this morning. It was bitterly cold, but she was surprisingly toasty inside. The rocks were even still warm against her feet and she wondered if perhaps Mr. MacDougall had replaced them recently. He seemed always to care for her, in small ways and overt.

She sat and stretched her limbs, then gradually stood to her feet and peeked through the flaps. Almost instantly she regretted it. Although it was a bright, clear, sunny morning, it was frigidly cold, the kind which makes the air painful to breathe, and she had just abandoned a wonderfully warm little nest.

The atmosphere surrounding her was most picturesque, worthy of being memorialised in a painting. The sky was a flawless field of bright blue, and the sun was a perfect golden orb as it continued to rise. The branches of every tree were blanketed with a thick layer of fresh, pristine snow, as was the field stretching between them and the treeline on the opposite side of the road. Were it not so impossibly freezing, she felt she would like to gaze at the scene forever.

The fire was already lit and happily crackling; a kettle hung on an odd contraption of branches, and the pan was occupied by even slices of apples off to one side awaiting the flames, but there was no Mr. MacDougall.

She quickly slipped away to complete a few brief morning ablutions, then hurried back, and saw no sign of her protector.

It was several minutes of waiting without so much as a noise, and her anxiety rose the longer she was left alone. If she were in trouble, would she even be able to call for help? She supposed she could scream, but she did not wish to alarm the man if he were simply relieving himself. After several moments of deliberation, and testing her ability to control her words, she cupped her hands around her mouth and called, "Mac! Mac!"

The snow swallowed her cry the second it left her lips, and she caught her hands against her breast in worry. If she left to try and find him, she feared she would only end up lost and cause even more trouble for him.

"Maaac!" She thought hard, willing her mouth to work properly. "Pl... Please! Mac!" Tears welled in her eyes as a sense of abandonment crashed over her, even as she continued to call for him. Her voice broke and she sniffed as emotions threatened to overtake her control.

A branch snapped and she spun around with a gasp, heart in her throat. The creak of heavy footfall compressing fresh snow grew closer, and Mr.

MacDougall's form at last appeared between the droopy, snow-laden boughs with a rope over his shoulder from which hung several fish.

With a sob she raced forward and launched herself at him, her arms locking about his neck as tears of relief flowed. "Mac. Mac! Alone... alone, alone. No! Stay."

He dropped the line of fish the moment Emmy leaped at him and his arms closed around her, one hand cupping the back of her head as she shuddered against him. "Och lass! I'm sorry. I thought ye'd be asleep yet. I dinnae mean to frighten ye. I'll not leave ye again." He finally scooped her into his arms, leaving the fish in the snow, and carried her back to the tent.

Taking a knee, he lowered Emmy down, but she stood on her knees and re-wrapped her arms about his waist, burrowing against him, her cheek pressed against his chest.

"No alone. No leave. Stay. Stay, me," she whispered between hiccoughs as the crying subsided.

He nuzzled his cheek against the top of her head. "Aye. I'll stay with ye, Miss Everleigh."

She tipped her head back and peered up at him. "Emmy."

He smiled down at her, taking time to tenderly wipe away her tears with the pads of his thumbs. "Lass, now that I ken how to address ye properly, it should be Miss Everleigh. I shouldna take a familiar manner with ye. Sharing a tent with ye is bad enough."

His smile always charmed her and turned her insides to warm porridge. Settling her hand over his heart, she shook her head lightly. "Emmy," she insisted.

Mr. MacDougall released a dramatic, long-suffering sigh. "Yer trouble," but his eyes sparkled and belied any truth to his words.

Stillness blanketed them, and the pair lost themselves in one another's eyes. It was Emmy who finally tapped her own lips. "Mac."

His brow creased. "I shouldna. 'Tis not proper betwixt us. I cannae be what ye need; I dinnae belong in yer set."

Emmy merely pouted at him, her thumb stroking the place over his heart beside where her hand rested. "Kiss. Please." His heart thumped against her palm, and she bit back a smile. So he was affected, after all.

"I'm trying to be a gentleman for ye," he protested, but it was most certainly not her imagination that his arms tightened about her, and his focus drifted from her eyes to her mouth.

Her expression softened. "Please."

That was evidently all the further encouragement needed to shatter his resolve. His hand cupped her nape, his other arm dragged her slight form flush against him, and with a soft groan he claimed her lips with his. Heat radiated outward through every one of her limbs in the most wonderful, dizzying way, and she floated away on the sensation of being in this man's arms until all else disappeared around them.

The line of fish was finally remembered and MacDougall slipped outside to fetch them, thankful that no other animals had run off with the catch. It didn't take long for him to build up the fire again, then to skin and bone the fish so his fine lady companion would have as easy a time eating without a proper fork as possible. He thought about giving her his knife to use, but he thought that might be even more distasteful to her sensibilities than using a simple pointed stick. However, she had proven time and again that she was stronger and more determined than he believed, and continued to surprise him in the most pleasant and astonishing ways. It was true that her verbal communication skills were still scant; however given her situation, she could have been quite pettish and ill-tempered. Instead, while she had expressed her frustration occasionally, she did not remain in that state of mind for long and rather behaved as if she were making the best of a troubling situation. It was impossible not to admire her spunk, a word he never before would have associated with a noblewoman who never lifted a hand in labour all her charmed life. Indeed, he had known seasoned labourers who did not conduct themselves as well under duress as she had.

They completed their meal and MacDougall made quick work of cleaning the cooking implements while she used some of the fresh snow to wash her hands and attempted to do the same to their wooden eating utensils, something he had to grin about. Even in the wilderness, she sought to maintain cleanliness whenever possible.

While the sky held at bay any further snowfall, the air was chilled enough that nothing had melted and the road was still impassable for their small simple wagon. A stage had rumbled by only once, and quite a bit slower than its usual swiftness. The conveyance was, of course, a bit higher from the ground and its wheels larger, so traversing the snowy terrain was far less of a problem. Themselves, however, would be forced to stay here. A stage would not stop for strangers along the road, and even if it would, he would not abandon the horse, nor would he allow Emmy to travel without a chaperone, not when danger still nipped at their heels. Thus, there was nothing more to do than to bed down, as it were, and make themselves comfortable.

He made a pot of strong, steaming tea then vanished into the temporary shelter where Emmy was already waiting, cocooned in her blankets. It did not escape his notice that, though she shivered and was clearly freezing, she had left his own bedroll where it was. His heart opened to her just a bit more. How could he not adore and admire a woman who sacrificed her own comfort for him? He could do without it, of course, but the simple fact that she did not wish to see him go without warmed his insides more than any wrap or hot beverage could do.

As he set the kettle and cups down, he quickly unravelled his bedding and swung the layers about her shoulders.

"No. Cold, you," she protested.

"What sort of knight would I be if I allowed the lady fair to freeze?" he countered gently, tucking the folds beneath her chin. "Truly, lass; I'm accustomed enough to the elements. 'Tis important to keep you healthy and warm."

He bit back the chuckle that threatened to escape at the dour expression upon her face, but she ceased her argument, though her displeasure at it was all too evident in her eyes.

"Now, where were we?" he asked, rummaging for the copy of *Pride and Prejudice* they had started the afternoon before their flight from the village.

He read well. She never would have believed it of a common working man, but she supposed that it should not surprise her overly much; everything about Mr. MacDougall was anomalous. Of course the accent of his birthplace hindered many of the words from being perfect, but she found that she far preferred his patterns of speech over the even, almost apathetic, cadence of her set in Town. There seemed to be more vibrance in the way he spoke, and she wondered if all Scotsmen were similar, or if it was a unique trait to her Scotsman alone.

Her Scotsman.

As he read, her cheeks pinked, and she found herself drifting in a waking dream of a life with him. A simple one, she decided, where they shared a country cottage rather than a stately manor in Town. Small children played in the fields around their house, climbed trees and ate apples from the branches, the sound of delighted laughter drifting on the breeze as she swayed back and forth with her hand smoothing over her belly, enlarged with his child.

"'In vain I have struggled. It will not do. My feelings will not be repressed. Ye must allow me to tell ye how ardently I admire and love ye.' What is this?" Mr. MacDougall suddenly exclaimed, and Emmy couldn't help but laugh outright at his genuine surprise.

"Have ye already read this?" he fairly cried, and she chuckled again and nodded. While it was a favourite with her, of course he would not have read it; how many men chose to read Austen's works unless they had a woman in their lives to persuade them to do so?

He hurriedly continued, his words coming more rapidly as the scene unfolded before him for the first time, with Emmy enjoying watching the play of expressions across his face more than she had ever enjoyed the scene in the book, itself.

The following moments were spent listening, in high amusement, as Mr. MacDougall read with as much enthusiasm and incredulity as any other lady had upon first experiencing the less-than-romantic proposal between Mr. Darcy and Miss Elizabeth. The language and outbursts from him were, of course, much more colourful than would have been proper within her own circle of friends, but the sentiments were the same. Emmy, herself, had barely suppressed her own astonishment when Darcy quite awkwardly declared his love for Austen's heroine.

"Man's a bampot. Hasna a romantic thought in his noggin. How could he propose marriage listing all that blather? I'd've planted a facer on him! Lizzy had better not say aye," he grumbled as he eagerly flipped the page to continue, with Emmy attempting to suppress the giggles that threatened to escape.

As the sun sank lower and temperature plummeted, Emmy moved steadily closer to his side in attempts to claim his radiating heat for her own. He finally closed the book and set it aside when she began to shiver.

She gave a little sound of protest and settled a hand upon his arm, but he merely took her hand in his and brushed a brief kiss to the back. "Ye'll catch yer death, Emmy my lass, and ye've not eaten for hours. We'll read more by and by."

And so, once their hunger sated and the fire nicely built up, he settled himself back against a log he had discovered and since dragged to their modest camp, book open in his hands. Emmy was at his side once more, curled up in coats and blankets, and when he casually draped an arm behind her, she leaned closer until she was nestled comfortably against him.

She must have drifted off to sleep, for she was next aware of a gentle jostling. She stirred to right herself but felt the ground vanish beneath her.

"I've got ye, lass. Sleep."

Thus, with such assurances warming her from the inside out, she slept.

She awoke most leisurely and for a brief sleepy moment she wondered if she were back in her bed at home, so comfortably she had slept through the night. But soon it became apparent that she was still in the cobbled-together shanty in the snow with a strong pair of arms wrapped securely around her, with her cheek resting over the steady thump of Mr.

MacDougall's heart. Pressing her elbow to the ground, she levered herself up and smiled softly into his face.

He was already awake and his eyes alert, of course. She doubted if the man ever truly slept. His dark eyes glimmered in the ambient glow of morning light.

"Did ye sleep well?"

"Yes," she answered confidently, and she thrilled at having another strong word at her ready disposal.

"It sounds as if the storm broke; we should keep travelling before another one settles over us."

Disappointment flickered across her features, and as if he guessed at her thoughts, he craned his neck up and kissed her forehead. "Aye, I know it. But I cannae keep ye to myself; ye belong with yer family." He paused. "I assume ye've family waiting for ye."

She nodded, albeit somewhat glumly. "Yes." She paused, her brain knowing the word and trying to force her mouth to obey her commands. "Uncle, no. C— co—"

"Cousin?" Mr. MacDougall hazarded.

Emmy nodded. "Cousin. Town. Town country. Wait. Me."

Mr. MacDougall wriggled until he sat up, and as Emmy sat back herself, he brushed a lock of chestnut hair back from her cheek. "We'll figure it all out, me and thee, once we're in London, and I'll not leave yer side until yer safe. Ye've my word."

It was the right course of action; she had spent enough time away from all that was familiar to her and she feared what sort of reception would greet her upon her homecoming. How would she be able to explain things? He would help, of course, but as she did not have every piece of information at her disposal, how could he? The hours, indeed even the days leading up to Mr. MacDougall's discovery of her in the street of that unnamed town were a blank for her. He meant her no harm; indeed, every moment spent with him ensured that, in his estimation, her safety was of the utmost importance. He sacrificed everything for her. A hundred times could he have left her to make her own way home, could have left her in the street, even, rather than intervene in affairs that were not his. But he did not. He was a shining example of a true gentleman, proof that birth and upbringing had little to do with the strength of one's character.

For as long as it seemed to have taken to create their shelter, it took no time at all to, what he called, break camp. Before too long, there was no sign of the fire that had cooked their breakfast, and everything was packed in the back of the wagon, ready to go. Even the trusted old horse appeared eager to travel.

Before they set out, she had held up the boy's trousers in question, and he had shaken his head. "As we'll be taking a train once we reach the next town, I think it would be better for ye to appear as ye are, even if yer dressed far below yer station."

She nodded her agreement. It had taken a bit to become accustomed to the coarseness of the material, but now that she'd been without her own finery for some time, she found she rather preferred the comfort of it. She felt more at ease in the garments of the working class. As fine as silks and satins were, she found they did not allow as much relaxation as the wool and linen that clothed her for a month's time. Now, she almost regretted that her time dressed in the disguise of a working girl was coming to a close. There was so much less pressure in this new life of hers.

Each knew their time together as it had been over the last weeks was drawing swiftly to a close. As such, Mr. MacDougall said little and there was only a scant attempt to engage her in any semblance of conversation. Instead, he stared stoically ahead of them while Emmy kept her hands folded in her lap, her fingers worrying at the folds of her skirt. The familiarity and intimacy that had blossomed between them now gave way to distance on both parts, each preparing for the return to their own normalcy in life.

And each was miserable.

Whether by stage or train car, there would be no more candid conversations, no more enjoying one another's company in tranquil solitude with her curled against his side. No, once they were again thrust beneath the watchful eyes of society, they would be weighed and measured, even if no one outside London knew of her elevated origins. No one escaped society's desire for gossip, whether low on the social ladder or at the top.

Chapter Thirteen

On the road toward Manchester, MacDougall discussed the importance of getting her to London as soon as possible. If there was some sort of plot against her as he suspected, they would be best served to travel by train so she could more swiftly reunite with her friends. She would be safe once she was with her own people again, and he would explain all his suspicions before leaving her. His chest felt too tight when he thought of their parting, so he pressed onward and ignored it.

They rolled into the trade city after the winter sun tucked itself into bed for the night, and the lamplighters had long since come and gone. The smell of human sweat and horse excrement was heavy in the air. Everyone seemed to be hurrying to their evening meals and to warm themselves after a long day exposed to the frigid cold of December.

Having eaten as they travelled, their first order of business upon arriving within the city's limits was to divest themselves of the wagon and horse.

MacDougall guided the tired horse through the streets until he finally reached a large coaching inn. A hand came out to take the horse, supposing they were there to dine and take a room, but he quickly explained his errand, and the hand went to fetch the manager.

The man who had charge of the establishment was younger than MacDougall had expected, and was stingy with his coin. The man's initial offer for their horse and wagon would scarcely pay MacDougall back by half, despite sweetening the deal, as it were, by adding all their travelling gear and supplies to the purchase. He just about accepted the almost insulting offer when Emmy intervened. After a bright, genuine smile and a sweetly spoken, "Please?" from the simply dressed but beautiful young woman, MacDougall walked away with money nearly equal to the original purchase of the horse and cart. His admiration for Emmy soared anew; it seemed she had even more hidden talents yet to be displayed, and never in one hundred years would he have expected haggling to be one of them. His girl was a riddle, indeed.

He stumbled over his own feet when that revelation struck him. *His girl.* At what point had his brain decided on proprietary rights over her? Indeed, there was deep longing and desire, but the shift in his thoughts shocked him. Despite all his inward arguing, she was not actually his to claim. Indeed, he had continuously reminded himself of the fact since the first moment he took her in. She had as much to do with him as a dove had to do with a tadpole. Yet there it was; he wanted her. Not only to warm his bed as the desire had admittedly been before, but to keep, to marry, to share his life. His hand tightened in a fist around the opening of the travelling sack he carried over one shoulder, and his other arm, in which was nestled her small, trusting hand, went rigid.

She would notice it, of course, and her gaze shot up to his as they wended their way through the crowds toward the train. Her hand gave his forearm a gentle, concerned squeeze. "Mac?"

He schooled his features to the best of his ability, giving a soft smile. "All is well, Miss Emmy."

Her expression said she doubted his words, but rather than pursue it, she allowed his answer to stand and instead turned her focus to the busyness of the merchant town.

They arrived at the station front in enough time to catch the last train to London, which would travel all through the night, and she stood to the side while he discussed ticket and seating details with the agent.

"Have ye any way for the lady to rest the night through?" He didn't want to offer additional information about her if it could be helped, but being that she was still healing from her injuries, he didn't relish her having to sit upright upon a hard bench from dusk until dawn. He hoped something would be available without divulging anything about her that might put her enemy onto her trail.

There was something called a bed carriage and he secured a ticket for her there. When they discovered where she would sleep in an entirely different car, he felt her start beside him, and he purchased a bed for himself, as well. While he was certain she would be perfectly safe in her berth, he dreaded leaving her alone, particularly when surrounded by so many strangers.

Even then, the idea chafed at him. It was becoming more and more difficult to face the reality that, within another day, she would be the responsibility of someone else, and he would see her no more.

They embarked and he helped her settle onto the lower berth, going so far as to give her his blanket so she would be warm enough. As she laid down and snuggled beneath the blankets, their eyes met, and the lovelight he was sure he saw in her eyes made his heart turn over in his chest. They were not alone, however, and it would not do to cast an ill light upon her, even if no one aboard besides himself knew her identity. He drew the curtain closed, shielding her from view, then climbed upon his own sleeping cot.

There were no emergencies through the night, and each time they changed trains, the transition was smooth and relatively uncomplicated. Given that he had never experienced a train journey before, it was all new and rather thrilling, travelling so swiftly, though a bit noisy. The train pulled into the station on the outskirts of London right on time, just as the early morning sun peeked its golden head above the rooftops and through the clouds. They disembarked and promptly hailed a carriage. It was only when the driver called down to them with his usual, "Where to?" did MacDougall pull up short with renewed realization.

Where was her home?

He glanced at Emmy, and her eyes widened a little.

"Can ye say, lass?" he muttered quietly to her.

Her face grew pinched with effort, her lips working but with no sound escaping. Her expression of helplessness tore at him, and he patted her hand. There was no way around it. "Tis an odd request, but will ye drive us 'round where the wealthy live?"

The driver blinked down at them, taking in their appearances with a dubiously arched brow. "You just want to… look at the houses?"

"Aye, for now."

After a moment's pause, the driver gave a small shrug. "Suppose that would be all right. The Mayfair district all right to begin?"

Her eyes glimmered in recognition and her hand tightened upon MacDougall's sleeve. "Aye, just fine. Our thanks."

He handed Emmy into the carriage and followed her in. Once the door was closed, the driver gave a snap to the reins and the vehicle lurched into motion.

No eyes could view them here, so MacDougall indulged in slipping his hand around Emmy's, clasping it close, going so far as to thread his fingers with hers. His stomach felt like a hollow void, and everything in him revolted at giving her up.

But it must be done.

"Mac!"

There it was: her dear home on the row across from Grosvenor Square, a place she had briefly wondered if she would ever see again. Her hand shot to Mr. MacDougall's sleeve and she gave an excited tug.

He thumped at the ceiling of the carriage to alert the driver, and before the carriage had fully rolled to a stop, Emmy was fumbling with the mechanism of the door to be let out. Mr. MacDougall intervened to open the door and Emmy darted out onto the walk before the monumental building, boasting its stately columns and rows upon rows of windows that stretched at least four levels into the air, the creamy stone facade displaying its wealth and cleanliness unlike anything she had seen in the villages.

Emmy was hurrying back along the street in the direction of her own door, knowing Mr. MacDougall would be right behind her if not at her side.

She marched up the stairs with the bearing of a queen and paused long enough for Mr. MacDougall to open the door for them.

"How dare you enter without an invitation?"

The pair had scarcely stepped through into the main foyer when the sharp rebuke rang out from down a hall, and a moment later, a well-dressed older gentleman came hurrying toward them. *Carter!*

"This is most irregular! I shall have you both arrest— Miss Everleigh!" His pace slowed as recognition settled in, then his steps hastened in their direction once more. "Your arrival is most unexpected; we did not anticipate your return for another few weeks, at least! And you are dressed… that is… it is rather unusual when compared to…" The man's eyes flicked to Mr. MacDougall before dismissing him as unimportant and returning his focus to her.

"Trouble, help. Mac, help. Ill, pain, snow… Mac help." Emmy gestured toward MacDougall in attempts to justify his presence, although the butler seemed more than a little off-put by him, as well as her broken way of communicating.

"Miss Everleigh? Are you quite well?"

"Allow me to explain a bit, Sir. My name is MacDougall. I came upon Miss Everleigh injured in a street in a small village beyond Manchester—"

"Manchester?" the butler exclaimed with a huff. "Such is impossible. Mr. Wainwright informed us they were destined for Newcastle."

Emmy heard Mr. MacDougall bite back a sigh. "I cannae say about Wainwright, but she was nearer to Manchester than anywhere. As I said, I came upon her after she had suffered a head injury, and she was unable to speak much. She still cannae say the words she means to; she struggles."

The wary butler eyed him suspiciously. "If she has such difficulty with basic communication, how did you discover where she lived?"

"It took some doing. Once she was recovered enough to travel, we pieced together that her home's here in London, and the driver took us 'round until she spotted the right place." He sounds as if he struggled to stifle a growl of annoyance.

"Well, we are of course appreciative for your assistance, Mr. MacDougall. I will confer with Miss Everleigh's cousin once he has returned and see if a reward might be owed to you," he offered coolly.

"Ye cannae put a price 'pon her well-being!" MacDougall thundered, his brogue thick with angry passion. "I helped for 'twas right an' I worried fer a lass to be by herself like that, wit' none to protect her when she was vulnerable! Ye can take yer money an—"

Emmy settled her small hand atop his forearm to soothe the obvious rage that had overtaken his senses. He was so unerringly gentle with her that she forgot what a forbidding man he had the potential to be.

"Ca— Ca— Carrr...t. Cart," she struggled. "Mac... stay. Mac, help. Help, good."

The butler watched his mistress's face with a mix of confusion and doubt, but at least her meaning penetrated enough. "If I am to rightly understand, Miss, you wish this man to stay so we might show our appreciation," though it was clear he wanted nothing more than to pitch Mr. MacDougall into the street. "If you would follow me, Sir—"

Emmy started forward, then stopped. "Where help?"

Carter paused and glanced back at her. "I beg your pardon?"

"Where— where help? Where... where..."

The butler's stiff posture relaxed as he watched his young mistress struggle, and a tender, almost grandfatherly light shone in his eyes. "Oh, Miss Margaret," he whispered.

Mr. MacDougall stepped in. "Is there someone that frequently assists Miss Everleigh? A maid?"

After a pause, the butler slowly nodded. "I see now; she is asking where her help is. With her new manner of speaking, deciphering her meaning is akin to solving riddles. As for her help, her lady Cossett is away with her family; the mother is abed and there are small children too young yet to work. The housekeeper is out for the afternoon, and the understaff had been dismissed until such time as we expected your return. I would be happy to send for Cossett immediately if she is required, although it will be a few days before she can return."

Emmy was immediately reminded of the sweet young girl who cared for her at the inn, her family's illness and troubles. Not for the world could she demand that Cossett return to Town when her family needed her. In answer, she shook her head. "Kitchen?"

"Of course; you must be famished after travelling. I'll tell our cook to—"

"No. Kitchen... kitchen help."

Carter paused, his gaze unfocused as if turning the words over in his head in the same fashion Mr. MacDougall had done countless times before, solving her riddled sentences one piece at a time. "Kitchen help," he repeated to himself.

"Kitchen help. Me. Help, me. Kitchen."

Fortunately, Mr. MacDougall had grown accustomed to interpreting her meaning. "Perhaps ye wonder if someone in the kitchen can help ye the way yer maid does?"

Emmy's smile blossomed, proof of his correct assumption.

"Ah, yes, of course, I shall send Cook to you at once to help you change into something... more suitable. Mr. MacDougall, if you would follow me, I will show you to one of our guest rooms." And Carter went off at the clip of a well-trained servant who expected obedience from those he deemed lower in station than himself.

Emmy glanced up at Mr. MacDougall, and the torment in his eyes as he glanced between herself and the departing Carter tore at her. She patted his forearm encouragingly. "Good. Trust."

He heaved a sigh and nodded, slipping his arm from beneath her hand. "Trust." And with that, MacDougall's long strides caught him up to Carter as the butler ascended the stairs.

The butler led MacDougall up a lavish staircase and then down a wide hall. Windows lined one wall and allowed so much light that not a single candle or sconce was needed despite the heavy cloud cover that hung over the city. Large paintings of past ancestors in ornately carved, gilt frames hung regally on the opposite side. Trees in large ceramic pots lined the passage, standing at regular intervals, beautiful golden spheres of fruit and brightly coloured blossoms nestled between the thick verdant foliage. The tiles underfoot looked remarkably perfect without a single scratch or crack anywhere to be seen, polished to a high sheen that caused him to wonder if anyone ever walked over it.

Carter opened a door and walked inside without preamble, and MacDougall dutifully followed. The butler went to the windows and threw open the heavy damask curtain that hung over each, allowing daylight to pour into the previously darkened room. "I will send someone immediately to light the fire for you, and have a tray sent up. If you have need of a bath, please inform one of the servants. I will leave you to freshen and rest, Sir." And without allowing MacDougall time to respond, Carter swiftly took his leave, closing the door behind him.

MacDougall had their bags in hand still, and dropped them unceremoniously to the floor at his feet. He stepped over them to cross to the massive windows that overlooked the famous square. It was still early; people had not yet risen from their beds unless they were of the working class, and they, of course, were not those who would take time to prance about Grosvenor Square. He imagined most of the swells would still be abed for several hours yet.

Turning, he put his hands to his hips and surveyed the room. The walls looked to have been done in some sort of paper, but upon closer inspection, he found it was a very thin fabric, a deep ocean blue with sweeping gold swirls. A few pastoral paintings hung on the walls along with an oversized portrait of a man and his hunting kit from a previous century. There were at least half a dozen sconces fastened to the walls about the room to say nothing of the many candlesticks about the room awaiting the strike of a match. At his side facing the park was a writing desk he was sure contained all the paper, nibs, and ink a person could need. The large bed sat upon a high frame between four solid wood posts, polished to a high sheen, a crimson canopy shot through with gold thread billowed above it. He imagined the cost of the fabric could easily feed a family for several years. A pair of chairs richly upholstered sat angled toward one another before the unlit hearth, a low marble-topped table between them. An armoire stood in one corner, and upon investigating, he found it empty; not even a speck of dust to be had. There was a chest of drawers, roses and vines carved into the legs of it. In one corner upon a pedestal stood a large, ornate vase, and in another was a small round table upon which sat a bowl, pitcher, and a short stack of neatly folded towels.

A pang hit him and his shoulders sagged. It was one thing to suppose the sort of wealth and family from which she originated; it was quite another to see it with his own eyes. He had created a decent bit of wealth for himself, by his standards at least, and if he emptied his savings it would be quite enough to begin a life wherever they decided. But this rose of society was a woman accustomed to donning a different silk gown every day, and every evening attending a different event open only to those who floated in the echelons of London. She could win the heart of a duke or a prince without even trying, he wagered, and surely her family would aim to make such a match for her. He would never be able to provide the style of life and luxury to which Emmy was accustomed, and she would never be satisfied to be the wife of a commoner. The fact ate a hole in his gut until he felt ill.

A small knock at the door interrupted his melancholy thoughts and, rubbing at the knot that had materialised in the centre of his chest, he answered it. There stood before him a girl in a house uniform, younger even than Molly from the inn, with a clean apron tied about her tiny waist and a bucket in each hand. The handles of odd implements protruded from the top of one bucket, the other was filled with water.

He eyed them curiously before his dark gaze lifted to the girl's face.

Her eyes widened as her eyes clapped onto him, towering over her with his height with a thick growth of dark beard, and she quickly ducked her head demurely. "You're in need of a fire, Sir?"

"Aye, thank ye, lass. Room is a mite chilled," and he stepped back.

She shuffled in and went straight to the massive, but empty hearth. Kneeling before it, she fished out a pair of iron tongs from the bucket and carefully removed several chunks of smouldering charcoal. The tongs were slid back into the bucket with a clunk.

MacDougall stood several paces away and watched her with interest. No matter where he lived as he grew up, the fire never went out. Then again, the kitchen fire was what provided heat for the entire dwelling, and while he recalled it being banked down in the evenings, everyone took care that it never went out completely. He hadn't realised how in depth such a task was inside a house, especially one as large as this.

It wasn't long before flames crackled and the wood popped. After standing, the girl took hold of the second bucket and carried it across the room, careful, well-trained movements filling the pitcher with water without a single drop dripping outside the vessel. With her tasks complete, she retrieved the hearth bucket, gave him a quick bob of a curtsy, and scurried out the door.

Another glance at the riches around him put his nerves on edge. He was never one to stay idle, and despite the luxury of his surroundings, he had no interest in remaining where he was. He quickly unpacked the few belongings and put them away. There would be no evidence to suggest he didn't know how to live properly if he had anything to do about it. Then washed his face and hands in the cool, clear water the young girl had just provided. He had no nicer clothes to change into and he saw little point in doing so, anyway, thus he strode from the room to explore the house. He knew it likely wasn't something that was 'done', but being confined to a strange room would be the end of him, he was certain.

Mrs. Edith Fray, the house's cook, was not a lady's maid. She had been with the family for as long as Margaret had been alive. Theirs was a rare household, one where, despite the differences in rank, there was mutual appreciation and respect between master and help, upper and lower servants. Mrs. Fray had been married once upon a time but was widowed quite young before she was fortunate enough to bear children. It was just as she emerged from her mourning period that her life at the Brookshire estate began. She came on as a second pair of hands to the main cook of the house, working alongside the elder cook—General Harrow as the woman was affectionately, and fearfully, called by the entire household. Once Mrs. Fray had become adept at running the kitchen, she was transferred to Everleigh House in London while General Harrow remained in the country at Brookshire to oversee things there.

Carter came bustling into the kitchen with unusual agitation for the usually stoic man. "Mrs. Fray, Miss Everleigh has returned."

"Oh! what a lovely surprise. She'll be wanting her usual tea then?"

"She has need of your assistance; Cossett has yet to return."

Mrs. Fray fluttered her lashes in surprise, but quickly wiped her hands on her apron. "Shame we are at half staff, but Miss Everleigh is so obliging I'm sure she'll not mind if I am a bit clumsy."

Carter hesitated a moment before crossing to where Mrs. Fray stood, and the woman's heart lurched. "What's happened, Mr. Carter?"

The tender old gentleman took the woman's hands comfortingly in his own. "There has been an accident, I gather." And he succinctly relayed the little bit of information he had gleaned from their young lady and her lowly companion, including her new, broken method of communication.

"Bless my soul," Mrs. Fray whispered.

"Her escort—I know not what else to call him—is in the Blue Room, and Miss Everleigh has already gone above stairs to her suite. If you cannot comprehend what she needs, continue asking questions until it is clear. That is all I can recommend you do. Despite her desire, I shall have Mrs. Pratt write to Cossett as soon as she returns from her outing."

Mrs. Fray nodded as she removed her apron, wiped her hands, and hurried to do Carter's bidding, fretting about their Miss Margaret all the way.

Once the cook joined Emmy in her room, it took some time and creativity to explain what was needed. At long last, however, Emmy was dressed once more in her usual finery, with her hair done up tolerably well for Mrs. Fray's unaccustomed fingers. She did not wish to be away from Mr. MacDougall for long; she knew to her soul that he would be ill at ease in a place like this, moreso without her by his side justifying his presence. Thus she was dressed and ready to go within an hour. It was time to discover why she had taken the trip north in the first place, and who better to ask than her oldest friend, Charlotte Bexley, whose family and friends affectionately called Lottie. It was fortunate, indeed, that their dwelling was but a street away and could easily be travelled to by walking. She dreaded the ordeal of attempting to explain her desires vocally, even if Mr. MacDougall had become rather adept at translating her nonsensical words. Even so, she rummaged through her writing desk's drawers until she discovered the calling cards for both Charlotte and her brother, William. These were slipped into her wrist purse.

Emmy returned to the main floor to break her fast, choosing to have it in the dining room with her protector and companion rather than having a tray sent to her room. She arrived just as Carter and Annie, the youngest of their servers, were bringing the meal to the table. "Mac? Where… where Mac?"

"I went to his room to inform him of breakfast but it was found to be empty. I discovered him in the library. Would you like me to bring him, Miss Everleigh?"

She shook her head, taking her leave to find him, herself. As she went, she reflected on the oddity of attempting to think of herself as both Emmy and Margaret, especially now that she had returned to Town. She had been Emmy in the company of Mr. MacDougall for so long, her mind was somewhat at odds with itself. Emmy, she decided. While he was still with her, she would be Emmy. Well, except to the staff, of course, and she could not very well correct them.

He was indeed in the library, and she discovered him comfortably seated in one of the wing-backed chairs before the fire, a small book open and cradled between his large hands. She took a moment to watch him, and it was impossible to stop the smile that curled her lips. Through their travels, they had completed Austen's novel, and she wondered what piece he had discovered now.

"Ye just going to stand there and stare at me, Miss Everleigh?" he rumbled, not even looking up from the page.

She laughed lightly and fully entered the room, coming to stand at his side. "Book?"

He closed it and glanced at the spine. "Can-died?"

Emmy's eyes gogged in astonishment. He was reading Voltaire's *Candide*. Not only that, he looked to be quite a ways through it. Had he simply opened it at a random place and was skimming the pages disinterestedly, or was he truly reading it?

He glanced at her face and evidently guessed at her thoughts. "Tis decent enough; a bit difficult to understand in parts, but I understand 'tis quite an older book from a different time."

She was unable to stop the surprised chuckle that bubbled forth and she shook her head incredulously. The man was a constant surprise to her. "Ah, food… table."

He nodded and the book was closed with a snap and set to the side as he rose to his feet. "Yer man Cart seems happy to have ye home, lass," he commented as he led her out into the hall, then allowed her to lead the way to the breakfast room.

Of course he would not know it was Carter, and she had no way of correcting it. "Cart… Cart… mhm!" She huffed and tried again. "T… t… Cart…"

Mr. MacDougall took her hand and gave the back a brief pat before releasing it. "Let the words come naturally, lass. It will not do to work yerself into a tizzy over it."

She huffed and frowned, and she swore she heard a soft snort; she glared up at him, and he just grinned. "Yer cute as a kitten when yer ire's up, lass," he muttered, which, of course, earned him a deeper scowl. This time he laughed openly.

Mr. MacDougall was not shy about his appetite, and once the meal was set before them, he feasted royally upon the breakfast that had been hurriedly prepared. Even Emmy ate with relish, albeit daintily. There was little point in conversing, and the servants who attended them continued to pass questioning looks back and forth at the silence that stretched, not understanding why their Miss Everleigh remained so quiet.

Finally, toward the end of the meal, he asked, "What is our first stop to be?"

In lieu of a vocal answer, she removed the calling cards from her purse, and Annie stepped forward to take the cards and carry them to where Mr. MacDougall sat at the opposite end of the table.

"William Bexley, Charlotte Bexley," he mused aloud as he read the pair of cards.

She smiled warmly and patted her heart.

"Ah, they're friends of yourn, of course. Should I remain behind then, so ye might enjoy yer visit in privacy?"

Her eyes widened briefly and she shook her head. "No. Mac, stay. Mac… Mac…" Not finding the words, she repeated the action of gently patting the place over her heart, a warmer, more gentle expression overtaking her features. She was thankful he was unable to hear the way her heart thumped loudly against her palm at that moment. Yes, he was quickly becoming the most precious person in the world to her.

Mr. MacDougall nodded as he finished his coffee. "Yer just in need of someone to speak for ye," he teased lightly.

Without thinking about the properness of it, she took her cloth napkin and lobbed it across the table at his face, which he snagged mid-air with a smirk.

The surprised gasp from Annie was impossible to miss, and Emmy glanced at her with shamed embarrassment on her face, cheeks blazing pink for a moment before she was able to continue her breakfast as if nothing at all had happened. She missed the wink Mr. MacDougall tossed in Annie's direction, not meant in a flirtatious way, but to acknowledge the bizarreness of the entire situation. Fortunately, she correctly interpreted it and giggled softly with her ducked down.

The meal concluded, and Emmy and Mr. MacDougall took their leave, unaware that eyes followed them as they went. The ease and comfort with which their lady of the house took with such a man caused quite a stir in the house. Carter caught Annie chatting with Catherine, the lower housemaid that had taken coal to the visitor's room, musing about just such a thing between themselves, and he reprimanded them for talking behind their lady's back. He informed them, in a firm, authoritative tone, that the stranger had saved their lady's life and that was the reason, the *only* reason, why she was so kindly disposed towards him. Duly scolded, the girls scurried off to resume their customary duties and responsibilities.

Chapter Fourteen

The moment Emmy stepped outside, she inhaled deeply, a peaceful smile curling her lips. It was so good to be home again! Even if things had changed irreversibly for her, the comfort of being somewhere safe and familiar was unparalleled. Tossing a smile up at her companion, she nodded her head in the direction they ought to go, and the pair set out at a slow, leisurely pace.

As they wended their way to the house of her friends, they drew a fair bit of attention. It was almost comical. While Emmy drew stares and gazes that implied wonder and admiration, those same people, in looking at Mr. MacDougall, seemed as though they'd just seen the troll that lived under the bridge in a child's fairy tale. It wasn't that he was homely; far from it. He was handsome to be sure, although in a dark, rugged way that lent to mind romantic fantasies of gothic highwaymen rather than the polished gentlemen to which society at large was accustomed. It was his imposing stature and his dark, penetrating gaze that seemed to cause such a stir. These obvious features seemed all the more noticeable as he stalked alongside Margaret's ethereal glide. She ignored the whispers and held her head with pride; not only was she proud to walk beside Mr. MacDougall, but she had long begun to prefer his rugged looks to the fair dandies that were so common in her set.

Upon arriving at Bexley House, Emmy presented her card to the footman, and the pair were shown directly into the parlour. The house servants knew Miss Everleigh was always permitted entrance to the house if the young master or mistress were at home, regardless of the hour.

The pair had not long to wait before Charlotte appeared. Her dark blond hair was done in ringlets at the sides of her face and bounced as she made a bee-line for Emmy, wide blue eyes dancing and hands outstretched in welcome. "Maggie!" cried Charlotte, using Emmy's—well, Margaret's—pet name. "I did not expect you back so soon! I had thought Mr. Wainwright would keep you north for ages!"

William Bexley, tall and slender with the same colour hair and eyes as his sister, snorted as he came in on his sister's words. "Come now, Lottie; Wainwright did not kidnap her. They would have returned within a few months, at most."

Emmy leaned back and eyed Charlotte, then Mr. Bexley, then Mr. MacDougall.

Mr. MacDougall's steely eyes were on Mr. Bexley as the latter entered the room, and Emmy looked from one man to the other. The pair looked as if they were prepared to throw fists.

"Who is this Goliath of a man, Miss Margaret?" Mr. Bexley finally bit out, clearly unimpressed with Mr. MacDougall's presence.

Emmy gasped and broke away from her friend, her eyes flashing. "Friend!"

Charlotte started and looked slowly between the other three. "Friend? Has 'friend' a name, Maggie?"

"Mac… Mac…"

"Arran MacDougall," he finished, stepping forward and offering his hand despite the cool, determined look in his eyes.

He was sized up before his hand clapped the extended one. "William Bexley." There was a pause. "Hold. MacDougall… The Highland Hammer?"

Mr. MacDougall nodded to confirm the man's memory as accurate. "Aye."

"Then you are most welcome, Sir. Have a drink," Mr. Bexley remarked as he crossed to the sideboard where stood a decanter and crystal cups. "I saw you fight once at the Pally. That was the bout with Maddox Bunting as I recall. I should have bet on you that night," Mr. Bexley handed him a snifter, "but a friend advised me to put five and twenty on Bunting. Not that it mattered overly much; I bet on you for the Cowley match in Barrow. I made two hundred fifty on that one, bet every penny I had on me that night.

"Glad I am that I dinnae disappoint ye," Mr. MacDougall replied distractedly, more paying attention to Emmy's attempted conversation with her friend.

"Maggie, you sly thing!" Charlotte exclaimed as she drew Margaret down beside her upon the sofa. The girl was so excited that she had yet to catch

Emmy's strange way of speaking, and Emmy knew well it would be a struggle to get a word in edgewise now that Charlotte had begun. "Running off to the north to be secretly wed! And you have not yet changed your cards, you goose!"

Secretly wed? Emmy reeled back and could practically feel Mr. MacDougall's gaze boring into her from across the room.

"It is quite all right, of course; we can remedy that today!" her friend continued, undeterred. "I am quite certain your husband will not mind if your oldest friend steals you away for a couple of hours! Indeed, where is Mr. Wainwright? Why are you here with this stranger when you ought to be parading about Town with your devoted husband on your arm?"

She stole a quick, horrified glance back at her Scotsman before fixing her stare on Charlotte again, fine tremors beginning in her centre and radiating outward. What was her friend going on about?

"And I hope you will let me help make decisions when you convince your new husband to allow you to renovate the hall," Charlotte continued undaunted. "It is just so old fashioned and dark. Of course if you prefer it as such, then leave it as it is, but I have always associated you with springtime flowers and sunshine. Or will you two make Grosvenor Square your home?"

"Lo–Lot.   Lottie—"
"How lovely and romantic the whole thing is. To discover that you and Mr. Wainwright were in love this whole time! You never said a word to me, and I feel quite neglected. But that is hardly a reason to

carry a grudge when you have achieved what so many of us wish: to marry for love. And he is so hand—"

Emmy surged to her feet. "No!"

Charlotte stopped mid-sentence, and the conversation Mr. Bexley was having with Mr. MacDougall ceased with the same sudden jolt. All eyes fixed themselves upon the recently returned socialite.

Emmy shook her head, trembling from head to foot, as pained eyes sought out Mr. MacDougall's; betrayal shone darkly from the depths of his gaze, and with his jaw locked, he looked away. She whimpered and nearly fled to his side, but just barely held herself in place for the sake of public propriety.

"Maggie? What is it?"

"No, no. Not... not, us. Not... Mac. Mac, stay." Tears of anguish glimmered in her eyes, and her chest tightened the longer he refused to look in her direction.

Charlotte's breath hitched and a shaky hand reached toward her brother. "Maggie, why do you speak in such a strange manner? What is a Mac?"

Mr. Bexley was there in an instant, lending the comfort his sister needed while staring in bewilderment between Emmy and Mr. MacDougall.

"Maggie?" Mr. Bexley pressed.

Emmy could only whimper. "...Mac?" Her focus drifted again to her Scotsman.

Mr. MadDougall held himself sternly, every muscle locked and his fists were clenched into tight balls at his sides until the skin blanched white. He looked absolutely furious.

She moved timidly in his direction, laid a hand on the back of his shoulder.

He jerked away, and her heart clenched painfully. "If yer married, lass—" The sentence ended as if he had choked on the words before he stormed out through the door. A few heartbeats later, a door slammed at the end of a hall.

Charlotte exchanged a concerned look with her brother, then rose and crossed to her friend. "Maggie, what has happened? I have never seen you in such a state. Pray, talk to me."

Mr. Bexley joined them and he slid a brotherly arm around Emmy's shoulders, tugging her into his side. "Indeed, if you are in trouble of some kind, you know we shall aid you in any way we can. If you need our protection from him, say the word, Maggie. I care not if he is a prize fighter; I shall bury him if he has harmed you in any way."

Emmy jerked and stepped away from the brother and sister, shaking her head adamantly. "No! Mac, Mac, friend. Mac– Mac–" She huffed in frustration and set her hand over her heart, her eyes begging the pair to understand her.

"Why do you not speak naturally, Maggie?" Charlotte pleaded.

"What of Wainwright?" Mr. Bexley demanded without giving her a chance to answer. "We were given to understand that the pair of you were so wildly in love that you could not bear to wait for the formalities, that you had eloped with the blessing of your cousin, Saxon. Indeed, Wainwright sent us word these three weeks past detailing that such were your true intentions behind leaving London when you did."

At that, Emmy fairly lurched back and stared at them, aghast. Wainwright again! The room spun and darkness crowded the edges of her vision. She was aware of her breath sawing in and out of her lungs, of the sound of rushing water in her ears. It was impossible! How could this be? There were days missing from her memory, but she knew in her soul she was not, and had never been, in love with Wainwright. It was unthinkable! If only she knew why she had left London with him in the first place… If only she could convey her meanings in a way that could be easily understood!

Brother and sister each took an arm and guided her to sit, then to recline upon the sofa, Charlotte instantly snapping open her fan to waft cool air across her friend's face. "William, what has happened to our friend?" she cried softly.

"I know not, but stay with her here. I will seek out answers from Mr. MacDougall myself,"he declared, and off he stalked.

He was in torment. How could Emmy have been so intimate with him when she was all this time a married woman? Surely she could not have hit her head so terribly as to have forgotten that prominent detail, could she? He thought back to every moment spent with her, and never once had she behaved like a modest woman recently wed to a love match. He shook his head and dragged a hand through his hair.

"Mr. MacDougall!"

He turned just in time to see a fist hurling at him, and he didn't even attempt to duck or block it. Perhaps a solid facer was just what he needed to knock the sense back into him.

It was a decent punch and he rubbed his jaw as he watched the fury rise in Bexley's face.

The young polished gentleman came at him again, and this time, MacDougall stepped easily out of the way, giving the back of the man's shoulders a light push away. "Ye only get one free shot," he muttered.

Bexley spun around, fists lifted and ready. "Well as neither her husband nor her cousin are here, I will defend our friend's honour! Put up your fists, Highlander!"

Forcing himself not to roll his eyes, MacDougall put his palms up instead and stepped back. "I've nae intention of fighting ye. I'll take my leave and none of ye shall ever set eyes on me again." He stalked his way to the door leading back into the house.

"You retreat like a coward and deny me satisfaction?" the man hollered behind him.

"Aye, just what I plan to do," MacDougall bit out.

"Have you injured our friend Wainwright, you knave?"

That had MacDougall stopping in his tracks. "I've not a thing to do with that… man. I've never laid eyes on him." There were many other choice words he wished to use for who he believed to be a blackguard, but he would refrain out of respect for Emmy; no, Miss Everleigh. *Nae, wrong again; she's Mrs. Wainwright.* His stomach went sour.

"Then why is it our friend cannot speak more than a word or two? Why is she in a state practically beyond consolation? Where is Wainwright?"

He was rapidly tiring of this young pup's prattle, but he supposed the young man had a right to know at least the basics of the last month. So with his back still turned, trusting the gentleman would be honourable and not strike him, he detailed whatever he thought Bexley ought to know about Emmy's injury and subsequent symptoms. At the end of it, he gritted his teeth, fighting for control over his emotions. "I had no way of knowing the lady was married. She wears no ring, and as ye witnessed yerself, she has precious few words at her disposal. At the start of it, not even that; it was all nonsense. At least her words have some bit of meaning behind them the noo." MacDougall sighed, deflating. "By heaven, I only wanted to bring her back to her friends. By heaven, nothing happened betwixt us to compromise her reputation. I did only what I deemed necessary to help her mend, and brought her back to the city as soon as the way seemed safe for her to travel without worsening her injury."

Bexley had remained where he was, listening intently to every word the Scotsman spoke, attempting to decipher the complexity that swirled around his sister's closest friend. The anger leached from him and no longer did he desire to pound this commoner into the ground. In fact, upon these new revelations, something did not sit quite comfortably with him. But he held his peace and said not a word.

MacDougall stuffed his hands into his pockets, his own anger giving way to a bone-deep grief for the loss of something he had not even truly possessed. "I'll take my leave of ye," and he started toward the house again. Instead of re-entering, he stopped and turned half way round to glance back at the young gentleman. "One moment. Ye said ye received word from Wainwright? How far back did it arrive?"

Bexley quirked a brow at him. "Three weeks, I should think. Perhaps slightly more."

MacDougall crossed his arms over his chest. "Has he returned to London at all since he left?"

"Not to my knowledge, no. I have not seen him at the club, nor heard that he returned. We were under the impression he and Miss Margaret were destined for Newcastle, as he informed us before they departed. He explained to us that Margaret had need of peace and quiet, that she had been rather emotional through the months before Christmas. As a result, Wainwright was taking her to a private retreat in the north, and he planned to propose once there. It was only after they left that we received word of their elopement. I suppose the cause of her emotional outbursts was a dislike for having to wait to wed her beau. Of course, to marry surreptitiously, their true destination was, of course, Scotland."

MacDougall swallowed down the sour surge in his mouth and focused on the facts. If what Bexley said was true, and he had no reason to believe otherwise, then Emmy was already in his own company when Wainwright penned the letter to their friends in London. And for that matter, it was impossible for her to have already married Wainwright—there was not time enough for them to travel all the way into Scotland to wed and then back south by the time her path intersected with his own. His scowl was like a storm cloud as he turned, marched back into the house, and went straight to the parlour.

The moment he strode through the doorway, his Emmy was on her feet and rushing across the floor to him. Pure instinct had his arms folding tenderly around her, despite her friend's shocked gasp and the sound of Bexley's footsteps coming up behind him. With this woman in his arms, all was right in the world and he could breathe again. At this point, he cared not if she was married to another man; he would fight the world and run away with her if it was what she wanted.

"Shh, lass. I have ye. Yer safe," he whispered against her hair, one hand travelling up and down her spine in slow, soothing strokes.

Bexley entered and joined his sister, who stared in open confusion, her hands wringing themselves together. "Something is amiss here, Lottie."

Charlotte turned her face up toward her brother's. "Were she wed to Mr. Wainwright, a man she loved, our Maggie would never behave in this way," she replied, giving the pair across the room a pointed look.

"You are quite right."

"I tried to persuade Maggie to tell me what troubles her, but I could not make sense of her words."

"And I fear you shall not, little sister, not without effort. MacDougall explained it; our Maggie suffered an injury, it seems, and what words she has are all a jumble now." He sighed and watched the pair across the room. He felt awkward at witnessing such an intimate display and finally cleared his throat, speaking loud enough for the pair to hear him. "Perhaps a bit of propriety?"

MacDougall released Emmy abruptly, as if he hadn't realised there were still others in the room. "Aye, of course. Lass, I should go. Ye've things to sort in yer life, and I'll be in the way. Yer friends can protect ye."

She peered up at him with liquid eyes and a downturned mouth and it took every ounce of willpower within him not to kiss the frown right off her lips.

"There seem to be holes in our understanding," continued Bexley. "Wainwright told me months ago he was actively courting Miss Margaret, and has been for a year."

At that, Emmy gave a cry and her hands pressed against her mouth, and her countenance was one of horrified astonishment. If that did not answer some lingering questions, nothing else would; her reaction could not be feigned, even if she were the most talented actress in the world.

Her friends seemed to take note of it, as well. "Does that answer yer question, Bexley?" MacDougall asked dryly.

Bexley strode resolutely across the room to refill his glass, and without asking, he did the same for MacDougall. The crystal glass was carried over and tendered into his hand, and MacDougall downed it in a single swallow. While he rarely partook of spirits, today was a day to make an exception.

"I'll not let that man get within ten paces of ye, lass," he ground out between clenched teeth.

A small tug on his coat sleeve had him glancing down into Emmy's upturned face again.

"Mac. Go."

He rocked back as if he'd been struck. It was long seconds that he stared at her, hoping he had misheard her, but no correction came from her lips. Finally, after swallowing the nails that had suddenly manifested in his throat, he nodded. "As ye say." Setting the glass down with a harsh clunk, he made for the door, his long strides devouring the distance to the front and out onto the street again.

If that was what she wanted, he'd do so.

And then he would go to the river and dig a hole at the bottom of it for his grave.

Emmy stared after him in alarm as he practically ran from the room. That had been unexpected, and she blinked. She felt as if a rug had just been yanked from beneath her feet.

Charlotte came to stand beside her, wrapping a girlish arm about her waist. "What an afternoon! Come, Maggie dearest. Let us have a seat by the fire and allow all this excitement to settle a bit. We shall untangle everything in due time. But fearful handsome as this Mr. MacDougall may be, I think you were perfectly right, sending him away."

She gave a start and her head whipped around in her friend's direction. "Away? Gone?"

"Why, yes. You said so yourself; you ordered him to go. I am sure he would never mean you harm, but with the lower-borne, one can never quite tell for certain."

Emmy threw her friend's arm off, and with that, she fairly sprinted out of the room and down the hall. That had not been what she meant at all! Foolish, foolish girl! And poor Mr. MacDougall; he would never trust her now. But perhaps she might catch him if she were very quick about it.

She threw open the front door and raced onto the street, her eyes frantically scanning the avenue to either side. Fortunately, the man did rather stick out, and she saw his tall, forbidding figure marching toward the corner, arms locked at his sides. She raced after him, her heart in her throat. She did not wish to call undue attention to herself, but more than that, she simply could not lose him!

Finally within reach, both hands wrapped tightly around one of his wrists and she yanked him to a halt, not caring if she made a scene that would set the tongues around them wagging. "Mac! Mac, no!"

He stopped short and remained where he was, his powerful body fairly vibrating with what she could only suppose was leashed anger. "Lass, ye told me to go. But dinnae expect me to stand by while ye and yer empty-headed friends berate me. I've some dignity, after all."

Emmy shook her head, fighting back her cry. "Mac! Go…. go, me. *Me*. Home me. Home!"

It took three full seconds before his posture relaxed. A sigh of relief rushed out of him with an audible woosh and he yanked her into his arms, holding her tight against him, his lips pressed to the top of her head. "Thank God, lass. Ye nearly ripped my heart from my chest."

She sniffled and buried her face in his shirt for a moment before she stumbled back and gave a fearful glance around the street. They were bringing disreputable attention to themselves, and she was well known and recognized here. For her cousin's sake, she did not wish to disgrace herself.

"Home, Mac."

He peered at the windows of the house they'd just abandoned before hurrying her in the direction of her own house.

"Aye, lass. Home. And then, we've plans to make."

Charlotte watched the odd pair sweep down the sidewalk for a moment before returning to the sofa, a scowl marring her sweet, babydoll face.

"Something troubles you, little sister," William declared.

She pursed her lips together and shook her head. "Does it not trouble you? Have you ever known Maggie to be so… fanciful like this?"

William threw himself casually into the nearest chair. "Now you say so, it is true Miss Margaret has always tended to be the most level-headed of our particular circle."

"Exactly my thoughts," she agreed, taking a small biscuit from the platter. But rather than nibbling at it, her fingertips broke off small, crumbling pieces.

The pair sat in silence, each alone with their thoughts. "Did she ever confide in you directly her love for Wainwright?"

"No, not once. The only time she ever mentioned any such thing was relating how tired she was of Mr. Wainwright's endless jests regarding joining their families. She said he would often tease, 'May as well get duty out of the way.'"

"But she never spoke regarding her own love for him?"

"Love, never. Annoyance, occasionally. But more than anything, she appeared to consider him a close, trusted friend. Never more."

William left his brandy on the marble side table and stood to pace, a sure sign his mind was untying some confusing knot.

"Wainwright told me before he left that she had been suffering from frequent headaches and volatile emotions. That his purpose of taking her to Newcastle was for rest at an estate he knew."

Charlotte frowned. "Now I think of it, he confided to me that he planned on finally proposing on that holiday trip. And I remember he specifically used that word: finally."

William pushed himself from the chair and went to the window, aimlessly staring out at the lavishly green square spread before their row. "Something does not match."

"Could we be mistaken, brother?"

"It is possible," he admitted.

Charlotte's gaze narrowed and peered more intently at him. "And what of our recent new acquaintance, this Mr. MacDougall?" she asked curiously of her brother. "You are much more adept at reading people than I am, you know."

"I only know of the man professionally," William answered. "However, I do not have the sense that our friend is in any danger being in his company. He is rather unpolished, perhaps, but he does not strike me as a liar or a swindler. If nothing else, heed Margaret's own behaviour; she seemed entirely comfortable in his presence, and even sought his strength and support when they were here with us. Did you notice that she continually looked to him for reassurance?"

"I did. At first I thought that she might be looking to him in some sort of subservience or duress, in the event that she had said something wrong before us. But she appeared genuinely frightened and concerned, and indeed she sought reassurance and comfort from him. She certainly did not behave as one who was forced to remain in his company, particularly the brazen way she ran after him."

"In addition, her reaction to being told that Wainwright made his intentions clear could not have been a ruse, I am quite sure of that. I have never known her to perpetuate any sort of falsehood."

"Nor I, indeed."

There was another long pause as the siblings sat with their thoughts. Finally, Bexley rose to his feet. "There are inquiries to be made, and I shall make them. Rest assured."

Charlotte's hands wrung themselves together in her lap. "I do pray she is safe! It is most distressing, not knowing for certain in whom to put one's trust."

"I believe she is in as good a set of hands as she could be, outside of our own. If MacDougal is half as capable and fearsome outside the ring as he is in it, she will be tolerably safe."

"I do hope that you are right about him, William," she said softly.

Chapter Fifteen

MacDougall led them back to Emmy's townhouse, having already memorised the number, the appearance of the front facade, and the direction between her home and that of her friends. He stole an occasional peek down at her as they walked, and was pleasantly surprised to see her striding confidently beside him, her head up, her eyes sparkling and prepared to greet the world. Given the grit she demonstrated to him again and again, he dared to hope there might be a future for them yet. Perhaps the impossible could happen.

There were more stares from the swells that frequented this part of the city, but as the lady at his side ignored them, he followed suit. Instead, while he kept his gaze fixed ahead on where they were going, his peripheral took in carefully sculpted gardens of Grosvenor Square. It was nothing overly special now, but he wagered it would be beautifully rich and verdant once the trees and grasses had opportunity to fully return to life. As it was, he could just make out tiny green buds beginning to erupt from nearly every branch. A far cry from the frigid snow storm he and Emmy experienced a mere two or three days prior.

"Yes, I expect the opera tonight to be one of rare delight. Perhaps if the weather holds, there will be fireworks like the old days!" a passing lady exclaimed to her friend.

Emmy glanced over her shoulder at the retreating pair, then turned her eyes upon him, their depths gleaming with anticipation.

"Hear something that interested ye, Miss Everleigh?" MacDougall asked with an amused grin. He wondered if she had the ability at all to mask what her true thoughts were or if she was always as easy to read as one of her books. Perhaps it simply took his getting to know and understand her better.

Her smile was wide and she hastened her steps toward home. "Hall. Hall. Music, hall," she continued to insist.

"Aye, I hear ye. Music hall," he agreed, leading her up the steps and into the townhouse.

"No. Hall. *Hall.*"

Did that differ from what he'd just said? "Aye. Hall."

Carter appeared a moment later to take Emmy's coat, and reluctantly, the man took MacDougall's as well. "Did you have a pleasant outing, Miss Everleigh?"

"Hall Cart. Hall. Hall."

Grey brows soared. "What was that, Miss?"

"She overheard a couple ladies speaking of a fine opera this evening. She has been repeating 'hall' for the past few minutes," MacDougall explained.

"Perhaps she means The Royal Gardens? It was known most as Vauxhall years ago."

Emmy's expression lit like a beacon in response.

"I recognize the name but I dinnae ken anything else about it."

Carter nodded. "The Royal Gardens used to be the height in entertainment of all kinds: music, operas, dancing, art galleries, fountains, dining, and some of Town's most beautiful gardens. There was even a reenactment of the Battle of Waterloo at one point if I recall correctly. The Royal Gardens have been unfortunately floundering the last several years. If Miss Everleigh overheard ladies conversing about an event this evening, it must be that they are opening a few weeks early due to the unseasonably warm weather we are having. Perhaps she wishes to attend?"

"I thought ye'd have need of a good rest after such a long and trying journey, Miss Everleigh. Would ye not prefer a quiet evening at home?" MacDougall prodded.

She shook her head. "You. You, hall."

"For certs, I can do without the grand spectacle at The Royal Gardens, even if they are so lavish. More than anything, I fear fer yer health, lass. Miss Everleigh," he corrected with a flick of a glance at the house butler who was hanging up their coats. "Ye've endured quite a bit of excitement since our paths crossed. Wouldna it be better to rest yerself?"

She scowled and straightened her back, pinning him with a determined look. "Hall. Gardens. You, me."

She was stringing more and more words together in cohesive sentences, and he could not help but smile at it, at her. "All right, if ye wish it. But I've not a proper thing to wear to stand up with ye, ye ken. I'll be sorely underdressed."

"No," she remarked, then a slow smile melted across her features. "Perfect."

And how was he expected to say nae to her? He would move heaven and earth to have her smile at him like that every day for the rest of his life. "Ye flatter me, Miss Everleigh. All right, I'll escort ye to these Vauxhall Gardens ye speak of. Do we supper here?"

She shook her head again, then gave the old, faithful servant a meaningful look before taking herself upstairs.

"Has she always gotten her way?" MacDougall drawled when she was out of earshot.

The old butler chuckled fondly. "Yes, Sir. Nearly always. But then, saying yes to her is little hardship." Carter paused then and eyed him, looking very much as if he wished to say something further.

MacDougall waited. He often found that, when one was quiet long enough, others would fill the silence with their thoughts.

"She is very... precious to us here, Sir," the man finally admitted. "We have watched her grow from girlhood. When her good parents passed on, God rest them, rather than disassembling the household, her cousin's family ensured the Everleigh staff remained here, remained together. And so we have, and continued to come in and out of her life as members of both the Everleigh and the Saxon households. It may not be proper to say so, but we all consider ourselves a part of her family, and I flatter myself that she thinks of us that way, as well." Carter pinned MacDougall with a direct stare. "I do not know how a man like you becomes so familiar with one like our Miss Margaret, but I shall be keeping a watchful eye upon you whilst you are here, Sir."

MacDougall wasn't a bit frightened by the man's distrust of him; on the contrary, it caused his respect for Carter and the staff to increase fivefold. "Sir, I am not here to cause any trouble; not to ye, certainly not to Miss Everleigh. I assure ye, I want nothing more than to see her kept safe and cherished the way she deserves."

Carter's brows arched. "And you, Sir, believe you are the man for the job?"

He fairly snorted. "Hardly, Sir; I ken I'm not fit for the likes of her. But neither do I believe Mr. Wainwright has her best interest in mind. I've never met the man, but the way things happened..." MacDougall paused, sighed, then shook his head. "We met Mr. Bexley today, and I think he said it best: there are holes in our understanding."

The old servant gave a slow, musing nod, and MacDougall took his leave. He had nothing nicer to change into than what he already wore, so he opted to return to the library and the book he had left behind earlier that day while Emmy made herself ready above stairs.

"Nothing I've seen compares to the likes of this," MacDougall commented quietly as they rose from their seats after the opera had concluded.

It had been a full evening of merry entertainment. Never in his life had he experienced the pleasures to be had at The Royal Gardens, and he could only imagine how it must have been at its height. He had since learned that everything at The Royal Gardens, formerly Vauxhall, happened simultaneously rather than one event after another. It was impossible to experience all the Gardens had to offer in a single evening, and he imagined that was the point of it. To fully enjoy the lavish debauchery, one had to return night after night; he was given to understand the programme changed with frequency. And the lights! The grounds were lighted such that the entire area felt like a fairyland. The effect was enchanting.

They had begun their evening at the Gardens with supper, and it appeared that many of the social elite had a similar idea. The dining room was abuzz with conversation and laughter, made easy by the limitless availability of punch and spirits. He had been rather surprised to spot a few in the crowd that, if their dress was any indication, were of a station or two below that of his beautiful companion. Indeed, MacDougall was even more astonished to discover that he was a recognizable entity. A pair of gentlemen approached them as they ate, calling him by his ring name and asking him to regale them with stories of his best boxing bouts and moments. MacDougall deferred, wishing to maintain a persona of anonymity instead of celebrity so he might enjoy a quiet evening with Emmy. He was certain their time together was coming swiftly to an end and he meant to store up memories of her to enjoy when he continued years in solitude. However, it was Emmy, herself, who encouraged him to share his stories, bestowing upon him a most charming smile that ultimately had him capitulating. Soon, half a dozen men of varying ages sat in chairs around them while he described this fight and that, and Emmy's eyes sparkled with pride as each tale was recounted, seeming to enjoy it as much as the men.

As he had gained an audience, and given Emmy's inability to tell him herself, he gleaned what information he could about the fabled pleasure gardens. There had, indeed, been a large reenactment using hundreds and hundreds of actors dressed as soldiers. Fireworks, described as colourful explosions in the air, had been regular occurrences for decades and many anticipated their return. Massive balloons would rise high above the city and those wealthy enough to afford it were even able to purchase rides in the basket suspended below it. The theatre boasted all manner of performers, from operas such as the one offered that very evening, to plays, dancers, acrobats, and strange characters from the Far East. There was a large, magnificent waterfall which they had crossed in front of on their way to dine. And that was to say nothing of the impressive gardens and grounds. It was easy to see the allurement of the gardens themselves, given how many shadowy corners and wooded groves existed for lovers to steal time for trysts away from watchful eyes.

Now they exited the theatre, with the final chords of the opera still echoing in his head, and a glance around proved just how many lovers took advantage of the area's reputation. He had done his level best to conduct himself with honour and respect while he and Emmy were in each other's company without a chaperone, especially once they began their travels to return her home. His blood heated immediately when he recalled how she felt pressed against him, the sounds of her soft moans when he kissed her, how her hair felt like silk ribbons when it slid between his fingers.

His body hardened and he fought to regain some control over himself. When he tipped a gaze down at Emmy and found her wide, sparkling eyes already adoring upon his face, it was everything he could do to keep from sweeping her into his arms.

He led her before the large waterfall, the Cascade he understood it to be called, and then beyond to the gardens and sprawling lawn. There were countless people milling about in groups and in pairs, some dancing, some singing rather drunkenly, and several enjoying rather amorous activities despite still largely being in view of other sets of eyes. It appeared that no one cared much about what others did while they experienced the Royal Gardens, almost as if the rules of polite society did not apply here.

Emmy was dressed quite simply, practically modest when compared to how many other women were clad, dripping with lace and ribbons and bedecked in jewels, some showing more skin than what they covered. It mattered not. She could wear dirty rags and still be fashionable. He largely ignored the masses around them and led her toward a stone bench with a vined trellis canopy arched over it. He hoped they would go overlooked. They would not raise any speculative eyebrows as he intended to continue treating her with the dignity owed her.

But surely some allowances might be permitted, here of all places.

He swept off his coat and draped it over the stone of the bench before guiding her to sit upon it, then he lowered himself to the frozen seat beside her. The lights overhead burnished her hair and it gleamed bronze. Her cheeks flushed prettily as he gazed at her. His entire heart was in his eyes, he was sure, and he could not bring himself to care enough to mask it.

"Lass… Miss Everleigh, Margaret, Emmy."

She grinned. "Mac."

He smirked. "I dinnae suppose there is chance of ye calling me Arran is there?"

Did her breathing catch? Did the colour flare to life in her face? It was only then that he recalled their differences in life and status, specifically how rarely a woman like her would call any man by his Christian name.

But her expression softened as she whispered. "Arr–Arran."

What a heady experience that was, his name on her lips, whispered like a prayer. Was it his imagination or did she lean closer? With his heart threatening to pound a hole straight through his chest, he gathered both her hands into his, marvelling at the delicacy of her despite the spine of iron he knew she possessed.

"Ye've tipped my world on its head, lass. Yer as kind and generous as ye are lovely, and yer far and away the most beautiful woman I've ever laid eyes on. I know ye can never be my wife, and I wish more than anything in the world that I could change my stars. But I cannae leave ye without confessing how deeply I—"

"What is the meaning of this!?"

Emmy's insides were naught but swarms of butterflies taken to wing within her.

The night had been magical, the stuff of fairy stories and romantic novels. Every bit of it would be etched in her memory for always, she was certain of that. How could it not be? She was back in her beloved London, wearing clothes familiar to her, but more than that, she was out with her Scotsman. When a handful of men recognized him and expressed their admiration of him, she had been only too pleased to allow them all to converse freely. It made her heart swell knowing how they honoured him. Of course, it was all due to his fame as a prized boxer, his accolades in the ring, his fierceness when fighting an opponent. It was but the athlete they admired.

That was but a small sliver of who he was, the person she had become so closely acquainted with over the last several weeks. But she could not care less about his athletic prowess or the number of fights he had won. It was not the athlete but the *man* she admired. She felt incredibly privileged to see the more intimate side of him, a side she wondered if many others even knew existed.

She felt not the cold, was no longer aware of the crowds around them. Only they two existed, *me and thee* as he was wont to say. From the very start, and without being requested to do so, he had thrown his lot in with hers, never wavering, and never once did she doubt his constancy.

And now... now! Would he speak the words her heart longed to hear? She held her breath, her eyes sparkling, her fingers nestled warmly between his own. *Arran. Her Arran.* Forever after would he be Arran in her private thoughts, and her heart danced for joy within her.

"What is the meaning of this?!"

She knew the identity of the interloper without looking. Ice sluiced through her veins at the malevolence lacing the words, and she visibly cowered, her body bowing in on itself as if to disappear from sight.

Wainwright.

Her lover's confession died on his lips, and information flew swiftly and silently between her gaze and Arran's. He was on his feet and shielding her from Wainwright's view before she could hope to intervene. Even when she stood, her palm pressed to his back, Arran had one arm behind him, wrapped about her waist and hip, securely protecting her from the threat that faced them.

"You blackguard! What is it you are doing with my wife!?"

Did he just say—

"Yer wife, my arse," MacDougall growled, and without preamble, he stepped forward and let his fist fly.

Wainwright saw his intention in just enough time to start back, and MacDougall's fist glanced off the man's cheek and nose; lucky that, as if it had been a punch that fully hit its mark, it may very well have killed them. Even so, the force of it the strike sent Wainwright crashing into the feet and lower legs of the trio of men that had accompanied him, and all went down in a pile of flailing limbs. Wainwright rolled about feebly as he strove to determine which way pointed upward.

"Wainwright!" one of his cohorts cried when he fell. Venomous eyes snapped up to MacDougall. "You bastard!"

Emmy watched in abject horror as all three of Wainwright's men scrambled to their feet and charged at Arran.

They had the attention of everyone in the vicinity now, curious onlookers forgetting their revelry and trysts in favour of something more scandalous and enticing. As if pulled by imaginary tethers, the crowd began to approach.

"Emmy! Run!" her Scotsman roared as he fought against Wainwright's men, thrashing against their detaining arms wildly, his fists flying this way and that faster than she could even track. There was blood on his hands, blood on his face and shirt, blood on the face of every man present. So much blood, and such violence. She stood as one frozen.

"Run, Emmy!" he yelled again. "NOW!"

That final commanding yell was enough to jar Emmy from her stupor and she took flight. Behind her she could hear men yelling that Wainwright was in trouble, that some commoner had gone mad, and while everything in her ached to go to Arran's defence and rescue, she knew doing so would make his sacrifice worthless. He had wanted her to run, to get away. It had only been a handful of days since they began puzzling out the scheme that had been closing in around her, but there was no doubt in her mind now. If Wainwright was innocent, it would eventually come to light. But for now, she had to escape!

The cries and grunts of the brawl and the cheers of the gawkers echoed through the gardens as she raced through the maze of shrubs and trees. She had been to the Royal Gardens on a few occasions, but not so many for her to be well acquainted with its twists and turns. What might be seen by some as a way to hide themselves from society was now her chance at evasion. If she could but manage to run all the way to the Gardens' exit without detection, she could fetch help. If not Carter then surely Charlotte and Bexley would aid her. They had met Arran, themselves, and Bexley appeared fond enough of him. She could only pray that Bexley would side with her and not whatever lies Wainwright had circulated about her.

In her depths, she knew she would not have married Wainwright, and never could. She was not fond enough of him to make such a commitment. Besides which, he had even spread amongst her friends the blatant lie that he had been courting her these several months. Wainwright had never pressed his suit, and she was certain he never once spoke with her cousin regarding his intentions. And if he lied to Bexley about that, then there was little reason to believe Wainwright about anything else he claimed.

She raced around a corner and nearly slammed into a hedge, a clear dead end with no way through it nor the fence on the other side leading to the street. She whipped around. The lights of the garden were no longer friendly; instead, the shadows they cast were deep and menacing, as if reaching for her to swallow her whole. The pounding of feet and the huffing of breath in the garden somewhere nearby spurred her forward again, and she took another turn, and another, her lungs screaming for air but she did not dare slow down.

Why did this feel so familiar to her?

"Margaret? Come out, come out," called a deep voice, sing-songy and almost playful if it was not so menacing. It was Wainwright; he was pursuing her. What had happened to Arran? Was he all right?

"I shall find you, my dove," he crooned.

My dove.

Her vision tunnelled and she stumbled as images flooded her mind.

Margaret was back on the train, lingering just inside the door leading to the next car. She could see Wainwright with the girl he had hired to be her companion for the train journey, speaking low between each other, his hands upon the girl's face in tender caresses.

"Does she suspect anything, do you think?" the girl, Miss Stewart, asked.

"Of course not, my dove. She is as trusting as a child, and you've played your part well. Our friends in London believe I am taking her north to propose, while the conductor and porter are thoroughly convinced she is my poor, mildly insane wife whom we are tenderly transferring to a private asylum off the coast of Scotland, and you are her devoted, loving nurse. Besides which, I have the marriage certificate

if anyone questions us. One day more and sweet, foolish little Margaret will be shut up for good, and we shall be free to live the life we deserve with her fortune in my control. Now, be a good girl, Hattie my love, and make our lady her special medicine."

Margaret whirled around and hurried back to her berth in terror. How could she have been so fooled, so blind not to have seen through the charade? Mr. Wainwright had been so permanent a fixture in her circle, she could scarcely remember a time when he wasn't there. And all the time, he was naught but a villain costumed as a trusted ally! His hateful voice played over and over in her mind. She glanced about the berth and snapped up her bonnet, taking just long enough to loop its ribbons across her throat. Her coat came next and she shoved her arms through the sleeves. Her dainty purse was snatched and she struggled to pin it inside her coat before pushing the buttons through their holes, one eye on the train aisle and the other on getting her coat closed against the frigid weather outside. She did not have much of a plan beyond getting off this train and away from he whom she now knew as her enemy.

The train was at full speed with no signs of slowing, the next town some distance down the tracks; jumping from the side of a car at this speed would be too dangerous! She crept through the cars until she arrived at the very back of the last car. She cared little if she drew much attention to herself just now; her only interest was escaping however she had to.

The wind whipped around her face and grabbed at her hair, and she was obliged to put one steadying hand over her bonnet to keep it in place. Buildings approached from the left as they came upon another hamlet, and the structures flew by as the train rushed passed. Peering around the corner, she caught sight of what appeared to be crates, or bales of hay maybe. Perhaps if she leapt onto them, her landing wouldn't be so bad. At any rate, she had no other choice. She had to get back to London before Mr. Wainwright discovered she was missing!

Holding her breath, she jumped!

The memory left her breathless and she fell to her hands and knees on the mossy floor of the Garden's maze. It was true; it was all true! Arran had not known all the details, but his instincts had been correct from the very start.

Miss Stewart! She was Wainwright's lover, the same woman he hired to be her companion, the one tasked with poisoning her. And that was the woman found dead on the train shortly after Arran rescued her from the street! That meant—

Oh dear God! Phillip Wainwright was a murderer! If he could commit such a heinous crime against a woman he professed to love, what horrors lay in store for herself? Surely he could not steal her away to the asylum in Scotland as he intended, could he? She was on her hands and knees, pushing off from the ground to run again, when she collided with an unyielding chest. A scream lodged itself in her throat and she flailed, her back arching, legs kicking, hands clawing frantically, desperately.

"Stop fighting me!" Wainwright roared as he struggled with her. "Stop it, I say!"

Emmy threw her head back and forth, and finally she heard it connect with a satisfying crunch. "No! Help! No! Arran! Arr—"

She was thrown down, landing flat upon her back with such force that all breath was expelled from her lungs at once, leaving her gasping.

Wainwright dragged a hand beneath his bleeding nose and across one cheek, further smearing blood across his already injured face. With a sniff, he reached into the inner pocket of his coat and extracted a flask.

"You will respect me, wife. I will not tolerate disobedience," he sneered, dropping to straddle her stomach and forcing the open end of the flask into her mouth.

Emmy sputtered, tossing her head until Wainwright's large hand clamped over her nose to keep her from breathing, and more of the bitter drink was forced down her throat. "Take your medicine like a good girl, my dove."

She coughed and wriggled in attempts to dislodge Wainwright from his seat, to push the flask out from between her lips, but it was of no use. She was no match for the strength of Wainwright's fury and determination.

"Arran. Need Arran," she begged, the words slurring around the flask.

The slap came out of nowhere and the blow stunned her. Something soft was stuffed into her mouth and a length of fabric was pushed between her lips and teeth then knotted behind her head. When she was tossed over his shoulder, her world spun and she nearly fainted. She kicked feebly, but his arm braced against the backs of her legs and kept her immobilised. The further they went and the longer she remained suspended upside down, the more her head pounded as blood rushed to her head. Emmy continued her attempts to struggle, but she had less and less control over her body until finally, her limbs slackened and darkness enveloped her.

Chapter Sixteen

Wainwright was secretly hoping his new acquisition would show a bit of spirit. His plans to shut her away immediately did not feel quite as appealing as breaking her slowly himself, but there would be more at stake if she was able to call upon her friends. Although, given how bitterly his face ached, it was just as well. Perhaps if he relocated them both to some out of the way country house he could take his time with her. But there would still be the annoyances from friends and her cousin, Saxon, who possessed a fearsome reputation.

While her cousin was a landed gentleman whose family was part of the first circle of society, Saxon had, in direct disobedience to his father, turned his back upon the life of a gentleman and took to the boxing ring as well as to the sea. It was a career that had not lasted long, but long enough for Saxon to become wealthy in his own right. When combined with the family's coffers, the income had nearly doubled. Not only was he a man of influence, but of action.He did not suffer fools.

That was why Wainwright's scheme had to be letter-perfect. And in his estimation, it was.

He trusted his men to detain the oversized ruffian Margaret had picked up over the last month, and meanwhile, he would spirit her away to Scotland. But first things first, he had to set the stage at her home before her servants and present himself as their new master.

The laudanum did its job well, and Margaret was rendered entirely insensate. Even when he rather clumsily transferred her into the coach he had arranged for, with one of his own men as coachman, she did not stir. The dosing with the laudanum was not exact, truth be told, but if she remained asleep until he loaded her onto a northbound train, he would be pleased.

Upon arriving at Everleigh House off Grosvenor Square, he lugged Margaret from the bench inside the carriage and hoisted her into his arms. She was slight enough, but as she was completely unconscious, the weight of her was trying. He jerked his head at his man, who jumped down and quickly lent his assistance by sprinting up the steps, pounding upon the door, then returning to take some of Margaret's weight from Wainwright. As the pair ascended to the front door, it opened and light from within spilled through and illuminated the darkness without.

"Good gracious, sir! Your face!" Carter cried as he threw the door wide, his alarm growing at the sight of his mistress being carried within. "Has she had a relapse?"

Wainwright's head snapped up and he glared at the old man. "A relapse of what?"

"She was greatly injured, Sir, while she was away. The Scottish gentleman, Mr. MacDougall, brought her safely home just this morning."

Interesting timing, that. Wainwright shuffled with his man into the house, his brain spinning a fresh web of lies as he went. "Well, that *gentleman* as you call him abducted her from my presence and I have spent the last month trying to find her. This was the state she was in when I came upon them at the Gardens. I fear what might have happened had I not discovered them when I did."

Carter's brows lowered over his eyes in puzzlement, clearly processing this new information. "I will go and fetch Mrs. Pratt to assist her," he turned to go."

"No, I will attend to my wife, myself," he insisted.

The butler paused. "That is most irregular, sir. Mrs. Pratt is—"

"You are not paid to question," Wainwright barked. "Now go and prepare her bed."

Carter's back stiffened and Wainwright wondered if the butler would argue with him. But the man spun on his heel and hurried up the stairs to do his bidding. All that needed to be done was to turn the coverlet down, but Wainwright had waited years to order the smug-faced old man around, and finally doing so filled his black heart with satisfaction.

They got Margaret into her room at last and rather unceremoniously deposited her on her bed. The coachman took his leave immediately, but Wainwright remained behind.

"Miss Everleigh's particular maid is still away, but I'll send up one of the undermaids," Carter replied as he left the suite.

"No need," Wainwright broke in. "I will attend her."

The butler paused and slowly turned round to stare at him through the doorway. "Sir, that is most irregular. The undermaids are perfectly capable—"

"I am her husband, Carter. If you worry so greatly for her, call this doctor. I have paid him to be here at a moment's notice for her care," and he pushed a card into the old man's hand.

"She has a physician in town that has seen her since she was a mere child, Sir. Surely he would be more—"

"Do you refuse a direct order?" Wainwright bit out. "I am her husband, therefore you answer to me. Now go, or I shall have you replaced." The door was slammed closed leaving Carter alone in the hallway, befuddled and more than a little concerned.

The young doctor slipped from the woman's room and made his way downstairs, his pocket much fuller than it had been when he arrived. Carter was waiting at the door with the man's coat, scarf, hat and gloves. "I beg your pardon, Sir," Carter began, "but how does Miss Everleigh do? Her household is greatly concerned over her."

The doctor had been well coached, and he paused to draw his mouth downward in an affected frown. "You mean Mrs. Wainwright? I am afraid the young woman is very ill, indeed. She was quite agitated when I examined her. She did not recognize her husband and showed signs of female hysteria, delirium, even to seeing and hearing things that did not exist in the room. I informed Mr. Wainwright that he should remove her from London with all haste, and he informed me he planned to return to Cumberland with her, as he had originally intended. I understand he was taking her to an estate that he knew of there. It is a wise decision, but even then, it may yet be too late." With a dramatic sigh, the doctor donned his articles, but held his hat in his hands for a moment longer. "It is a regrettable situation, however she is most fortunate to have a husband so devoted to her care." Pressing his lips together in an attitude of dismay, he slung his hat upon his head and took his leave, plodding slowly along so as to further display his disappointment in the deteriorating state of his patient. It was only when the carriage turned the corner that he allowed a self-satisfied grin to tug at his lips, and he fingered the notes folded in his pocket.

Carter watched the carriage pull away from the front of the house and only closed the door when it turned the corner. He had yet to find his bed, and with what the doctor had just shared, his heart was troubled all the more. His steps were slow, dejected, and he ran a hand over the top of his balding head. Poor Miss Margaret. How could it have all come to this? And Mr. Saxon would be devastated; he doted upon his young cousin so!

Rather than taking to the servants' stairs, he headed for the kitchen for a cup of tea, and wasn't at all surprised to see Mrs. Fray seated at the kitchen table along with Mrs. Pratt, their housekeeper. A plate of cake sat in the centre of the table, untouched, and there was an empty teacup waiting for him. The pair of women looked up as one, expectation shining in their eyes.

He smiled gently and slid into the chair across the table from Mrs. Pratt, and she filled his cup. "What news?" she asked softly as she sat, and Mrs. Fray's hand slid into hers for support.

"The doctor said she must be removed from London immediately and suggested Scotland."

"Poor little dear," Mrs. Fray cooed. "I cannot understand what could have happened. She has always shown such a strong constitution, just like young Master Saxon."

Carter chuckled. "He is not 'young' anything any longer, Mrs. Fray. He is well on his way to thirty."

She sniffed and took a sip of her tea. "He will always be young Master Saxon to me."

"Ought I to send for Cossett?" Mrs. Pratt cut in gently. "I'm sure Miss Margaret would improve with having her lady with her."

"I have done so already; I sent an express calling her back my first available moment. You were still out," he explained. "I hope you will forgive my overstep."

Normally, Mrs. Pratt may have taken offence with Carter acting in so high-handed a manner as to send for one of her girls. But this was Miss Margaret, and exceptions could be made where she was concerned. "Of course. I am thankful you did; then Cossett might return as soon as may be possible to aid our Miss Margaret."

Carter quickly finished his tea and stood. "We three should try to rest at least a little before morning dawns, don't you think?"

Mrs. Fray gave an unladylike snort as she, too, rose to her feet. "As if I would sleep a wink tonight. Did Mr. Wainwright allow you to help prepare Miss Margaret for bed at all, Mrs. Pratt?"

The housekeeper shook her head. "I did attempt it but was denied entry. He claimed that right for himself." She shuddered, the thought abhorrent to her.

Carter shook his head. "I cannot make out what Miss Margaret sees in him. He has always behaved as the most self-important hanger-on I have ever met, and Miss Margaret is the apex of generosity and kindness. They do not suit."

"Matters of the heart are often nonsensical," Mrs. Pratt offered.

"If her heart is involved with someone like like Mr. Wainwright, I believe she may need a surgeon," Mrs. Fray grumbled as she blew out the sconces and handed Carter a candlestick.

Mrs. Pratt bit back a chuckle. "The remainder of the staff should return just after breakfast, Mr. Carter. With any luck, Cossett will be with us day after next. Surely Miss Margaret would not deny her."

"No, but her new husband may," he countered, leading them all up the stairs to the top level of the townhouse.

"If he does so and Miss Margaret does not give that man a piece of her mind, I will be very much surprised."

"The doctor said she was practically nonsensical," Carter reminded.

"Then all the more reason she would need her lady."

"Let us revisit this on the morrow. I'm sure they have gone to bed by now after such excitement, and we'll see what is to be done when the sun rises."

By nature, Wainwright was not a hard worker. He preferred to coast through life on his good looks and charms, taking advantage of every opportunity that would enhance his lifestyle with the minimal amount of effort. It was rare for him to be up before noon, and often was even later on mornings that followed a ball or other event. But this morning was different, special.

This was the morning things would at last be within his grasp. Within a few days, Margaret would be a resident of Moorsgate Lunatic Asylum and he would be free to live out his days with the comfort of her immense fortune at his disposal. He could take as many lovers as he chose behind closed doors while outwardly playing the part of the devastated young groom whose insane wife would have to remain shut away for all her life. There would be such beautifully tragic articles written about him, about his care of her, how grief-stricken he was, how difficult it was for him to see his beloved locked behind bars for her own safety. But it had to be done, of course. One could not allow a madwoman to move freely about society. What would her family think? It would be scandalising.

Once he had her fast and tight in Scotland, all loose ends would be effectively tied off, at least until such time as her cousin returned to Brookshire. But he would not bother himself with that eventuality until it was time.

First, however, Wainwright had to get Margaret out of London and onto a train. Again. And it would be all the more difficult this time; she was kept quiet due to the regular doses of laudanum-laced wine he had plied her with throughout the early morning hours. Whenever it seemed she began to return from her stupor, a bit more was given from the flask stored out of sight in his coat pocket, and she would sink into sleep again. It was tempting to wrap his hands around her neck and be done with her permanently, but he needed time for the story of their marriage to take hold as fact in the minds of society as well as her household.

He frowned as he rose from washing his face. Her servants, especially the three old ones, questioned him in a way he was not at all accustomed to. Did they not know their place? Did Margaret never set them right? Well, that would be one of the first changes he would make upon his return from Scotland. He would arrange for an entirely new staff for his house. Although, perhaps, he would keep on a few of the younger girls who might please him. He would see.

But first things first: they had a train to catch.

Normally he would require one of Margaret's servants to pack her things, but he did not want to involve them any more than was absolutely necessary. Speed was of the utmost importance just now, and he wanted nothing more than to be on his way once more. He had been in Town a few days prior and stayed at his club; his luggage was still there and he sent word through one of his accomplices last night to have his things sent to the railway station. As for Margaret's things—

A knock interrupted his plotting. "Mr. Wainwright? Forgive the intrusion, Sir; we have breakfast prepared and wondered if you and Miss Ev– Mrs. Wainwright would like a tray sent up."

He wasn't so familiar with the voices that he knew which servant stood on the other side of the door; it was female, and it was young. At least whoever it was remembered to use Margaret's new surname, and he grinned to himself.

"I will take a tray: three minute eggs, ham, good hot rolls, a slice of cake, and coffee with sugar and cream. Oh, and bring me a trunk for Mrs. Wainwright's belongings. We will be taking the train at quarter past ten."

There was a pause on the other side of the door before footsteps retreated down the hall and finally down the stairs. Wainwright nodded to himself, pleased that Margaret's servants recognized him as the master of the household. He would not be here for long, but it was important for them to know their place, and know *his* place, as well.

Breakfast was longer in coming than he preferred, but a glance at his watch confirmed there was still time. When someone finally came with his tray, he unlocked the door and allowed them to enter. It was one of the undermaids; he did not recall her name, just that it was the pretty quiet one with yellow hair. His favourite.

"Where is the trunk I ordered?"

"It will be brought up by a footman shortly, Sir," she explained. She bobbed a quick curtsey and moved to take her leave.

"No, you stay. You will pack your mistress's things," he commanded as he sat down to partake of the food she'd brought him. "But not until I have finished eating."

"But, Sir, I—"

Wainwright waved a hand, and she fell silent. Rather than leaving as she so clearly desired, she stood just inside the doorway against the wall, hands folded in front of her, head down.

"I cannot see you well when you stand over there. Move. To there," he said, pointing in the direction of the wall near the window where he sat.

She did as she was told, but kept her eyes fixed on her boots, even when she took her place.

Wainwright ate slowly and leisurely, his gaze hungrily wandering over the girl's slender form. Occasionally it flicked over to the bed where his wife slept, and his mind compared the two. The girl was pretty enough, although in a plain and understated sort of way, but she would never be as stunningly beautiful as Margaret. However, Margaret was too stubborn and outspoken to be really pleasant. Perhaps this girl could be a new dalliance for him when he returned. He decided, as he completed his breakfast, that she would be one of the few servants he would keep on after releasing all the others. And when she ceased to please him, there were scores of others in London he could hire.

Just as he gulped the last of his coffee, hiding the wince as the drink hit the open wound on his lip, a footman arrived with the trunk, and the maid quickly got to work transferring Margaret's things from her closet and bureau to the depths of the trunk. The footman, meanwhile, was ordered to prepare a carriage to take them to the station.

He watched her carefully, enjoying the flit of anxiety across the girl's face as she hurriedly packed Margaret's things. The girl did not know all that was needed for her mistress; she was not that sort of servant and he knew it well. It wouldn't matter; whatever was taken to Scotland would likely be sold by the asylum doctor as soon as Margaret was admitted. But it would make the story of their swift departure all the more plausible to her friends. Indeed, there would be no farewells between her and her friends. He eagerly anticipated having the burden of Margaret's life upon someone else's shoulders. Her money, however—that was a burden he was happy to carry.

Carter held his hat in his hands, shifting his weight from foot to foot. He was not accustomed to making social calls, particularly not when the recipient was one of wealth and position on par with his own mistress, however duty trumped anxiety. The Bexley footman had started just the smallest bit when he'd opened the door to admit Carter to the house, and then led him to the parlour, but to his credit, he said nothing beyond saying he would see if Mr. Bexley was available to receive visitors.

"Please tell him it is Mr. Carter of Everleigh House, and it is most important that I see him at once," he had added just before the footman shut the parlour door.

To his surprise, Mr. Bexley did not keep him waiting long, and greeted him with a surprised smile. "Carter! What brings you over in the middle of the day. Nothing amiss at Everleigh House, I trust, although I cannot imagine what else would bring you to my door."

"Mr. Bexley, thank you for seeing me. I'm afraid I am in need of your advice, and perhaps your assistance, Sir."

"Of course. Please, do sit and tell me your errand," Bexley offered, seating himself and gesturing to the other chair.

Carter had been a butler for the Everleigh household for nearly fifteen years, and had held such an occupation for the last thirty. He was well versed in social etiquette and conventions and had never been at a loss for words before. Now, he struggled to formulate his thoughts, and it took every ounce of willpower to remain seated when he desired to pace. "Miss Everlei– Mrs. Wainwright returned to us suddenly yesterday morning. I understand she came to see you."

Bexley at once snagged onto the new title, and his eyes narrowed. "She did. Forgive me, but did you say Mrs. Wainwright?"

Carter nodded. "I did, Sir. She was returned to us very late last night after having enjoyed the evening at The Royal Gardens with Mr. MacDougall, but was not in Mr. MacDougall's company. Rather, it was Mr. Wainwright who brought her home. She was… well, it is difficult to tell if the lady slept or if she was injured… but she was not awake. Mr. Wainwright behaved as if he was unaware of her previous injury; surely you noticed her odd and disjointed way of speaking."

"It is impossible not to," Bexley replied. "It is any wonder she can communicate at all, but Mr. MacDougall seemed to puzzle it out well enough. But you say she did not return with him, but with Wainwright. Indeed, I was not aware he had even returned to Town."

"I was not aware of it, myself, nor was I aware that she had married Mr. Wainwright during the time in which she was away from London. But that is just what Mr. Wainwright claimed when he returned with her, Sir."

"When she and Mr. MacDougall visited yesterday, and Lottie in her exuberant way congratulated Miss Margaret on her marriage, she certainly did not behave as an excited bride would. Indeed, she was rather aghast when Lottie mentioned it, and was even more surprised when I shared what I had assumed was common knowledge: that Wainwright had been courting her for a year."

Carter straightened in his seat. "Mr. Wainwright courting Miss Margaret? That is as difficult to believe as the fact that she eloped with him. If they were courting, we would know it. Mr. Saxon would know it. She would not hide such information; there would be no need to."

Bexley nodded. "I was not under the impression it was a secret. Wainwright casually spoke of it as if it were known to everyone. Although he did confide in Lottie and me that he planned to propose while they were in Newcastle, and that he wished to surprise Miss Margaret with his offer."

The butler blinked then and his gaze shifted away, his mind turning facts over and over as if solving some puzzle in his mind's eye.

Bexley watched in silence for a moment before he interrupted the man's thoughts. "You have something?"

"Perhaps, Sir," Carter answered slowly. "Mr. Wainwright sent for a doctor when he brought Miss Margaret home from the gardens, but he refused to call on her usual physician and instead demanded we send for another. He provided the name and where he could be located. When the doctor left, he said Wainwright was going to take her to Cumberland as originally planned. But—"

"But Wainwright told us they were destined for Newcastle. Cumberland is on the opposite side of the country."

"Just so, Sir; we were informed of the same. And it comes to me now that Mr. MacDougall said they were near Manchester, not near Newcastle at all."

"No, Newcastle is far north to the east side; Manchester is closer to the western coast," Bexley mused, then nearly shot to his feet. "I need to speak with Mr. MacDougall. Where is he now, Carter?"

The butler stood. "I know not. He left with Miss Margaret yester night after she insisted they go to the Royal Gardens, but I've not seen him since, Sir. It was Mr. Wainwright who brought her home, insisting the Scotsman abducted her during their journey north."

"I find that rather doubtful. On the contrary, if her actions were any indication, I would say she is quite fond of him, and he seemed fiercely protective of her. Not at all the way a kidnapper might behave. And if he were, in fact, a kidnapper, why return her home?"

"There is something more, Sir."

"Good God, what else?"

"She is not at Everleigh House any longer. Mr. Wainwright left just after breakfast with her. According to the undermaid, who was forced to help carry the trunk to the coach, Miss Margaret was still asleep, said she did not even open her eyes when she was placed within the conveyance."

Bexley's hands were on his waist, his jaw tight and his eyes flashing in anger. "Have you the afternoon free, Carter?"

"I will make it so, Sir. What do you need?"

Chapter Seventeen

Emmy could almost perceive her surroundings after struggling to claw her way back to consciousness. Her throat was parched and her tongue stuck to the roof of her mouth. Her head felt muzzy, and there was a severe lack of obedience from her limbs. The rhythmic rocking side to side paired with the rushing of water in her ears made Emmy's addled brain wonder if she were on a boat. But that made no sense. She last recalled being at the Gardens with Arran, showing him the delights of the entertainment venue. Then… then…

The rest was but a void, with no recollection except MacDougall's beloved face.

Arran. Her heart gave a joyous little leap.

But where were they now? What had happened that they were travelling again?

The sound of waves faded and gave way to wheels rolling over packed earth and horses hooves clopping close by, and her previous boat theory was exchanged for the more likely reality of being spirited away by carriage, a stagecoach if she were able to judge by the swiftness of movement. She finally pried her eyes open. Fields and trees flying by the window lent credence to her presumption; they were, indeed, travelling by coach.

"She lives, more's the pity."

She knew that voice. Turning her head took far more effort than it ought, but she was finally able to force her gaze to focus upon the hateful visage of the man who had haunted her dreams. His face was badly swollen on one side, his lower lip split and still oozing. Satisfaction blossomed within her knowing the pain he was likely in; he deserved every bit of it. "You."

Wainwright grinned. "Me. Did you enjoy your rest, my love?"

Emmy groaned and tried to straighten her slumped posture. He looked awful, not at all the polished and put-together gentleman she had always seen before. The side of his face was horribly swollen and bruised, and there was an ugly glint in his eyes. She clenched her jaw angrily for a moment. "Not love."

He tipped his head to the side as he regarded her. "Would you prefer Wife, then? Or perhaps Mrs. Wainwright?"

Her blood ran cold even as her temper flared to life. "Not wife. Not yours."

"But I have a signed certificate and reliable witnesses that say otherwise," he preened. "Once we arrive safely in Scotland, you will be someone else's problem, and I shall take great pleasure in enjoying the luxuries provided by your fortune. Which is, of course, my right as your legal husband."

"Not. Yours," she repeated slowly, disdain dripping from each syllable.

Wainwright lifted a shoulder. "It really does not matter what you think or say—what's done is done. Now then. I know it has been some time since you've eaten anything, and I imagine you shall need your strength for whatever the good doctor has in store for you once we arrive at his asylum. We should be approaching a town shortly where we might sup. Are you going to be good and behave yourself, or must I give you more wine to ensure your obedience?"

Wine. Was that why she could not remember anything after the Royal Gardens? She wriggled until she successfully sat straight, her shoulders strained from her wrists being bound at the small of her back. She would not allow him to win. She would fight! More than anything she wanted a life with the handsome Scotsman that had won her heart, and the only way to be reunited with him was to escape the leech before her.

But overcoming him with force would never work; she was far too weak of limb and senses just now to put up enough of a fight. However, might that not work in her favour?

She dropped her head forward and even slumped a little in an attitude of defeat. "Behave. Be good."

"Excellent, my dove. You are learning quickly. You may survive Moorsgate with your sanity intact after all, but I doubt it." He glanced out the window for a moment before his gaze swung back in her direction. "What on earth is the matter with your speech, Margaret?"

As if she would be willing to explain it to him even if she had the ability. Rather than attempt to answer, she turned her face away and fixed her gaze upon the countryside through which they drove. She prayed he would not insist upon conversing with her, either here or at any inn. She instinctively felt it would be safer for her if she could hide the aftereffects of her previous injury. In their very brief conversation, he had made mention of a doctor and an asylum, neither of which boded well for her. Let him believe her to be submissive and docile. MacDougall would come for her, and somehow all would be well. It had to be.

It was only when the carriage rolled through a village and stopped before a coaching house that Wainwright made any move to unbind her. He set a hand to the top of her shoulder, gave a small tug to urge her forward, and with a fine blade sliced through the ropes looped securely around her wrists. She gave a soft cry when her arms fell free, and her hands massaged at the aches that radiated down each limb, hissing as thousands of pins pricked at her nerves.

"Such a dramatic little pet," Wainwright tutted as he replaced the weapon.

A pair of boots landed hard on the ground outside, and the door swung open a moment later. Wainwright stepped out, then extended his hand just inside the door to help her down. She was loath to accept it. *Submissive and docile,* she reminded herself. While she did not smile, she did gracefully slide her hand into his and allowed him to assist her to the ground, and from there, they entered the building which housed both rooms for rent and dining for travellers.

She hoped beyond hope that they would not be staying the night here. Being rendered insensate under Wainwright's power, as must have befallen her between now and their row at the Royal Gardens, was lamentable, but being awake for any of his repugnant attentions would be far worse. She could do this. She could play the part of a doting young wife, or at least a young wife who tolerated her new husband.

They were seated quickly. Due to the relatively empty room, she guessed it was not a usual mealtime. He ordered for them, and she sat silently by, offering soft, demure smiles across the table and lowering her eyes whenever the server happened to glance at her. Let Wainwright believe he had triumphed over her, arrogant man that he was.

Her stomach felt full of stones, but she forced herself to eat what was brought to them. If she wished for this to work, she had to behave as if nothing at all were amiss, as if she were subservient and perfectly content with the situation at large. She ate what she was able, delighted in the soothing sensation of the hot tea upon her throat, and even managed a soft, "Thank you." While there, she glanced surreptitiously here and there for any sign that might inform her of her location, but to no avail.

Over an hour later, with fresh horses at the ready, Wainwright helped Emmy back within the confines of the carriage and revealed another long length of rope. She demurred silently, one hand clasping the other against her chest, her body twisting away from him while she eyed him pitifully. "No. Please. No." Her wrists were still rubbed raw from so many hours of the coarse rope chafing her delicate skin.

The man's icy gaze flicked briefly to her wrists, narrowed, then returned to her face. He leaned slowly across the way, bracing his forearms on his knees. "Will you behave yourself? If you cause me any further trouble, you will feel the effects of it. I have been kind until now, but I guarantee you will not appreciate my anger if you stoke it."

She swallowed and nodded her head. "Yes. Husband."

That seemed to soothe him and he smiled, looking almost like the charming friend he had been for all those years prior. "Very well, my dove. Since you have answered so pretty, you may remain unbound as you are. But at the first sign of any disobedience…" He waggled the end of the rope back and forth.

She nodded and settled against the cushioned back. One thing she had learned while in MacDougall's company was the delight found in not sitting erect every moment of the day. True, the boning of her unmentionables didn't allow for much movement, but even relaxing her posture was a welcomed change. Additionally, as she found Wainwright absolutely detestable, there was no reason to stand on formal ceremony with him, nor any reason to impress him. Thus, she slouched as much as her garment permitted.

Wainwright snorted. "Comfortable, are we?"

She said nothing and did not even deign to glance his way.

With what sort of doctor was Wainwright leaving her? What fate awaited her at this asylum? Was it some sort of hospital at which physicians and surgeons tried out different medical methodologies upon their patients, or was Wainwright simply shutting her away never to be found? She was unsure which was preferable.

She must have drifted off, for when the carriage suddenly lurched and her eyes snapped open, she was at some sort of shipyard, albeit a small one. Emmy leaned forward to peer this way and that, again with the hopes of determining where she might be, not that it would do her much good. Then again, facing a known entity felt far less daunting than agonising over the unknown.

To her surprise, the carriage rolled to a stop, and seconds later, the door opened. Out Wainwright stepped, and she followed dutifully. They faced the ocean, and nearby was a small transport vessel, large wood crates stacked upon the deck with at least a dozen men scurrying to and fro to ready it for travel. She blinked and unconsciously retreated.

A hand fell to her lower back, propelling her forward. "None of that, now. Come, be a good girl," he replied almost affably as he ushered her toward the boat. When she resisted, his long fingers closed around her arm just above her elbow and he began dragging her along. She wrenched her arm once with a grunt of protest, and quickly found both arms pinned to her sides. Emmy was about to kick out when she felt Wainwright's lips brush against her ear. "If you continue to fight me, I will simply allow *all* the men aboard to keep you company while we are at sea."

The threat of it was enough to douse the fight out of her, and she stilled instantly.

Wainwright chuckled, a low, sinister sound that made her skin crawl. "I am tempted to allow them to become more intimately acquainted with you regardless. Perhaps it would save me some money." He laughed outright and dragged her across the dock, up the gangplank, and onto the deck.

Hurry Arran.

Chapter Eighteen

"He just sits there," remarked one guard. "He's scarce moved a muscle in two days. Some Highland Hammer he turned out to be."

The second guard chortled. "Good thing, that. I heard he tossed five grown men like they was nothin'."

After another moment lingering by the cell which held him, along with half a dozen other prisoners, they continued on their way, evidently not finding the entertainment they sought.

MacDougall flicked a glance in the direction of their departing backs, then heaved a sigh. It was true; he hadn't moved from his spot on the straw-covered floor, beyond relieving himself, since he'd been brought in.

At least not that anyone on the other side of the bars had seen.

"Clear," one of the inmates mumbled, and MacDougall was up on his feet again and headed for the bars. Every moment he was unobserved, he was working at the bars, alternating between prying them apart until the mortar cracked and picking at the stone that had just begun to crumble.

"Think it will work?"

"I've got to try," he muttered as he yanked at the bars again, a grim smile tipping his mouth upward when they groaned under his hands.

"As if a hole in th' wall'll go unnoticed, ye balmy redshank," another criminal remarked from his place against the bars, one eye on the hall.

"Dinnae care if they notice, long as I'm gone by the time they do," MacDougall countered, brushing at the stone holding the bars in place before giving them another hard pull in opposite directions. A loud, metallic screech echoed through the cell as the ends of two bars gave way, chunks of mortar dropping to the floor, the bars bent outward.

The eyes of several men gogged. "How did—"

"Someone's coming," the lookout hissed, and the men returned to their previous position, with MacDougall taking his spot on the floor again.

"Yer being sprung free, Highlander," the guard announced as he walked up. "Some swell paid your— What's this?" His attention snapped to the now inefficient bars protruding from the opening on the opposite wall. "How– Were you– Did you do that?"

MacDougall wisely remained silent, as did the rest of the inmates, but his gaze snagged on the well-dressed man that stepped into view.

It was Mr. Bexley, the older brother of Emmy's friend, and he looked simultaneously amused and displeased as he stared at the damaged window. "You could not wait for bail? Were you attempting to bring down the entire place around you like Samson of old?"

"Nae, just the window."

"Just the window? We're three stories up! Did you plan to ascend upon the wings of the angels?" Bexley suppressed a sigh and shook his head, setting his hands to his hips; the guard continued to stare at MacDougall as if he'd just grown a second head. "Well, let us go. I've posted for you, and evidently I shall have to pay for a new grate, as well. You may reimburse me at your leisure."

MacDougall didn't bother hiding his surprise or befuddlement as he climbed to his feet and crossed to the bars separating them. "Sure and I'm thankful, but—"

"No time. Guard?"

"Yes, Sir," said the guard, shaking himself. He unlocked the barred door and it swung open with the grating of rusty hinges.

MacDougall stepped through the frame, the cell door slamming shut behind him. He extended a hand to his saviour. "My thanks, Sir."

"Bexley," the man corrected as he clasped MacDougall's hand, offering familiarity over formality. Bexley pivoted smoothly on a heel, guiding the way through the maze of halls and corridors that would lead them out. MacDougall easily matched his gait to keep up. "I've much to acquaint you with, and time is of the essence. That scoundrel Wainwright has quite the lead, and if we have any hope of bringing Miss Margaret back—"

"Back! Back from where?"

"Miss Margaret's butler, Carter, came to inform me that Wainwright left with her yesterday morning for the north. Their coachman dropped them at the station leaving for Manchester, and when questioned, the station agent recalled an unconscious woman being loaded onto the train. Fortunately for us, there is no way to do so inconspicuously so they were easily remembered. At any rate, the agent supplied that their ticket destination was Liverpool—as far as the line goes." Bexley flicked a glance his way as they turned a corner. "As I understand it, there was a confrontation between you and Wainwright at the Royal Gardens."

"How did ye hear that?"

"Society pages."

"Naturally," MacDougall muttered. He hated London, but in this particular case, he sent a brief prayer of thanks heavenward for the Town's appetite for gossip about its neighbours.

Bexley was continuing. "I informed Commissioner Rowan of our situation. I also paid a man from the Bow Street Runners to ride up to Carlisle and attempt to find out more. He has the descriptions of both Wainwright and Miss Margaret, so perhaps Fortune will be with us and someone will have noticed them."

MacDougall doubted he could have organised such a search as quickly and efficiently as this man had, and he was stunned. Were it left to him, he would have ridden hard following whatever trail he discovered like a fox chasing a rabbit. This was much more promising. "Tell me all ye've uncovered. Betwixt us, we should be able to puzzle it out."

Bexley spent the carriage ride from the Horsemonger Lane Gaol back to Grosvenor Square outlining what he and Carter had learned, allowing MacDougall to begin sorting the information into piles in his brain, connecting the dots from one to another.

"I've already visited the clubs to check the betting books, and while Wainwright made plenty of wagers where he was a member, nothing stood out as something that would help us discover their whereabouts now."

MacDougall shook his head, having no idea of the significance of any of those names. But with Bexley's narrative now over, he took his turn in supplying facts where Bexley's were missing, particularly the suspicious timeline Wainwright provided that contradicted his and Emmy's. And that was when a certain memory tugged at him. "Have ye already spoken with Miss Stewart's old employer?"

That brought Bexley up short. "Who the deuce is Miss Stewart?"

MacDougall quickly explained the potential link between her and Wainwright. "If we're able to gain an audience with the family she worked for, we might learn something new." He lifted a shoulder. "Could be worth the time. She worked in Woodbridge according to the newspaper article."

Bexley considered this for a moment. "It is an excellent thought, though Woodbridge is on the other side of London from us. Let us dig around Wainwright's townhouse first. It is only half of an hour from here and it may yet provide much needed information. If it is not enough, we shall hie ourselves off to Woodbridge. Agreed?"

"Long as we're quick about it," MacDougall assented.

After giving the coachman a new destination, the pair fell silent, occasionally adding bits and pieces to what they already knew, twisting the puzzle pieces this way and that, examining them to determine what fit together.

Upon their arrival, Bexley convinced the footman at the door that he was acting as Wainwright's attorney regarding legal matters in Wainwright's new marriage, which promptly gained them access to his master's library. The footman eyed MacDougall warily, but Bexley thanked the man and dismissed him before he could raise much question. Behind closed doors, the pair began a methodological search through drawers, books, and piles of papers.

MacDougall was glancing over the shelves of books lining the walls, each spine in perfect condition as if the book had yet to be cracked open. His lip curled; so Wainwright liked the appearance of knowledge and culture but did not care one jot for expanding his own sphere of it. He wasn't surprised. One volume was turned backwards and he tugged it free. It was a book of English law. Already his pulse quickened, and when he opened it, the pages naturally fell open at a chapter on marriage, a scrap of paper marking the section.

"Bexley."

Charlotte's brother had been flipping through a leather-bound ledger. The pair met in the centre of the room to compare their respective finds.

"This was tucked in the pages," MacDougall explained, handing Bexley the piece of parchment that was sandwiched between the pages, dozens upon dozens of alphabet letters written repetitively, lowercase and upper. "And look what it marked." He turned the book around to show the page's title.

Bexley's gaze narrowed, gears turning in his mind. "Marriage law. And look at this. There are odd notations in the margins, and at a glance, I cannot make heads nor tails of the numbers themselves. Additionally, the initials M.L.A. continuously appear."

They puzzled over their finds in silence for a moment before MacDougall asked, "Can ye take it with ye?"

Bexley shook his head. "The wisest course of action is to leave everything as we've found it. We can return at a later date when needed and allow the proper authorities to happen upon them... once we offer pointed suggestions." He was absently glancing over the repeated letters on the scrap, slowly shaking his head in confusion before he replaced it between the pages of the book and handed the volume back to MacDougall to replace.

Bexley was sliding the ledger back in its drawer when wood at the bottom shifted. After prodding at it, one edge tipped up to reveal a shallow false bottom hiding another stack of papers. He withdrew them and cursed under his breath. "I believe I know what that bit of paper was for."

MacDougall joined him at his side. "What did ye find?"

"Love letters written in a lady's hand, signed by Miss Margaret. But look here," and he held two nearly identical letters side by side. "Do you see the difference between them? Observe the signature."

Surely enough, there were minute variances between them. MacDougall's eyes quickly scanned the pages, disgust sparking and quickly blazing into an inferno. "This is claiming she's always been in love with him, that *she* wants to elope to Scotland. He's making it out as if it was her idea!" He would have snatched the pages and ripped them to shreds if Bexley hadn't jerked them out of reach. As it was, he broke away to stalk the length of the room and back again, indignant rage boiling within him.

"We should go. We do not wish to call more attention to ourselves than we already have." Bexley cast MacDougall a wary eye as he replaced the falsified letters and ledger back in the drawer. "And if we stay any longer, I fear you may raze the place to the ground."

Chapter Nineteen

Michael Saxon released a long sigh as he finally stepped down from the carriage in front of Everleigh House. He had been away too long this time. He rolled his head on his neck to stretch the muscles and felt them loosen. Rather than travelling straight to Brookshire, which would have taken him around London, he chose first to check in with his dearest girl: his cousin Margaret. She was always in Town this time of year, and he sorely longed for a sight of her after the months of separation. Even when he'd left home and hearth to experience the world, leaving the luxury of his father's estate behind him, he had written regularly to his Little Rose, the pet name he had used for Margaret since babyhood. According to his family, young Master Saxon leaned over his infant cousin in her bassinet and declared she was 'pretty as a rose', and the name stuck. Of everyone in the world, she was the most precious to him. Of all the people in his life, she alone had always loved him, always championed him, always desired to see him happy above all else.

All through his life, he had clashed with his father over a number of topics, practically limitless in number. Being the only son came with expectations and responsibilities, none of which had interested young Saxon in the least. When it was discovered that he was sneaking off to mills to box rather than attending his classes, his father had been furious. The elder Saxon was determined to take the young man to task and force him into the mould meant for him, going so far as to threaten disinheritance if his son did not give up his fanciful ideas of becoming a champion pugilist.

That ultimatum had not gone well. Rather than yield to his father's command, Saxon had simply left.

For the next several years, Saxon made his own way: boxing and fencing his way up and down England, then across the western continent, accepting odd jobs on ships and learning to sail, and eventually helping to manage a small fleet which ferried goods back and forth across the English Channel.

When he was four-and-twenty, after years spent amassing quite a bit of independent wealth by business and by his fists, word reached him by letter, penned by the family steward, that his mother had suddenly died and his father had suffered an apoplexy. Saxon had hastened home for the first time in six years and stubbornly posted himself at the old man's bedside, never once deserting his post except to relieve himself. He held the weathered hand for hours at a time, read quietly from books and newspapers, and kept constant vigil as his father slipped from this world into the next, following his wife into the grave only a fortnight later.

Despite the threats, Michael had not been disinherited, after all. In fact, upon clearing the man's study, he found clippings of newspapers with his own name printed in every one, each lovingly taking a page in a large ledger evidently meant for that express purpose. For all his purported disappointment, the old man had proudly followed every fight, every win, every decision his son had made while away from Brookshire.

Now grown and without parents, Michael and Margaret were all each other had in the world by way of close relations. Oh, there were likely distant relatives somewhere, but they had not been in Michael and Margaret's direct sphere as they'd aged, so it was them against the world.

Figuratively speaking, of course.

He trudged up the steps, unsurprised when the footman opened the door before he reached the top stair. "Welcome home, Mr. Saxon."

Saxon offered a kind but weary smile as he handed the footman his articles.

"Afternoon, Marks. Is Maggie at home?" In answer, the young man's face fell and grew rather ashen, and Saxon's heart stuttered. "Marks."

The footman had opened his mouth to speak when Carter's purposeful footsteps clicked on the tile floors, and Saxon left Marks where he stood to intercept the butler. "Carter, I've just arrived. What is it?"

"We are at sixes and sevens, Sir. Mr. Bexley and a recent visitor, a Mr. MacDougall, are scouring

London for clues regarding Miss Margaret's whereabouts. I have heard nothing since—"

Saxon's throat closed. "What about Maggie?" he demanded.

Carter fired off the curious details of what had transpired in his younger cousin's life since he had left to oversee some prospects in France. By the end of it, Saxon was torn between his desire to turn the British Isles upside down in search of her, and heading straight to Jack's to pummel something. Or someone.

"They have instructed me to wait here for further word, but that was early this morning, Sir. Perhaps they have returned to Bexley House—"

That was all Saxon needed. Forgetting hat and coat, he ran from the room, flew down the stairs and practically jumped back into the coach, which was still awaiting to have his luggage unloaded. "To Bexley House. Now!"

Bloodlust roared through him and he found it incredibly difficult to contain himself, nearly impossible. If he were a man of lesser steel and calibur, he might have succumbed to the rage. If anything happened to her— But no, he refused to entertain such dark thoughts. Instead, he forced his focus to narrow to a pin's point intensity until all that existed was the problem before him. He would haunt Bexley House until the man returned, and then he would bring his Little Rose back.

It was a fortunate turn of events that had him arriving just as Bexley was stepping from his own carriage.

"Bexley!"

The man spun, surprise and relief both evident in his expression. "Saxon! You're here! Did someone send for you?"

"If they did, I travelled ahead of the missive. I've just come from Carter. Tell me all that you know."

His dark gaze flicked in the direction of the carriage as another man stepped out, and he was momentarily stunned at the man's height. He wasn't a giant, but he was nearly a head taller than Saxon, himself, who was already the tallest in their circles. The commonly dressed man sauntered over, expression hard and unreadable. Vague familiarity teased his brain for half a heartbeat, but there was no time to waste on something so trivial when his cousin was missing.

"Saxon, this is Mr. MacDougall. MacDougall, this is Mr. Saxon. He is Miss Margaret's cousin and guardian."

The pair sized one another up and came to silent acceptance, shaking hands before following Bexley up into the townhouse.

Over a hastily prepared meal of bread, cheese, and cold meat, Bexley and MacDougall repeated what they had gleaned from their search of Wainwright's study and everything that MacDougall had witnessed, himself. By the end of the narrative, Saxon was seething.

"I'll kill him," he vowed.

"Not if I reach him first," MacDougall added.

Saxon's eyes flew to the stranger and narrowed inquisitively.

"Have something to share, MacDougall?"

The Scotsman remained silent, as did Saxon, leaving Bexley to glance back and forth between the pair of statues, inwardly wondering who would crumble first.

It was a full two minutes before Saxon finally broke the silence. "I am Miss Everleigh's legal guardian. Now, have you something to share, Sir, or shall I have Bexley escort you to the street?"

He heard the man give a frustrated sigh before it appeared he made the decision to acquiesce. "I come from nothing, not even a family left to call my own. I've made enough to have a comfortable living for myself, but I ken 'tis not what a lady such as yer cousin deserves, or is accustomed to."

"I don't believe that is what I asked." Saxon swore he heard the man growl at him, and he straightened in his chair, gaze levelled and near menacing, daring him to lash out.

He didn't, though, and Saxon's estimation rose a degree or two. Instead, MacDougall ran a hand through already dishevelled hair. "I'll not speak truths I've yet to confess to her directly, but if I cannae have her at my side, I'll live my days alone."

More silence followed, the only sound the distant tick of the large clock standing in the hall.

Saxon inhaled slowly, time slowing as he processed. Finally, he gave a short, curt nod and the tension in the room eased. "All right then. What is our next course of action?"

"If we can locate the family Miss Stewart worked for before her death," Bexley started, "they might have some idea where she was headed, even if she had quit her position. If not the family, perhaps other servants in their employ."

"Have you searched the clubs?"

Bexley nodded. "Yester. I looked through every betting book to see if mention was made concerning either Mr. P.W. or Miss M.E. I found nothing."

"And Wainwright has quit Town?"

"As far as we can tell. A train agent said he saw Wainwright loading Emmy onto the train headed for Manchester, and their tickets were for Liverpool."

Saxon blinked. "Emmy?"

MacDougall waved him off. "Tis a long story, that."

Seemingly satisfied, Saxon nodded. "What of any of Wainwright's friends? Surely one of them would know; Wainwright is a braggart and would never be able to keep it a secret among his intimate circle. Why not see if we can find one at a club or at Jack's?"

MacDougall's mouth pressed into a line. "Nae good."

"How's that?"

"None'll be frequenting anywhere over the next weeks."

Bexley snorted, and Saxon glanced between the pair. "And why is that?"

"They're all in hospital, broken," MacDougall offered casually. "Tis why Bexley dug me out of gaol. Wainwright and his cohorts surprised Emmy and me the night we came to London. While Wainwright ran after Emmy, I had his men on me like a pack of rabid dogs. Sure all of them are still abed, unable to walk."

Recognition lit behind Saxon's eyes; the Scotsman was a fellow fighter. That was why he'd seemed familiar to him. Though they had never shared the ring together, their careers had somewhat danced around one another, both well known for their almost inhuman strength when throwing a punch. "And that's what you do to those who threaten my cousin?"

"Every time."

Saxon paused, processing the statement. "I wholeheartedly approve." With that, he rose to his feet. "Let us away to the hospital and see what further information we can persuade these broken men to give up."

Chapter Twenty

How long would one continue to live if one simply lay still?

Unable to track her time spent here, she counted the number of times she awoke from what she assumed to be sleep, opium induced or otherwise. It had been eighteen 'wakes' since she first arrived, and already it felt as if she had endured decades. She longed for the sun, for the moon, the stars, anything that would allow her a glimpse of the world beyond the hell of her life here.

No, not life. This was not living. Indeed, it was barely surviving.

Reality. Perhaps that was a more appropriate word for what her world had become.

Emmy heaved a sigh as a fresh wave of despair washed over her, threatening to drown her. Her tears had dried up days ago, months ago, possibly years. There was no passage of time in this tomb of grey stone. Her room was essentially a box. No windows, just a bed to which she was lashed with leather restraints. Evidently, her captors had taken offence at her insistence in leaving this dreadful place when she was first brought to them, and so they made escape impossible for her.

It surprised her to discover that the doctor and his nurses were not cruel, nor abusive, nor even as mad as their patients. Rather, she found them to be frighteningly sane and logical, and perhaps that was what unnerved her most. Everything that was done was for a purpose, scientific in nature. The doctor did not derive any sort of twisted pleasure from inflicting discomfort or pain; he merely studied it and scribbled away at a book open and at hand at all times. He was a man of knowledge and learning, he had said when she had first met him. All that he did was for the purpose of understanding the human condition, its strengths and frailties. He did not view her as human, not in the same way he viewed himself, and therefore, it was impossible to reason with him. He had a mission, and she was but an instrument used to fulfil said mission. That was all.

The last three sessions had involved a tub of freezing water in which she was submerged for long periods of time. She had stopped crying out for mercy after the first session, learning quickly that to appeal to their humanity was useless as there was no humanity left in their souls. It had dried up somehow, sucked dry in the name of knowledge, leaving behind heartless husks that only physically resembled their once human forms. It was depressing and disheartening, and she almost felt sympathy for them.

Almost.

She had eaten but once since the meal at the coaching inn with that detestable man responsible for her fate. The nurses had plied her with some sort of cold porridge, but food held no interest for her. One only ate to live, and she had decided that living was finished for her. However, they were inventive creatures and some horrific contraption was wheeled in that forced food down her throat with no ability to do otherwise. She was not even swallowing it and yet it ended in her stomach.

To pass the time, she retreated into her memories: living and re-living the happy times of her childhood when her parents lived, the afternoons playing princess and knight with her cousin, dancing at balls, choosing beautiful fabric for new gowns each Season, and of course, her short but beautiful weeks with MacDougall.

She sighed. *Arran.* He had asked if she would call him Arran, and she both loved and hated the way her heart warmed in her chest when she whispered his name to the cold, dark room. With her eyes closed, she could almost hear the thick Scottish burr when he said her name.

"Emmy, my love."

Arran. She smiled, unable to help herself.

"Come back to me, *mo chridhe.*"

He hadn't used his native language around her much; there was no reason to as she could not understand a single utterance unless he then translated it. She had heard him murmur the phrase a few times, and while she had no way of knowing its meaning, somehow it always caused her heart to skip with delight. Perhaps when she arrived in heaven she might ask God what it meant. Surely He would know.

Her face warmed with the memory of his palms cradling her face. She could almost feel his thumbs stroking the tops of her cheeks.

"Please, lass, wake up. Please be well. I need ye more than my next breath. I love ye. I refuse to live without ye, Emmy, my lass."

She gave a happy little coo of pleasure, determined to savour every moment of this beautiful fantasy. Her lashes swept upward, and there, hovering over her, was the most beloved face in the world. "Love you," she whispered.

MacDougall gasped and his fingers dove into her hair, wanting to crush her to him but being mindful that she was likely even more fragile than before. "Emmy! Thank God and all His angels, yer awake! And yer speaking, lass!"

Her eyes twinkled as if she were laughing at him. "Always speak in dreams."

What sort of things had she endured that her mind couldn't tell the difference between awake and asleep? "Yer not dreaming, lass." His hands worked furiously to undo the restraints that strapped her to the bed, first her ankles, then her wrists. The areas were raw where she had clearly fought against the restraints, open and weeping, unable to scab over to heal. He wanted to tear the doctor apart for treating her—or *any* human—with such callousness. MacDougall vowed to himself to spoil her every waking moment of every day to make up for not rescuing her sooner. "I'm here."

"Arran always here in dreams. Favourite part." She was almost speaking fluidly, though somewhat slurred, as if she weren't entirely awake. Perhaps she wasn't. Perhaps that was the reason she was able to finally communicate: her brain was sleeping and no longer obstructing her tongue. Whatever the explanation, hearing her voice was sweeter than an angel's song and he would never tire of it.

He slid his arms beneath her and cradled her against his chest, his heart nearly bursting when he felt her burrow into him. She was lighter than he remembered, and while she was clothed, the garment was so threadbare he'd been able to see the outline of her body through the cloth. He didn't want to ever set her down, and he knew he would have nightmares for weeks about losing her again.

"So warm," she murmured, rubbing her cheek over the spot where his heart thumped.

"Ye'll never be cold again, Emmy, my love."

He hurried through the building of horrors, forcing himself to ignore the cries for mercy and rescuing. They would all be set free. He would see that the local laird took responsibility for what was happening there. But for now, Emmy was his only focus. His logical brain argued that it was not fair to leave all the wretches creatures behind even for a short time, but his heart didn't care. She was his whole world. Everything else could burn as long as she was safe and in his arms.

As instructed, Bexley had waited at the wagon with the drayman MacDougall hired, and they straightened in alarm the moment the front door of the fortress-turned-asylum was thrown open. All it took was one look at Emmy's bared legs and they leaped into action. Bexley snagged a blanket from the back and ran to meet MacDougall, unfurling the fabric as he went. Meantime, the driver shook out a second blanket and spread it over the wide flat surface of the wagon's bed. MacDougall and Bexley continued their jog toward the wagon, the blanket haphazardly tucked around Emmy's shivering body as they went. She was gently laid down, the second blanket folded around her like the first, and between the three of them, they carefully settled her between MacDougall's knees as he sat with his back against the seat. The moment everyone was safely seated, the driver snapped the whip above the horse's flank and the wagon jumped forward, setting a rapid pace toward the village.

Emmy continued to shake and tremble in the circle of his arms, her teeth chattering audibly, and he pulled the blankets closer around her before tightening his hold, willing his body heat to chase away the chill. She had already endured so much, he feared she would not be able to recover from another fever if one took hold of her again.

He thought he heard her whisper, and he bent his head. "What was that, love?"

"Where going?" Emmy mumbled, eyes closed and face relaxed as one asleep.

"Home."

"Home," she repeated with a smile on her lips. "Arran home going?"

He pressed his lips to the top of her head. "Ye couldna keep me away."

Chapter Twenty-One

As eager as MacDougall was to marry Emmy at once, she still had quite a bit of healing to do, emotionally and physically. He would not rush her, and Emmy expressed a desired to be whole for him when she began her new life as Mrs. MacDougall.

MacDougall would have been quite happy to run away with her without all the pomp and circumstance her social class expected, but it was clear how much she wanted a ceremony which would include all her loved ones, and one elopement in her life, albeit a false one, had been quite enough for her nerves. He had waited for her this long, and he would gladly wait for years if that was what she needed. So, he gladly conceded, spending hours at her side, day in and day out, content to simply be with her and ease her journey back to health. Again.

Saxon, for his part, had not thought he would like the man who was taking away his Little Rose. In the quiet recesses of his heart, Saxon had, in fact, always expected to marry his beloved cousin one day.

However, despite his intentions, it was clear that Margaret adored the Scotsman and would not be happy unless her life was spent at MacDougall's side. Thus, Saxon forced himself to get to know the Highlander for his cousin's sake. With the man's code of honour and white-knight streak, Saxon liked the man in spite of himself, and it wasn't long before the two needled one another like brothers. With their common training in the ring, they even took to sparring against each other, although neither had any plans of re-entering the boxing world.

There was a short stretch of time, just as the weather turned from pleasant spring to warm summer, when all three men vanished for several days and nights in a row. While neither Lottie nor Margaret nor any of the staff spoke of it, all knew it was to tie off the end of the final rope. When the trio returned a week later, the shadows that had lingered around the eyes of betrothed and cousin were finally gone, and Margaret felt as if she could take a full breath for the first time since she leaped from the train platform all those months before. MacDougall had even returned with a special gift for her: Molly and her entire family had been relocated to the country to join the staff at Brookshire. There was even talk of sending little Freddie to school.

There would be whispers among the servants and Emmy caught them huddled over a newspaper on more than one occasion, stealing furtive peeks at her before bustling off about their business. No doubt it regarded the fate of the man who had wreaked so much havoc in her life, and she would shiver when she thought of how close she came to being shut away from the world because of Wainwright's jealousy and avarice. But then, if not for that most despised person, she would never have met her other half. Perhaps God above could turn all things for good, after all.

It was August now. Margaret—or Emmy, as MacDougall would always call her—was making her slow way from the manor house to the sprawling natural gardens behind the house, her favourite place to spend the heat of the afternoons. The grass was lush and green underfoot, the trees overhead provided deliciously cool shade, the flowering shrubs gave a riot of colour that could not help but cheer one, and knowing their mistress's preference for that particular area, the servants ensured there was always a pitcher of cool drink standing at the ready on the small outdoor tea table.

On this day, however, her usual oasis was decorated with much more than nature's usual beauty.

Intricate vines with large lush leaves had been trained around the trunks and branches of the trees. The tea table had been lavishly set for two and a small cart nearby held an array of delicacies and dainties. Lanterns hung from here and there, though darkness had not yet fallen. Gentle harp music wafted on the breeze from somewhere unseen, tones so soft that it almost felt as if it were part of the garden. The overall effect was almost fairy-like, much like the Royal Gardens.

And of course, there were roses everywhere: roses strung together to make cascading curtains around the tea table, roses standing in bowls and vases, roses of all colours woven and braided with the vines until they seemed to be part of it.

Emmy's breath caught at the sight of it, but what arrested her attention most was Arran MacDougall, her Scottish knight without the armour, standing in the midst of it, clad in the clothing befitting a prince. Even when she had offered a new wardrobe, he had politely deferred, saying he was much more comfortable in what he owned, although he did allow the purchase of additional clothes in the same style. But now, with his hair freshly combed back, a freshly pressed cravat tied about his neck, a waistcoat of beautiful midnight blue hugging his torso and a pair of buff trousers hugging the contours of his legs, her heart raced as if she had run to town and back again without stopping. It was the first time that his inner princely demeanour matched the outside, and while clothes were merely surface level, the genteel lady in her sat up and took notice. Her throat grew dry and, though much of the language was at her disposal once again, words utterly failed her.

MacDougall smiled and closed the distance between them, his hands taking hers in a tender clasp. "Emmy, lass."

"Arran. What this?"

He kissed her tenderly on her forehead before he leaned back to peer down into her face. "It came to me that I have neglected something verra important," he drawled, the burr of his accent thick, his voice deep. "I've told ye how I love ye, how I would give up my life to keep ye safe, to see ye happy. I've told ye how much I admire ye, admire yer strength and determination. I've told ye how I long to be at yer side the rest of yer days, and we have discussed marriage betwixt us. But there's aught I missed."

"Missed?"

He smiled. "Aye, lass. It seems to me that ye've been told what to do most of yer life. I dinnae want to be just another man ordering ye about, so I'm *asking* ye, lass. Margaret Rose Everleigh, the very beat of my heart, my darling Emmy... Will ye do me the great honour of marrying me and becoming my wife?"

Tears sprung to her eyes unbidden and her heart felt as if any more happiness would make it burst. She threw herself into his arms with a joyous ripple of a laugh and kissed him with all the love in her being. "Yes! Arran, yes! I marry you!"

September was half gone by the time Margaret was fully healed and recovered, and the wedding was set for a perfect late-September morning. With Cossett's assistance and Charlotte's eye for detail, the bride was lovingly dressed in an exquisite ivory satin gown, the wide neckline swooping gracefully from one shoulder to the other, short puffed sleeves hovering above her elbows, and a full skirt over layers of fluffy tulle. Her wealth of hair was pinned up in an elegant sweep away from her face, and a garland of pink tea roses sat atop her head like a crown with her mother's gauzy veil trailing down her back like mist.

As the morning sun streamed through the church windows, it caught the tawny locks of her hair and glorified them into tones of gold and bronze. She walked to the altar on the arm of her cousin, entirely oblivious to every whisper around her as her gaze locked upon her husband-to-be, awaiting her with a smile on his face and a light in his eyes.

Though the clergyman was appropriately solemn, joy and excitement fairly radiated from the faces of the lovers as they gazed at one another. Neither could recall anything about what was spoken during the brief ceremony, and they were utterly oblivious to the dear friends who joined them in the church that day. All that existed were the two souls that, at long last, were joined together as one.

Acknowledgements

The process of creating this, my very first book for publication, most definitely took a village of family and friends. That said, I am so beyond thankful for my 'village', more than any words can express.

The first tier of thanks goes to my cheerleaders, my amazing supporters who have been there since the very start of things: my wonderful and patient husband who wasn't ever bothered when I would disappear to write no matter how many times I did so, who encouraged me to keep going, to not give up, who loves me despite how much I've talked his ear off since... well, since we started dating in 2002; our amazing kids for loving me, for believing in me, and for sharing me with two very needy fictional characters; my mom—my first and forever friend—who has unfailingly cheered me on in every aspect of life including my love and pursuit of various artforms, whom I love 'more than tongue can tell'; my dad who always knew I could do it; my late grandmother Helene who was so incredibly excited when I told her I wanted to be a writer, and who wanted so much to see me publish my first book—I hope there are libraries in heaven and that God will set this one aside for you.

The next group of thanks goes to the close friends who acted as my editors, my beloved second-string cheerleaders: Noby, Melanie, and Devin. Thank you so much for carving out time in your hectic schedules to support me, to push me to be better, for correcting my errors in love, and celebrating the milestones along the way.

And thank *you*—yes, YOU—for buying or borrowing this book, for taking a chance on an unknown author. There are millions of books out there, and the fact that you picked up mine means more than I have words to express. Truly, from the bottom of my heart, I thank you.

To my "Favorite", whose face I've never seen but whose friendship I value and cherish as much as any other. This literally would never, could never have happened without you. You are indispensable, so I hope you don't think you're done yet. Twenty years of writing, and we still have stories to create!

To the Most High: it is all and always for You.

About the Author

Lily M. Winters has been creating stories since she was old enough to lift a pen. A left-brained artist in every sense of the word, she informed her mom at age five she wanted to be an actress. Years later, she went on to receive a university degree in theatre arts and performance. She also makes jewelry for her company, Stardust Trinkets, sings at the top of her lungs, and loves making people laugh.

Above all, she loves her Yeshua, her husband Daniel, and their two amazing kids who are growing up way too fast.

Her other characters are already demanding to have their stories told, so check back with her on Facebook and other social media platforms to see what she's up to. As always, honest reviews are *much* appreciated.

Made in United States
Troutdale, OR
05/27/2024

20165762R00193